INTERCEPTION

A HALL OF FAME ROMANTIC COMEDY

EVA HAINING

COPYRIGHT

ALSO BY EVA HAINING

The Cardinal Brotherhood Books 1&2 Box Set

Luxure

Kadedus

Gier August 26th 2021

PROLOGUE

NOTHING GOOD CAN COME from letting a guy ride you bareback.

Since the day I lost my virginity in the back of my high school boyfriend's Camaro, I've had one rule:

If you're not gloving it, I'm not loving it.

It's a pretty simple rule, but you'd be surprised how many times I've broken it when faced with a raging lady boner, tequila, and a hot guy saying all the right things. I've been lucky.

But luck has a way of running out eventually...

CHAPTER ONE

ZEE

GUYS CAN BE SUCH ASSHOLES. I'm about to spend the next week of my life making sure a tiny man, who I'm sure has a tiny dick, keeps his grubby little fingers to himself in the future.

My best friend, Faith, called me last night, panicking and begging me to help her. Of course, I got the first plane out to Seattle to be by her side. There isn't anything I wouldn't do for her. She's like a sister to me, even more so than my actual sister. Hearing her upset and knowing she's hurting got me all riled up. I spend the entire flight planning what I needed to do to help her deal with the situation quickly.

Faith isn't like me. She's lived a sheltered life with overbearing parents trying to keep her as their 'little girl' for way too long. I know she finds it frustrating, but it's not the worst thing in the world to have parents who care too much. I had the opposite problem. My dad has never given a damn what I do, he never has. And my mom's a door-mat, and that's me being polite.

When I left for college, I swore I'd never let anyone make me feel as worthless as they did. Holidays are the only time I see them. I perform my duties as a daughter, and they pretend they actually want me around. To be honest, I think they'd be relieved if I just stopped visiting.

My sister is the kid my parents planned. They only wanted one child, and I was a mistake long after they were over the novelty of being parents.

Faith is all the family I need. We've been inseparable since the day we met. Fate made us roommates, and although we're polar opposites in so many ways, we just clicked. The idea of someone hurting her in any way makes me want to go on a bloody rampage. One thing's for sure, I'm going to make this guy pay for hurting her.

When I arrive at the hotel, Faith is there waiting for me with a heartfelt hug and bloodshot eyes. She's been crying.

"Thank you so much for coming, Zee. I didn't know if I should just forget about it, but I can't."

"Let's sit down and order some food. You can walk me through everything that happened, and we'll make a plan from there. Where's Hunter in all this?"

"He broke his hand after I told him what happened. He's recovering from surgery at his friend, Cooper's house."

"Cooper Danford? The Titan?"

"Yeah."

"He's so unbelievably sexy. All rugged and bad boy, and just sex on a stick."

"I haven't met him, but Hunter speaks highly of him."

"So you told him what happened, and he broke his hand?"

"Yeah. And at this point, Malcolm isn't his manager anymore."

"Tell me everything." Faith walks me through weeks of this guy making suggestive comments and warning her about messing with his precious cash cow, Hunter Vaughn. When she gets to his actions on the flight, I'm about ready to explode.

"Is there even any point in trying to do something about this?"

"Of course, there is. He's a weasel and deserves everything he gets."

We spend the next few days tracking down flight numbers, staff names, passenger manifests, and contact details for people who were in the surrounding seats and may have seen something. Our methods may be somewhat questionable, but it paid off. *Jackpot!*

When we have enough information, we go to the police, and I'm glad to say they take Faith's complaint seriously. It turns out this guy has numerous prior claims against him, though nothing they could take to court and charge him with. By the time the detective finishes taking Faith's statement, she seems exhausted by the whole thing. She has a naturally bubbly personality—she has to be when she's a klutz of comedic proportions.

Today, she seems weary and downtrodden. It doesn't help that Hunter Vaughn isn't in the picture right now. She's been pretty closed off about him since I arrived, but I know she'll tell me everything when she's ready. For tonight, I'm going to spoil her with room service, trashy movies, and all the candy she can eat. Throw in a bottle of champagne, and we're good to go.

The sooner we put this maggot of a human being, Malcolm, behind us, the better.

My head is pounding.

I shouldn't have indulged in that second bottle last night. Faith clatters around the room like a bull in a china shop, tripping over anything in her path. I give myself a few minutes for the room to stop spinning before I venture out of bed and stand upright.

I'm *never* drinking again... at least not today.

When Faith appears as fresh as a daisy from the shower, her voice is like a gong ringing out in my ears.

"Morning!"

"Do you have to be so loud and perky?"

"What's wrong?"

"It's called a hangover, Faith. You should try it sometime, then maybe you wouldn't be screaming at me right now. Can we drop the decibels, please?"

"I told you to take two aspirin and a full glass of water. It works every time."

"Oh, go shove aspirin up your ass. I'm hurting, and 'I told you so' isn't helping." I grab the pillow next to me and press it over my head, blocking out little miss sunshine.

"Why are you in such a good mood today, anyway?"

"I'm just happy you're here. Is that okay, or do I need to shut up?"

"Well, now you've made me feel like a colossal bitch. Yes, it's fine that you're happy I'm here. In fact, why don't we go out today and do some retail therapy?"

"Sure. What do you have in mind? Shoes? Handbags? Jewelry?"

"I'm thinking lingerie. You need some hot lingerie now that you're a sex siren. No virginal bride stuff for you." Her expression turns sour. "I meant it as a good thing. You did what you came here for... right?"

"Yes, but I thought it would be followed by a heck of a lot more sex."

"It will be. Hunter will be chomping at the bit to get in your panties again when the pain meds wear off, and he can get his dick to stand at attention. Those drugs don't generally lend themselves to raging boners." I thought that would get at least a smile out of her, but she's not up for me poking fun or talking about her getting a good poke!

"I've messaged and called Hunter countless times, and he won't reply to either. I wanted to stay with him that night at the hospital, but he didn't want me there."

"How do you know where he is now?"

"His bodyguard. He let me know when he got out of surgery, and I may or may not have probed him for Hunter's whereabouts."

"So, you and he did the nasty, and now he's not returning your calls?" I want to slam his already broken hand with a sledgehammer right about now.

"Something like that." I don't know whether to hug her or shake her.

"You did what you set out to do. The training wheels are off. Why don't you just leave it at that?"

"Because..." God, she's hopeless. I told her she wasn't cut out for all sex, no feelings.

"He makes your panties tingle?"

"Zee, I had no idea it could be so amazing. Now I know why people are obsessed with sex. I just want to climb him like a spider monkey every minute of the day, and he won't even talk to me."

"You really like him, don't you? It's more than just sex. Am I right?"

"Yes. I'm clearly incapable of the meaningless-sex thing."

"You know what your problem is? Your heart is linked to your vagina. It happens. In fact, I think most women have that problem. Not me, obviously."

"I don't believe you. How can you have such an amazing physical connection with someone but not feel anything for them?" Faith is the only person who can make me feel bad about my sexual appetite. She doesn't mean to, but we're just so different in that respect. When she asks me questions—even though I know it's just her being inquisitive—I feel like Julia Roberts in *Pretty Woman*.

"I feel plenty at the time... appreciation for their mad skills and excitement and exhilaration for that new experience along with spine-tingling joy from all the amazing orgasms. Just because I don't instantly fall in love with a guy doesn't mean I'm heartless. I can separate sex, infatuation, and love. It's a gift." Faith breezes past my statement. I don't think she knows what to do with me half the time.

"So how do I get him to talk to me?"

"If you know where he is, then go there. He can't ignore you if you're standing right in front of his face."

"Will you come with me?" I walked straight into that one.

"What?"

"Come with me. You always make me stronger than I feel. I need you. I know I don't have the right to ask you for more help. You've already done so much for me this week, but what if he slams the door in my face?"

"Of course, I'll come. If he tries to slam the door in your face, I'm going to slam it on his balls. You're amazing, and he's lucky that you want to give him the time of day!" Her smile brightens, and I can't be annoyed as she pulls me into her arms.

"You're a legend, Zee. What would I do without you?"

"It doesn't even bear thinking about! You'd be a mess."

"You mean more of a mess?"

"Hey, don't put yourself down. That's my job." She tickles my side. She knows I hate being tickled more than anything else in the world.

"You love me."

"I do. Now, please, for the love of God, get me some coffee."

———

"What do you think?" Faith holds up some super freaky red panties.

"Put the hooker panties back. Red is a rookie mistake. I don't know when the idea was planted in women's brains that red is what guys find sexy."

"They don't?" Her expression is so bewildered, it's cute.

"Oh, my sweet, innocent friend. No. Red is tacky. Black is always the better choice. It's sexy, it looks good against any skin tone, and it flatters any size curves."

"Then I'm doing something right! Ninety percent of my underwear is black." She dips the back of her jeans just low enough to show me the tip of her panties and a whole lot of ass-crack.

"I did NOT need to see that."

"You've seen my butt plenty. We live together."

"Do we? You've barely been at the new place. Your shit is still in boxes in your bedroom." She scrunches her nose before giving me her best puppy dog eyes.

"I'll get around to it. After the Hall of Fame, I'll be done working for Hunter and will probably slob around the apartment in my granny panties and sweats, depressed that my epic sex is over and done with."

"No slobbing! Don't let a man dictate your mood. Ride him and side him." I start picking out some bras and panties for her to try. She's hopeless on her own.

"What does that even mean?"

"It means... fuck 'em and chuck 'em. Hunter Vaughn does not get to be the one to walk away with your cherry and make you feel bad about it. You ride him, and then you *side*line him." She rolls her eyes at me as she gravitates toward all manner of strange-colored underwear.

"What about this?" She holds up a super cute teddy, but that's not the look we're going for. Faith needs less cute and more siren.

"Step away from the girlfriend lingerie. This stuff is sexy when you're dating. You need variety. For straight-up, can't say no, drop to his knees begging to bury his head between your thighs sex, we're sticking to black."

"When did you become the Hitler of my underwear?"

"Since you asked me to help you seduce one of the hottest men in NFL history." I grab her arm and drag her toward the changing rooms, thrusting a whole bunch of items I picked out at her. "Now go try these on."

"Yes, ma'am."

While I'm here, I may as well treat myself to some new undies. It's not until I'm on the other side of the shop that I hear Faith shouting my name.

"Zee! I'm stuck." For God's sake. Everyone within earshot is trying not to laugh as I scurry across to my best friend shouting like she's at a football game. "I'm stuck!"

"Jesus. Keep the hollering down to a roar, Faith." I reach for the door to her changing room, but it's still locked. "Open the door, genius."

"Hang on. I can't reach it. My arms are stuck. This stupid teddy is tangled in my hair."

"How can I help you if I can't get in?"

"Can you fit under the door? Hang on, let me try to get the lock." She bangs against the door, but it's still locked. "Seriously, Zee, I need you to shimmy under the door. I'm freaking out, and I'm about to rip a clump of hair out trying to get free."

I look to the bottom of the stall. There's probably a foot between the door and the floor. Fuck. I'm going to have to lie down on a store changing room floor and push myself through into a stupidly cramped space.

"I hate you right now. My stomach is already churning from the hangover, and now I'm going to gag crawling under this door. You're so paying for my new underwear, and I'm going to buy the most expensive thing in here."

"Deal. Just get me out of this." If all eyes weren't on me before, they are now. I drop my purse on the floor, along with the items Faith is now going to be buying for me, and lie down. Ugh. This is so gross. I'm going to need five showers after this. I'm not a germaphobe, but I might be after today.

"Move away from the door, Faith. Otherwise, I'm about to get an eyeful of your snatch. The objective was to find you something that would get Hunter in this position, not me." I grab the bottom of the door and pull myself through, and sure enough, Faith is a sight to behold. I can't contain my amusement.

"Stop laughing at me!"

"If you could see you right now, you'd be laughing, too."

"There's a full-length mirror in here, and I can see how ridiculous I look. Now, get me out of this."

When I manage to squirm into the room and shimmy my legs so I can stand up, I'm pretty sure I just peed a little, I am laughing so hard. Hunter Vaughn in a tutu would be more graceful than Faith is right now. I don't even know how she's managed to contort herself like a pretzel in such a small scrap of fabric.

Her arms are up over her head, one of the straps is tangled in her hair, and the other is across her face, smushing her nose like a pig. I'm fighting every urge I have to snap a picture of her right now.

"Holy shit, woman. How do you get yourself into these messes?"

"I don't know. Help me!"

"Well, I guess we're buying this one." I grab the thin scraps of lace and rip. With a sigh of relief as the teddy is left hanging from her hair, I'm accosted by her breasts.

"Thank God. I think I pulled a muscle."

"Thank God? Thank me, the best friend a woman could ask for. I've seen way more of you than I needed today. Tell me at least some of this looked good on you before you made yourself a teddy straight jacket."

"Yes. I'm buying everything."

"Maybe they won't notice that this is torn to shreds," I say as I untangle it from her hair. "It's a shame. I bet you looked great in it. I'm sure Hunter would appreciate it."

"I can't even get him to call me back."

"Well, we're going to remedy that tonight when we fly back to Nashville. He'll be the one ripping off your underwear... with his teeth." Her cheeks blush. Damn, she's got it bad. Turning up on his doorstep better work.

What the hell was I thinking? Faith and I are five minutes away from our destination—a stranger's house that we're not invited to. Scratch that. We're going to a *celebrity's* house, one who I've conjured in my fantasies to flick the bean on more than one occasion.

I'm reminding myself that I'm about to make a jackass of myself for Faith. If nothing else, I'm a stellar best friend. If she's going to make a fool of herself chasing after Hunter Vaughn, then I'm going to be the dipshit at her side, ready to give him a piece of my mind if he doesn't let us in.

Hunter Vaughn may have had a bad week, but unless he's dead or his dick literally fell off, he shouldn't be ghosting my girl. She told him she was a virgin. He knew the score. You don't quit answering a woman after you pop her cherry unless you're a fucking teenage boy, and I know enough about this guy to know he's not lacking in the experience department. He's an NFL legend with a legendary sex life—not who I'd have chosen for Faith to take her maiden voyage with, but she's a grown-ass woman, and no one gets to decide for her.

I'm a little nervous as we edge closer to our destination, and anyone who knows me knows that I don't get nervous—ever. I've been a Titans fan since I was old enough to talk. I never miss a game, and Cooper Danford and Hunter Vaughn were the dream team, the all-time greatest duo in Titans history. *I'm starstruck.*

I don't want to make an ass of myself in front of either of them, but if Faith gets the cold shoulder or they turn us away on the doorstep, I'm going to make a scene. It's inevitable. No one messes with my best friend and lives to tell the tale with their manhood intact.

As we pull up in the driveway, it's just as ritzy as I imagined it to be. This place must have set him back a few million. Just what you'd expect from an NFL star. I tip the Uber driver and grab our bags from the trunk. Faith looks like she's going to blow chunks any second.

"Are you ready for this?" I wrap my arm around her shoulder, trying to calm her nerves, but I don't think I'm helping.

"This was a bad idea."

"Where's the Faith who set out with a goal to get laid good and proper this summer? He does not get to turn you into a simpering idiot."

"You're right." She stops and grabs her phone from her pocket, typing out a quick message. There's a sly grin on her face that tells me she's up to some mischief.

"Are we going to stay out here, or are you going to knock on the door?"

"Just wait a minute." It's raining, so obviously, she'd want to stand outside. What the hell? Her phone beeps, and I realize what she's up to. Well played, Faith. She's texting him.

When she's ready, I follow her to the doorstep and wait anxiously for Hunter to answer the door. He doesn't disappoint. The second he sees Faith, he's on her like white on rice sucking face in the rain—all chick-flick fantastic. I have ceased to exist in her world.

I'm severely out of place right now, so I move to sidestep them and head inside, but I'm stopped in my tracks.

Holy Jesus, Mary, and Joseph.

My breath hitches, my chest constricts, and my knees almost buckle beneath me at the sight of Cooper Danford standing in the doorway, devouring me with his ice-blue gaze.

CHAPTER TWO
COOP

HOLY SHIT.

I don't even know her name or why she's standing on my doorstep right now, but whatever brought her here, I'm happy for the sudden turn of events in my day.

Hunter has been hiding out here since he had surgery on his hand, but if I'd known Faith was going to show up with a smoking hot friend in tow, I would've called her myself and drawn a map to my place.

"Hi, I'm Zoey. You must be Cooper. Mind if I come in and leave this feral pair to snack on each other's faces?" So this is the best friend. *Damn!* Hunter and Faith are too wrapped up in each other to set foot inside the door. Zoey is getting rained on while waiting for them to stop sucking face, so I hold open the door and welcome her in.

She strides past me like she owns the place. I like her already. Leaving Hunter to do his thing, I follow behind Zoey, enjoying the view.

"Make yourself at home. I wasn't expecting guests, so you'll have to excuse the mess."

She drops her bag at the side of the couch and wanders over to the kitchen island before turning to look at me—really look at me.

"You're even hotter in person than you are on TV. The football gear is sexy and all, but fuck me, wow..." She doesn't finish her sentence, leaving me hanging. I get the impression I could be in for a lot of that in the next twenty-four hours.

"I'll take that as a compliment. Can I get you a drink?"

"Sure. Wine if you have it."

"Red or white?" As I walk past her toward the fridge, anticipating she'll ask for white wine, the scent of her perfume hangs in the air between us. She smells good enough to eat, and right now, the thought of feasting on her makes my cock twitch. "Chanel?"

"I'd rather not drink my perfume. Red wine will do just fine, thanks."

"I had you pegged for white, maybe even sparkling." She gives me a sly grin.

"You'd do well to avoid pegging me at all, champ. I'm not the kind of girl who fits into whatever cookie cutter you think I came from."

"Sassy. I like it." I grab a bottle and pour her a generous glass of pinot noir.

"I bet you do." Oh, this girl is a minx. This weekend just got *very* interesting.

When Hunter finally comes up for air, I can tell he's giving Zoey a wide berth. I find it supremely amusing—the mighty Hunter Vaughn, scared to come and talk with his fuck buddy's best friend. In his defense, she's glaring at him something fierce as he disappears, dragging their bags to the guest room. I'd help him, but I think he needs a few minutes alone to compose himself.

"So, how did you guys meet?"

Faith drops down onto the couch across from her friend, and as I grab her a glass and pour her a drink, I see why Hunter is so smitten. She's beautiful. He never stood a chance of holding out on her.

"Are you going to stare at her all night? Creepy much?" Zoey slings back her wine like it's grape juice.

"Careful, Zoey, you sound a little jealous." I don't know why, but I want to ruffle her feathers a little.

"In your dreams." I top up her glass. Getting just a fraction too close, a buzz of electricity runs through my veins when her breath catches ever so slightly. She's quick to mask it. "Do you not understand personal space?"

"The lady doth protest too much. I think you enjoy having me up close and personal. You already admitted you think I'm hot. No need to backtrack now."

"You have a high opinion of yourself, Cooper Danford."

"Those were your words, not mine." There's a twinkle in her eye. She likes the bravado. It's written all over her face.

Faith breaks the tension, launching into some funny stories about her dad. It's always good to get the dirt on Coach, and she's definitely got a flair for comedy. As much as I'm enjoying listening to her, I can't take my eyes off Zoey. She's stunning.

When Hunter finds his balls again, he strides into the living room and straight over to Faith before sitting down next to her and pulling her into his lap.

"Your room is set up, ladies. What have I missed?"

What the ever-loving-fuck? I have never seen Hunter doing any kind of PDA with a woman he's dating. Come to think of it, I don't think I've ever seen him dating. Picking someone up at a club or after a game—sure. Watching him with Faith right now is some *Twilight Zone* shit. Zoey looks as shocked as I feel.

"Fuck. You guys aren't fuck buddies. You're legit into each other."

"Thanks, bro. No pressure." Holy shit. Zoey's stare snaps to Hunter, her eyes burning a hole right through his forehead.

Faith recognizes the warning signs from her friend and jumps to Hunter's defense. "There's no label."

"She's not my fuck buddy. This is real." I'm not about to poke the bear. I know when my best friend is serious and when I should keep my mouth shut. I'm speechless. When Hunter rocked up here last week with a busted hand, I thought there might be more to this fling with Faith than just sex, but I wasn't prepared for him to have real feelings.

Zoey doesn't have the same problem as me. She's not backward in coming forward when it comes to advocating for her best friend.

"You get one chance. Hurt her or ghost her the way you did this week, and I'll break your other hand, and your legs, and your face. Got it?" She's feisty as fuck, and I just want to jump her right now.

"Yes, ma'am." Hunter isn't going to mess with her, that's for sure.

"Well, all right then. Enough of the Spanish Inquisition. What have you boys got for entertainment around here?" Hell, yes. If she wants to be entertained, I'm more than happy to oblige.

"Boozing, banging, and boxing." The three Bs of a good night, and if I play my cards right, I can add the fourth B to the equation —breasts.

"Boxing?" Seriously, that's what she heard?

"X-Box. That's what you chose to pick up on?" She gives me a sly grin.

"Well, I already have the booze, and these two are the ones who are going to be banging." The glint in her eye and the way she bites her bottom lip gives her away. She's teasing me.

"I'm a gracious host, Zoey. I wouldn't want you to feel left out. I'll happily provide you with as much banging as you can handle." My cock twitches at the thought of getting her underneath me. I like her sexy little mouth.

"You couldn't handle me, Coop." There's an undertone to her words. If she wants to challenge me, I'm up for it, or I'd happily die trying.

Hunter whispers something in Faith's ear before taking her hand and leading her down the hall. One thing's for sure, Faith isn't sleeping in the guest room tonight.

And then there were two.

"Can I get you another drink?"

"Sure. One down, right? Just the banging and boxing to go. Do you have anything harder?" There are so many things I want to say right now, but I hold my tongue. I guess my face didn't get the memo. "I mean liquor. You have such a dirty mind."

"I said nothing. If anything, you're the one with the dirty mind. Tell me, what *hard* thing did you assume I was thinking of?" Her eyes rake the length of me, her gaze coming to a standstill when she reaches my crotch.

"Vodka. Do you have any vodka?"

"Sure." I can feel her eyes on me as I walk over to the liquor cabinet. "You want it straight up or with a mixer?"

"Mixer. Do you mind if I go check out the options in your refrigerator?"

"Have at it, girl. Mi casa es su casa." The ease with which she navigates my place is sexy as hell. There's no insecurity or trepidation. She knows what she wants, and she's not afraid to ask for it. I wonder if that translates to the bedroom.

With a double shot of vodka for her and a scotch for myself, I go to where her fine little ass is sticking out from behind my refrigerator door.

"Would you like ice?"

She grabs a bottle of cranberry juice from the fridge and closes the door, twisting her body to face me. "No ice. I like it... hot."

The heat in her eyes is all the encouragement I need, but I sense she likes a game of cat and mouse. We both know how tonight is going to end. She's going to be spread eagle with my face buried between her thighs. I brush past her, dropping a few ice cubes into my glass, and she watches me as I take a sip, pulling one of the cubes of ice into my mouth. The spark in her eyes lets me know I'm on the right track.

Dipping my head down, I brush my lips against her neck, letting the tip of the ice slide over her skin before pulling back ever so slightly. I need her permission. Seconds feel like hours as I hover millimeters from her lips. Her scent is intoxicating, but I quell the urge to hoist her up onto the kitchen island and bury myself deep inside her.

She's even more beautiful up close. There's a vulnerability in the way she drops her gaze. The rapid rise and fall of her chest are betraying her cool, calm exterior.

She takes a step back, putting some distance between us. She doesn't bother adding the cranberry to her drink, instead slinging it back in a single gulp.

"So, Cooper, we both know you're a player." Something in her eyes tells me she's a bit of a player herself.

"Does that bother you?"

"Not at all. I'm a firm advocate of the one-night stand. No pesky attachments. No strings. Just hot, sweaty sex and plenty of orgasms. Can you handle that?"

I move toward her, stopping just shy of her lips. I can almost taste her, her breath soft and shallow as she fights the magnetic pull between us.

"If you want it, Zoey, take it. You can have whatever you want from me tonight. All you have to do is take it." I rest my arms on either side of her, bracing the cold granite in an attempt to hold back. Who am I kidding? There's no way I'm going to be able to stop myself once I get a taste of her. Every nerve ending in my body cries out for her touch, but I don't even know her, yet she's in my home, invading my space. Unless she makes it crystal clear what she wants from me, I'm going to tear myself away, lock myself in my room, and crack one out in a less-than-satisfactory self-inflicted release.

She slides her hand between us, running it down my chest, her lips still just out of reach. As her fingers trail over the waistband of my jeans, I can't hide how much I want her. It's evident in my erection straining to be unleashed, my cock twitching as she rubs up and down the length of me.

"Fuck me, you have quite the anaconda." She bites down on her bottom lip, her eyes staring up at me through hooded lids.

"What are you waiting for, Zoey? It's yours for the taking." I press my hips forward, letting her get a firm grip on me.

"Maybe I don't want you."

"The way your hand is palming my cock right now, I call bullshit. You want me." It's taking every ounce of self-control I have not to fist my hands in her hair and take her in what I know will be an explosive first kiss.

"And you want me. Your cock tells me everything I need to know."

"Then kiss me. What are you waiting for?" She wants the upper hand. I'd guess she's used to guys begging her for it. I hold her gaze, my body on fire at the desire I see reflected back at me. "You've got your hand on my cock. I'd say you've already shown your hand."

"If that's the case, it's your move, Cooper. Show me what you're made of. Kiss me, ravage me, strip me naked, and fuck me." *Holy shit.* It's been a long time since a woman has turned me on this much without so much as a kiss.

I press my lips to her cheek, ghosting the faintest of kisses on her skin before moving my lips to her ear, whispering softly, "Tell me you want it. You take it, or you say it. Your choice. I'm ready and waiting, but you already know that. What's it going to be, Zoey?"

Before I get a chance to step back, she pulls me close, her hips replacing her hand, grinding against my cock in a desperate plea. Fisting her hands in my hair, her lips crash down on mine, our tongues twisting and tangling in a frenzied fuck. In an instant, my hands are all over her, exploring every tight curve and lifting her into my arms.

"Wrap your legs around my waist." She does as I ask, tugging on my hair, forcing me to look at her.

"Now tell me you want me, Cooper."

"I fucking want you." I practically run down the hallway to my bedroom, eager to lock the door behind us and lose myself in this woman for hours. This wasn't how I expected my day to go, but I'm really fucking glad she showed up on my doorstep.

I lay her down on my bed, a little roughly, as I pull my shirt over my head and discard it on the floor.

"Take off your clothes, Zoey. I want to see that body of yours before I give in to your demands and 'ravage' you." She oozes self-confidence, her gaze fixed on mine as she strips down to her underwear.

"Cute panties. You always wear Hello Kitty?"

"I wasn't exactly planning on dropping trou today."

"You're fucking hot."

"Are we done discussing my underwear? I can think of better things for you to be doing with that mouth of yours."

"Not one for small talk?"

"It's not necessary. I don't need to be wined or dined. You don't need to whisper sweet nothings to me or pay me any compliments. I'm already close to naked on your bed, and you have something I want. It's as complicated and as simple as that. Now lose your pants."

"Yes, ma'am." I unzip my fly and push my jeans down, letting my erection spring free. I'm rewarded with a dark and sensual smile as she takes in the sight of me, rock hard and ready for her.

I move over to my nightstand, grabbing a condom packet and dropping it on the bed before reaching for her ankles and pulling her toward me.

"Is this what you want, Zoey?" Without a word, she unhooks her bra and throws it at me. "Fuck me, your tits are perfect."

"Yeah, I know," she says, letting her hands drift up her torso, cupping her breasts. *Jesus Christ.* I'm going to come before I get anywhere near her if she keeps this up. I position myself at the bottom of the bed, sliding my hands up her legs, hooking my fingers under the waistband of her panties. I've never understood the allure of boy shorts on a woman until now. Even with cartoon characters on them, she looks sexy as hell. Anticipation unfurls in my stomach, causing a strange flutter of nerves I'm not used to.

She lifts her hips just enough for me to pull her panties off and throw them on my bedroom floor. Holy fuck, her body is glorious. I drop between her legs, pushing them open as my lips crash down on hers, the soft swell of her breasts pressed tight to my chest. Her lips are so full and pouty, and her tongue—this girl's mouth was made for sin. Every lick and stroke have a direct line to my cock, and my brain is on overload.

Zoey is ravenous, her hands roaming my body as she hooks one leg around my waist, grinding her warm skin against my junk. God, she's already wet for me. I kiss and nip my way from her lips, down her neck, enjoying the shiver that runs through her when I hit a sweet spot behind her ear. Her nipples tighten, and I can't wait any longer to taste them.

While I suck one into my mouth, she pulls on the other, sending me into a tailspin. Every flick of my tongue has her writhing beneath me. I make my way down her body, my fingers trailing between her legs, my mouth following hot on their heels.

Wrapping my arms underneath her hips, I hold her in place as I take her with one long, languorous lick. Fuck, she tastes good—sweet, warm, and better than honey.

She lets out a raspy moan as she circles her hips, pushing against my mouth, forcing me to take more of her. It's so fucking hot. I want to be everywhere at once—kissing her lips, tasting her arousal, sinking my cock balls-deep inside her to feel the warmth of her core as her muscles tighten around me.

Her body responds to my touch, quickly reaching a fever pitch as I continue to lick, flick, and kiss her clit. It's not long enough for me—I could do this for hours and never tire of the taste of her—but there's no way in hell I'm going to deprive her of what she so clearly craves. Fisting her hands in my hair, she takes control, riding my face to an intense orgasm.

I want to hear her screaming my name, but she doesn't give me the satisfaction, instead shouting to the heavens as she crashes over the edge.

"Oh God, yes! Don't stop... holy shit... God, yes!" Even her low and raspy voice is dripping with sex, a seductress in every way possible. When she attempts to shift out of my grasp, I press down on her hips, holding her in place.

"Not so fast, Zoey. One orgasm isn't going to be enough. You're going to scream until you are hoarse, coming over and over again until you can't take it anymore. Then and only then am I going to give you what you really want... my cock."

She bucks wildly, losing herself to the pleasure I inflict on her body, but she resists calling my name, making me want it even more. Zoey takes it all, time after time, riding my face with reckless abandon. It's not until her legs are shaking uncontrollably that I reach for the condom packet. She pulls it from my hand, ripping it open with her teeth before sliding it over the head of my cock, her hand gripping me tightly as she rolls it down the length of me.

"God, you're hard as a rock." She continues to caress me, positioning me at her entrance. I stop myself, teasing her just a little and for as long as I can stand it. "What are you waiting for? Fuck me."

"Say my name."

"Is that what gets you off? Having a woman scream your name?" She looks me dead in the eye, her gaze oozing sex appeal. She knows she's sexy. She owns it with no apology.

"No. I want to hear *you* saying my name as I sink balls-deep inside you. You think my mouth is skilled? I haven't even begun to show you what I'm capable of."

"Then do it. Take me. You know you're desperate to feel my tight little pussy around your cock."

"Not until you say it."

"And if I don't?"

"Then I guess I'm going to have blue balls. It's one little word, Zoey. Just... one... word. I want to hear my name tripping off those pouty lips of yours." I don't even know why I'm challenging her. My cock is screaming at me to shut the hell up and fuck her, but she's got all the power here, and this is the only way to even the playing field.

"Come on, champ." She wraps her fist around the base of my cock. "You know you want it." It takes every morsel of self-control in my body to pull back, but the second I move to get off the bed, she grabs my wrist.

"Get back here and fuck me, Cooper." Holy shit, her sultry rasp is even sexier than I thought it would be as my name falls from her lips. "Are you happy now? I said it. I want you, Coop. Now finish what you started." She doesn't have to tell me twice.

I push her legs open and take her in one hard, punishing thrust of my hips. Jesus Christ, she feels good, and the way she moans as I hammer into her over and over again, it's fucking music to my ears.

"That's it, baby. Let me hear you." I wrap one arm underneath her, around her waist, tilting her body to just the right angle to take all of me.

"Oh fuck! Yes, Coop! Oh God... harder." She throws her hands up, gripping the headboard as she writhes beneath me, grinding her hips with every thrust of mine. My lips crash down on hers, our tongues setting the same punishing rhythm—thrusting, fucking, and desperate for more.

When I can't hold back any longer, I chase my release, rearing up on my knees, watching as Zoey falls apart, her body so fucking beautiful.

"Come with me, baby. I want to hear you come again." I grab her hips and thrust, angling myself just right so that she feels every stroke of my cock, hard and fast, pushing her over the edge. The moment her muscles tighten, I know she's right there with me, and I take her harder and faster until I come with a fucking roar.

"Coop!" Our bodies are slick with sweat as we ride out the after-shocks together before collapsing in a heap of tangled limbs. Her breath is ragged, her breasts heaving with every labored rise and fall of her chest. I already want more of her. I slide my hand into her hair, pulling her lips to mine in a lazy, sensual kiss, taking the time to explore her.

"Zoey..." I realize I don't know her last name. Maybe I should've asked her that before fucking her senseless.

"Call me, Zee. And don't talk. You'll ruin it." I'm not sure what to do as she slinks out of bed and reaches for her clothes. When she can't locate anything more than her Hello Kitty panties in the dark, she grabs my shirt and pulls it on. *Fuck me!* She makes that shirt look better than it ever has on me.

My phone starts blowing up, giving me something to focus on other than dragging her back into my bed, which is what I really want to do right now.

"What the fuck?"

CHAPTER THREE

ZEE

WHAT WAS I THINKING? If there was one guy not to have a one-night stand with, it's this one. Faith is going to kill me when she finds out. I've just made her complicated relationship with Hunter even more so. I'm stuck here with Faith until she's ready to go home, and worse, this is Coop's house. Do I just go sleep in the guest room as if nothing happened?

I don't usually sweat the goodbye after a quick fuck, although there was nothing quick about what just happened. He's got skill. I mean his mouth is just—I could ride his face for days. I lost count of how many orgasms I just had, each one more delicious than the last. Every muscle in my body is going to hurt tomorrow.

Where the hell are my clothes? I definitely had them when I came in here. After shrugging on my panties, I just grab his discarded shirt and slip it on. Coop's phone keeps pinging, followed by a thunderous, '*what the fuck*' from him.

"Everything okay? Girlfriend blowing up your phone?" I need to stop talking. *Idiot.*

"Your best friend just grabbed the headlines of literally every gossip column on the internet."

"What? She's upstairs with Hunter."

"No, she's not." He holds his phone out to me, letting me see a picture of Faith in a car with Hunter. "Apparently, she's driving my car around town, and well, you can read the rest." He drops his head back on the bed, the sheets slipping just low enough to show his mouthwatering happy trail. God, he's hot. I could jump him again right now, but I won't. I try to focus on the breaking news blast.

"Holy shit." I drop the phone on the bed and run out the door. I need to get my phone and call Faith. How the fuck does she manage to get herself into these kinds of situations?

I almost take a nosedive up the stairs I'm moving so fast. When I find my phone, I call her, but it just rings out. I try texting, but I don't get a reply. I seriously don't understand how she manages to cause mayhem wherever she goes. Making my way back to the living room, I suppose I just need to wait for her to come back.

Coop emerges from his room, looking as freshly fucked as I feel. His hair has that sex-mussed yet styled-to-perfection look about it, and I just want to grab it. I can still smell his cologne on my skin and feel the chafe of his stubble on my thighs. In nothing but a pair of low-slung sweats, he's impossibly handsome.

"Your friend is a one-woman wrecking ball. This could end Hunter's Hall of Fame nomination. Do you have any idea how much interference I'll need to run on this? And that's just the tip of the iceberg. He doesn't have a manager right now."

"I don't give a flying fuck about your friend. What about mine? She just announced that she dropped her V-Card with him. Do you have any idea how pissed her family is going to be?"

"She should've thought of that before shouting it from the rooftops."

I barrel over to where he stands and poke him in the chest. "Say another word about her, and I'll kick you in the nuts."

"I doubt that. You seemed rather partial to them twenty minutes ago." He's infuriating as fuck, and I hate that he's not wrong.

"Shut up. Why couldn't your friend just keep his dipstick to himself?"

"She was all over him like a rash. He's been trying to hold her off since the day they met. A guy only has so much willpower. You ever think maybe she should've just taken him at his word and left him alone?"

"Right, because guys are known for walking away from a willing pussy."

"Is this about them, or are you just pissed that you jumped into bed with me?" I'm about to slap him in the face when he grasps my hand.

"Let go of me. You're an asshole."

"That may be the case, but I think you like it. I think you *hate* that you like it. Tell me I'm wrong. Your body told me everything I needed to know, Zoey. I can still taste your arousal."

"You weren't exactly having a bad time, big boy." I find myself smiling at his wry grin, and it bugs me. I don't like that he sees right through my nonchalant demeanor.

"We're not talking about me. I'll freely admit that I thoroughly enjoyed fucking you." He loosens his grip, his other hand caressing my cheek. "You don't need me to tell you you're a great lay."

I don't know what comes over me. I launch myself at him, my lips finding his in a passionate kiss. There's something animalistic in my desire to feel his body against mine. He throws me down on the couch, about to embark on a repeat performance when we hear the roar of an engine pull into the driveway.

I scramble to my feet, suddenly all too aware of my lack of clothing. At least his t-shirt is long enough to cover my ass. Whatever the hell just happened, it'll have to wait until we deal with Faith's latest clusterfuck.

Coop and I are standing in the doorway when they appear. I'm surprised that Hunter looks pretty chill until he catches a glimpse of his friend's steely gaze.

"What the fuck?"

"Where did it break?"

"*TMZ*. Pictures *and* about half of the audio recorded on a phone."

"Fucking hell." He heads inside, leaving me to grill Faith.

I pull her behind me, heading straight for the guest room, slamming the door shut behind us.

"What were you thinking?" She has the good sense to realize I'm not kidding around. This is serious.

"How bad is it?"

"Bad. Coop says he's going to get his manager to step in and run interference while Hunter organizes some PR to mitigate it. It's not going to be a good look for him. It'll take about three seconds for people to do the math when they see your last name. The minute they connect the dots, they're all going to think he's a cradle robber who deflowered his mentor's daughter. There's no good way to spin that." I hate to see the hurt in her eyes, but this is no time for sugarcoating. We need to get ahead of this. She needs to be prepared for the backlash coming her way and will most definitely be heading in Hunter's direction.

"I should've left him alone when he asked me to. I shouldn't have pushed him to be with me." There's nothing I can say as she takes in the sight of me. She can tell exactly what I've been doing in her absence. It doesn't exactly leave me with a leg to stand on. "Seems I'm not the only one who's been up to no good."

"Girl, I can categorically attest to the fact that what I was doing was good. Insanely good. Really, unbelievably, toe-curling amazing." I didn't want to admit that. I seem to be contracting her verbal diarrhea.

"Okay, I get it. TMI." She didn't just say that to me. I grab my phone, pull up *TMZ*, and hold it up to her face.

"I don't think you get to say TMI ever again."

Faith goes deathly silent, reading the article, her eyes going wide as saucers as she takes it all in.

"I need a drink." That I can help with. I rifle through my bag for some shorts before heading downstairs in search of the hard liquor. Coop and Hunter are deep in conversation as I shuffle past, aware that Hunter is now getting an eyeful. He whispers something to Coop that gets him a glare and a 'shut the fuck up.'

I grab the vodka off the counter, ready to head back upstairs, but Faith appears in the living room, her phone to her ear. Shit—it's her dad. The boys go quiet as Faith attempts to diffuse the situation, but her dad is yelling so loud, we can't help but overhear the entire conversation.

"I have to go. I'll call you in a few days once this all calms down. Don't worry about me, I'm okay. Zee is with me."

He doesn't relent, calling her disgusting, shaming her for wanting to have a physical relationship, which frankly is none of his goddamn business. I hate seeing Faith so upset, and in the end, I grab the phone. I know her better than anyone, and his tirade is going to crush her.

"Hello, Mr. Fairchild, this is Zoey. I don't want y'all to say anything else that you might regret, so I'm going to hang up the phone just now and let you and Faith calm down a little. I'll be right by her side while this plays out in the media. I'm sorry you're upset, but I need to think about Faith. I don't intend to be disrespectful, but I'm hanging up now." I shut off the phone and throw it on the table. I hope Faith isn't mad at me for doing that, but shit, she's the nicest person you could ever meet. She doesn't deserve any of this.

Unfortunately, my best friend has a knack for putting her foot in her mouth. No one could anticipate what happened tonight, but berating her about it will not change anything. It'll only make her feel worse. She doesn't say anything but turns to Hunter, looking positively lovestruck as he stares back at her.

Coop breaks the silence. "Zee, I think I love you. That was hot as fuck. Let's leave these two to digest today's events. I need you in my bedroom. Now." A thrill courses through me at the prospect of following him back to bed, but I take Faith's hand in mine.

"Do you want me to stay with you tonight? We can go to the guest room."

"No, you go get yours, girl." I can't help the giggle that escapes me. Is it wrong that I'm so relieved she doesn't want to bunk with me?

"Love you, friend." Before I get a chance to hug her, Coop grabs my hand and practically drags me down the hall like a caveman.

Faith is in good hands with Hunter. There's nothing else we can do tonight. It's late, and this problem will sure as shit still be here in the morning. As soon as the door shuts behind us, Coop flips the lock and pushes me back against the wall.

"What you just did for Faith... that was fucking hot." He slides his fingers under the hem of his shirt I'm wearing, trailing his fingers up my side. "I'm going to lick every last inch of your body. You good with that?" A jolt of electricity shoots straight to my core as his eyes find mine, smoldering with the promise of a night I won't forget.

"Only if I get to lick yours." Without another word, I reach for the waistband of his sweats and let my hand follow his happy trail.

"Deal." He lifts me into his arms, walking me over to the bed with a reverence I find disconcerting.

We explore each other's bodies for hours, the sun rising by the time we fall into an exhausted slumber. I'm not the girl who wants to snuggle or fall asleep wrapped in a man's arms, but I let myself, just this once. His shallow, even breaths are comforting, and I'm too tired to drag my ass upstairs for the sake of what's essentially a power nap at this point.

All hell is sure to break loose when the world is awake, and people hear Faith's drive-thru confession. She's going to need me, and Coop seems like the kind of guy who's going to get behind his friend and do whatever he can to help. We can allow ourselves a few hours to forget that we're strangers who had one incredible night together. I'll deal with my own clusterfuck once I get Faith back on track.

Faith has been a wreck these past few days. I took a couple of days off work to support her, and we've been laying low at Coop's the entire time, but today, I need to get back to reality and back to work.

Watching how she and Hunter interact, it's clear that they are so much more than a wager. They are completely smitten with each other, and I'm confident after probing him more than once about his intentions when it comes to my best friend, he's more than capable of taking it from here.

It's been a strange couple of days. Coop and I have fallen into bed more times than I can count as well as in the shower, the tub, the kitchen floor in the middle of the night. It's not exactly been your typical one-night stand, and we're bound to see each other again now that our closest friends are officially a couple.

When I pack up my things, I look around the guest room. I left my bag in here under the ruse that I was just sleeping in Coop's bed for convenience after long nights of fucking, but I wasn't kidding anyone, not even myself.

Faith and I hug it out before I leave, and she holds me tight. "Thank you, Zee. I couldn't have gotten through the past few days without you. You're a legend."

"I think you would've been just fine. You're strong, kiddo. Don't let anyone ever convince you otherwise."

"I love you. Call me when you get back to the apartment."

"Will do." As I head out the door to wait for my Uber, Coop comes bounding out the front door.

"Why did you call an Uber? I can drive you home."

"You're busy. I don't want to be an inconvenience." He slides his hands into my hair, pulling me in for one last kiss.

"When will I see you again?"

"I'm sure we'll see each other around. Our friends are dating, and we're bound to bump into each other every once in a while." As my Uber arrives in the driveway, I force myself out of his arms even though my heart is hammering in my chest.

"Zee..." I pick up my bag and open the car door.

"Later, Coop. It's been fun. Thanks for the hospitality." I don't look back as I slide into the back seat and slam the door shut. I've never had a three-day one-nighter before, and I won't be doing it again. It's too messy, and besides, my vagina needs time to recover from the great Cooper Danford. That man is hung like a horse and knows how to use it.

By the time I pull up at my apartment across town, I'm happy to be home and in my comfort zone. It's time to get back to real life. Falling in love and having epic sex with an NFL god is perfect for someone like Faith, but not me. It was fun to dip my toe in the water and forget about my problems for a few days, but reality waits for no man—or woman.

I soak my aching muscles in the tub for well over an hour, remembering every second of toe-curling passion that made me sore in the first place. I'm a little sad when I can no longer smell Coop's cologne on my skin, but it's time for this Cinderella to get back to normal.

When I rented this place, I was expecting that Faith and I would make a ton of happy memories here, and we'd make this our home. I get the distinct feeling that she may not end up living here after her summer job is over. Something tells me she'll have a new roommate by then.

It's nice to crawl under the covers of my own bed and switch on the television for some background noise. *Entertainment Tonight* is still running the audio on Faith's drive-thru faux pas. I can't help but chuckle at the excitement in her voice. God, I love that woman to bits.

I drift off with the television still on, but my dreams are of someone else entirely—someone I have no desire to fantasize about from this point on.

The girls at work have been on me for days, looking for all the gory details that didn't make it onto *TMZ*. They know me better than to think I'd actually give them the dirt on Faith. If there's one thing I'm good at, it's keeping my mouth shut. If only I were as good at keeping my legs shut.

I hate to admit that I've flicked the bean with Coop in mind more times than I can count since I got home. Faith has been messaging me, asking if she can give him my number. She's not supposed to have told me he asked for it more than once, but she hasn't given in yet. I begged her not to hand it over. If he calls me, I'll agree to meet up with him, and one thing will lead to another. I'm not getting tangled up in a fling with him. He's too good between the sheets, and it's already going to take all of my self-control not to jump him on the occasions we'll inevitably be thrown into each other's company through our friends.

Faith has started sending me every cute GIF known to man, begging me to give up my number. She and Hunter are still laying low at Coop's place, so she's living in cloud cuckoo land, enjoying the bubble, and I know her—she's playing out some fantasy that we'll all live happily ever after together. I think she's going to get her fairytale with Hunter, but she needs to get the idea of Coop and me out of her head.

One of my colleagues ducks into my office.

"There's a delivery for you at the front desk."

"Thanks, Josie. I'm sure it will arrive with the rest of my mail." I have so much to get done today, I don't have time to chat.

"It's not a work thing. You need to go get it." She's wiggling her eyebrows at me, and to be honest, I just want to lock my office door and dispense with the cryptic clues.

"Sure, I'm busy right now. I'll swing by the front desk and pick it up when I have time."

"Why do you have a bug up your ass today, girl?"

"I don't. I just have a shit-ton of work to finish."

"Okay. Why don't we go out for a drink after work? Maybe you can fill me in on what's going on with you... and with Faith?"

"I'll take you up on the drink, but you're shit out of luck when it comes to Faith. You know I'm not selling her out. She gets in enough trouble without me making it worse."

"Fair enough." She disappears, leaving me to break the back on my workload for this week. I've been a little distracted with everything that's been going on, but my clients won't wait for my personal problems.

An hour later, I get a text from Faith.

Faith: *Did you get anything nice today?*

    Me: *What? I'm at work.*

    Faith: *OK. Will you come over this weekend?*

    Me: *Where are you going to be?*

    Faith: *Still at Coop's.*

    Me: *Why don't you come spend the weekend at our place? You know you have a room, right?*

    Faith: *Hunter wants me to keep a low profile until everything calms down. Please, please come here for the weekend.*

    Me: *No can do. Talk soon.*

I put my phone on silent and throw it in my purse. I love Faith, but I'm not going back to Coop's place. This job is kicking my ass, but for some ungodly reason, I thought it would be a good idea to become an accountant. Could I find a less sexy profession?

When my brain is scrambled, I remember there's a mystery package at reception for me. I wander down the hall, stopping to make myself a much-needed coffee. As I round the corner, I can feel my cheeks flush at the sight of the reception desk. Why didn't Josie tell me to come get this package because it's embarrassing as hell? That would've gotten my ass out of my office a heck of a lot faster.

The receptionist gives me her brightest smile as I walk up and grab a giant balloon phone, weighed down by a box. Jesus, this is what Faith was talking about when she messaged me earlier. I'm going to kill her.

"Gift from someone special?" I don't even make eye contact as I clear her desk of this monstrosity.

"Nope. Practical joke." I drop my gaze to the floor and hightail it back to my office. There's a card attached to a brand new iPhone box. Are you shitting me? This guy can't take a hint.

I rip the envelope and expect some smart-ass note from Coop, but there's a small part of me that's a little disappointed when I flip open the card and see that it's not from him. It's from Faith. I am going to kill her for this.

I gave Coop the number of this new phone. If you change your mind and want to talk to him, you can switch it on and probably find a few texts from him already. What's the worst that could happen?

Faith x

She's relentless, I'll give her that. As for Coop, I doubt he'll be messaging a random number. I try to leave it alone, but my intrigue gets the better of me. The phone is fully charged when I switch it on, and sure enough, there's a message from one of only two numbers programmed into the contacts—Cooper Danford. Expecting some digital-age equivalent of a love letter, I'm not prepared for the message that awaits.

He's such a jackass. A stupid, funny jackass!

CHAPTER FOUR
COOP

IF I NEED to spend another week with the lovebirds, I'm going to shoot myself in the face. It was my suggestion that they remain at my house until we get Hunter a new manager and some much- needed damage control, but man, they are loud as hell when they fuck. I've told Hunter to quit with the porn soundtrack, but it would seem Faith is unable to keep her mouth shut. If I weren't sporting some blue balls, I'd be more understanding, but holy shit, I need to go out tonight and find a hot girl of my own to make scream for a few hours.

Faith still won't give me Zee's number, and I'm assuming that's at her request. Then yesterday, she gave me a random number and told me to message it. When did I get relegated to a burner phone? Does Zee think her pussy is so magical I'm suddenly in love with her, or I'm going to become some crazy stalker? I'm Cooper-fucking-Danford. I don't need to beg for it.

It's pissing me off that I'm even thinking about Zee almost a week after she left. I caved and sent one message to the number Faith gave me—a dick pic but without my dick. Just enough of my happy trail to get her excited, but when she scrolls down, I photoshopped my johnson and replaced it with Mr. Hankey, the Christmas poo from South Park. No reply.

Showered, shaved, and looking sharp, I grab my keys and leave Hunter to defile my home some more, but at least tonight, I won't need to listen to it. I called a few of the guys on the team to meet me at a bar downtown. A few drinks, laughs, and a hot girl will make this day a damn sight better.

My score sheet is flawless when it comes to picking up chicks. When I go out with a game plan in mind, I have yet to leave empty-handed. If my Titans rap sheet were that good, I'd already have a garish Hall of Fame blazer hanging in my closet.

The music is loud, and the drinks are flowing when I arrive. My teammates have already drawn a crowd of admirers, and when I spy a sexy little redhead looking disinterested as she stands next to her fawning girlfriends, I set my sights on her. A challenge. Not too easy, but the second we make eye contact, I know I can thaw her icy demeanor.

Before I get across the room, I'm accosted by half-a-dozen girls asking for my autograph. There's always one who wants you to sign her bra. It's a tough job, but someone has to do it! Maybe the redhead can wait. A sexy pair of signed breasts trumps a challenge any day of the week. By the time I reach the bar, I have a handful of napkins with first names and phone numbers. For tonight, Boobs McGhee gets my attention and a drink on me.

The newest Titan sidles up next to me.

"Hey, Declan. What's shaking?"

"How do you do it, Coop? The girls are hanging off your every word." Declan is fresh out of college, and the way he's looking at me right now, I feel like some old geezer. I'm twenty-nine for fuck's sake. I'm not about to sit and explain my animal magnetism to the guy. I whisper in my lady friend's ear. Shit, I've forgotten her name already. Megan? Mandy? It definitely begins with an 'M.' She disappears for a few minutes and returns with a handful of friends in tow.

"Ladies, I'd like you to meet Declan Ryker. He's the new rising star of the Titans, and you're about to be seeing a shitload of merchandise with his handsome mug on it. Who'd like to buy him a drink?" As expected, they all scramble over each other to get to him, each batting their eyelids and giving him their best sex-kitten smiles.

"Does it get me brownie points that your teammate is about to bag one of my friends?"

"Sure does, M..."

"Megan." She rolls her eyes at me, but it doesn't hold much weight when she's brushing her entire body up against me.

"I knew that."

"Sure you did, hot shot." She pulls out her phone and snaps a selfie next to me.

Suddenly, I've lost all interest. Shit, sometimes I think these girls would post a picture while they're riding me. Would they even care that their snatch was on Instagram for the world to see? No, probably not.

My phone vibrates in my pocket, and I take the opportunity to extricate myself from her clutches. As I head outside to escape the noise, it makes me laugh to see Declan already heading for a dark corner with a sexy brunette. Boy's got game after all.

"Hey, man. How are you?" I haven't spoken to my buddy, Anders Verbeck, for months. He got traded to the Yankees at the beginning of this season and has been absolutely crushing it.

"I'm in town for the weekend. Just saw your ugly mug out on the town." I look around me, wondering where he is.

"Are you at the bar?"

"No. At Firefly. There are pictures of you signing some girl's tits on social media. Grab the guys and head over. We've got the VIP section to ourselves tonight. Bring some of the adoring throng with you, too."

"Sounds good. Give me thirty minutes. I'm ditching the girl. Fuck me, I only met her twenty minutes ago, and she's already posting pictures. You know that's going to get old really fast."

"She's hot. Bring her. I'll take her off your hands."

"I'm sure she'll be more than happy to let you scrawl your name next to mine. Later, bro."

"Hurry up." I shove my phone in my pocket and head back inside. It doesn't take much to convince the guys to move onto a club, especially when I invite the swarm of women surrounding them.

A few calls and a limousine later, we're pulling up outside Firefly, attracting even more attention from the line of people waiting to get inside as we stroll on in. Declan saunters up to a woman waiting in the line and asks her if she wants to join us. The guy I assume was her date isn't happy at being ditched for half the Titans starting line-up. I guess they won't be going out again any time soon.

Anders wasn't kidding. They have the entire VIP lounge to themselves with servers bringing food and bartenders mixing every drink known to man. When he sees me, he grabs a bottle of scotch and heads my way.

"Cooper Danford! How the hell have you been, bro?"

"Good. I'll be better with two fingers of that scotch." Megan is still attached to my side like a limpet. He looks her over like she's the next entrée.

"Two fingers, you say? I'm told I have some skill when it comes to my fingers."

"Anders, this is Mandy."

"Megan. My name is Megan." She holds her hand out to greet my friend, releasing her grip on me. I'm going to make a sharp exit and leave him to it.

"Anders Verbeck. Pleased to meet you, Megan. Can I buy you a drink?"

"Sure." He snakes his arm around her waist and leads her toward the bar.

"Nice catching up with you, bro. You could at least leave me the scotch!" He sets the bottle down on the nearest table before flipping me the bird over his shoulder.

I grab the bottle and head for a dark corner. I'm just not feeling it tonight. Hunter has always been my wingman, and now that he's retired and 'in love,' I need to change up my game. Dispensing with the need for a glass, I take a long gulp of scotch as I sit back and watch everyone grinding to the music. A few moments later, a bartender appears with a glass.

Fuck, she's cute, really rocking the tight jeans and cut-off shirt—the bread and butter of every hot bartender in the city. And the belly-button ring has just earned her a bigger tip tonight.

"You know you're not supposed to swig from the bottle, right?"

"It's been that kind of night so far."

"Well, at least use this." She hands me the glass. "Can I get you anything else, Mr. Danford?"

"You know who I am?"

"Really? Does the playing-dumb thing usually work for you? You're a legend in this town. I watch every Titans game. Of course, I know who you are."

"You're a Titans fan?"

"Don't sound so surprised. It's possible for a woman to enjoy foot-ball and not because of the hot guys."

"You think I'm hot?" I give her a sly wink.

"Get over yourself."

"Trust me, I'm over myself this week." She's about to respond when my phone vibrates. What now? Faith's probably set my house on fire by accident, or Hunter has a broken cock from too much sex.

My phone seems to be my self-made cockblock tonight. Holding it up, I send her on her way with the universal signal of 'I've got to get this.' I'm seriously off my game. I should already have a woman writhing beneath me, and yet I literally handed her over to Anders. There are at least twenty girls in here I could be seducing right now, and I'm not.

Well, fuck me! She finally decided to deign me with a reply.

Z: *You're a regular Shakespeare, Danford. I've obviously been missing out on some thrilling conversation.*

. . .

It strikes me as a little too coincidental that Zee is messaging me now, right after some chick posts shots of us together on social media.

Me: *Who is this?*
   Z: *You know fine well who it is.*

I know I shouldn't, but she makes it too easy.

Me: *Brandy?*
   Z: *Is that the name of the bimbo you're with right now? I can see why you think she'd be texting you. She probably got lost on her way back from the restroom.*

Bingo! Those three little dots appear and disappear so many times, she knows she gave herself away. I can't help smiling as I type my reply.

Me: *You cyber stalking me? Miss me already?*
   Z: *You wish.*
   Me: *And yet you're messaging me.*
   Z: *Only because of your woeful photoshop skills.*
   Me: *I really had to size up Mr. Hankey to cover my junk. I'm blessed in that department. I don't need to tell you that. You've seen the goods up close and personal.*
   Z: *The only thing bigger than your cock is your ego.*
   Me: *You know it, beautiful.*

. . .

Those pesky dots keep disappearing, but after five minutes of staring at my phone, I force myself to shove it back in my pocket. I'm not letting myself get in knots over this girl. We had some fun, but Christ, it shouldn't be this difficult to have a conversation.

I last an hour and half a bottle of scotch before I'm ready to call it a night. The sexy bartender reappears as I stand to leave.

"Leaving so soon?" I reach for my wallet and grab a hundred-dollar bill.

"Yeah. Thanks for the glass."

"Keep your money. Your friend Anders has an open tab and a healthy tip for all the staff. I get off at midnight if you want to... hang out?" The desire in her eyes would normally be a red rag to a bull for me, and she's just my type—tall, leggy, and blonde—but I can't seem to shake the last girl I spent the night with.

"If it were any other time, I'd be totally up for hanging out with you."

"Say no more. Nice meeting you, Cooper Danford."

"You, too." She scurries back behind the bar, and I watch in disbelief. What the fuck is wrong with me?

Anders' voice pulls me back to the moment. "Did you just blow her off? Bro, what's up with you tonight?"

"Hey, man. I'm heading out. Thanks for the invite. Call me when you're back in town, and we'll grab dinner."

"Sounds good. Later, Coop."

"Later, Beck."

As I make my way through the crowd, the thought of going back to my place and listening to Hunter and Faith getting freaky is wildly unappealing. Instead, I call my favorite hotel in town and reserve a suite for the night. By the time I take a cab over there, I'm starting to feel the effects of the scotch.

I've always enjoyed staying at hotels. It's part of the job. You travel to play, and some players hate it, but that has never been me.

The moment I get in the room, I strip off and slide under the crisp sheets. My phone vibrates on the floor, still in my jeans pocket, but I'm too tired to answer it. Just one night without everyone else's issues. It's not too much to ask.

———

My head is pounding when I wake up, disorientated that I'm not in my own bed. I look to the standard alarm clock you find in most of the hotels across America. It's ten thirty? The last time I slept that late, I think I was in college. I'm an early riser by nature.

There's a stale stench of last night's liquor on me, so I head straight for the shower. I'm not looking forward to putting on the same clothes, but at least I'm only thirty minutes from home.

I should be sated and relaxed this morning, but instead, I'm cracking one out in a hotel shower. The moment I get home, I'm dragging Hunter out, kicking and screaming. I need to get my mojo back up and running, and I don't have time to vet a new wingman. Faith will need to do without him for a few hours tonight.

My fresh, clean feeling is short-lived when I grab my jeans off the floor. I can't put the same underwear on, it's just gross. I throw them in the trash and figure going commando is marginally better. After carefully zipping my fly—you don't want to risk catching the General when you're sans boxer shorts—I instinctively reach for my phone.

Hunter has been calling me. What's up now? I quickly call him back.

"Hey, Vaughn. Everything okay?"

"Where you at?"

"The Hermitage."

"Are you alone?"

"Why do you care?" It's not like Hunter to grill me.

"Come on, bro. You know the team is all over Instagram when y'all go out on the town. Faith saw pics of you and some girl's boobs."

"Good for her. No offense, Vaughn, but who I spend the night with is none of your girlfriend's business. You've never given a shit about my nighttime activities before now."

"I get it, but you banged her best friend senseless last weekend, so you brought this on yourself. I thought you liked Zee."

"I brought this on myself? Are you shitting me? You turned up at my door, then they turned up at my door. I had some very much consensual fun with Zee, and then she went home. It's no big deal. She doesn't care, so neither should Faith. I'm happy for you guys to lay low at my place, but I don't answer to anyone. I'm hanging up now."

Why is it that when Hunter complicates his life with a chick he had no business hooking up with in the first place, my cock activities have come under scrutiny? I'm pissed that he'd call me about this. I didn't even get my rocks off last night!

There's a message on my phone from Zee.

Z: *Was Brandy everything you hoped for?*
    Me: *Why do you care?*
    Z: *I don't.*
    Me: *Bullshit.*

I don't understand this girl at all.

Me: *If you want my cock, all you have to do is ask.*
    Z: *Have you even washed off last night's skank?*
    Me: *What do you want from me, Zee? Is this your attempt at friendship? You want to hear about the chicks I bang? I sure as shit don't want to hear about whatever guys are floating your boat.*
    Z: *I haven't slept with anyone since you.*
    Me: *Neither have I.*

.   .   .

It seems like an eternity before she replies. I don't know why she gets under my skin. What does it matter if she thinks I was out fucking another girl last night? She made it clear when she left my place that she wasn't up for going on a date with me. I was her one-stop cock shop for a few days. A convenient fuck.

Z: *Apt 106, 3429 W. Darrow St.*
   Me: *You want flowers or something? A food delivery?*
   Z: *I want your cock. You said all I had to do was ask.*
   Me: *Then ask...*
   Z: *Fuck you.*
   Me: *You're about to.*

I'm out the door before my shirt is buttoned. The old couple in the elevator gives me a sideways glance as I ride down to the lobby, but I couldn't care less right now. I grab the first cab and bark the address at the driver, throwing a fifty at him.

"Get me there in under ten minutes, and there's another fifty in it for you."

"Yes, sir." My cock twitches at the thought of being inside her again. Fucking traitorous appendage. I should've ignored her, but holy shit, she does something to me. I'm aching to nestle myself between her thighs, and I hate that I want her so badly.

When the cab pulls up outside her building, my pulse is racing and whooshing in my ears, drowning out whatever the driver says to me as I slide another fifty into his hand.

I press the button for the elevator about ten times, willing it to come faster. When I see it's still going up floors right now, I head for the stairs, taking them two at a time. This is when training comes into its own!

When I see the door to her apartment, I'm coiled so tight, ready to pounce. Before the third knock, she flings open the door, devouring me with her eyes.

"You were wearing that shirt in the photos from last night."

"It's about to be on your bedroom floor, so it really doesn't fucking matter."

CHAPTER FIVE
ZEE

COOP KICKS the door shut before backing me against the wall, his lips crashing down on mine as his hands fist my hair. God, he tastes good. As much as I hate to admit it, my body has missed him this week, and right now, I don't care about anything else but the pleasure he can tear from me.

"Bedroom." His voice is dark and commanding between kisses. "Now." As his lips caress my neck, I can barely think straight. "Zee, where's the fucking bedroom?"

"I don't know." A knowing laugh escapes him.

"I haven't even started yet, and you've already forgotten where your bedroom is. You really have been jonesing for me." I swallow his words with my tongue. I pull him aggressively down the hall, stopping along the way to taste him, greedy in my unbridled desire.

"If you don't shut up, I'm going to kick you out. Your mouth is here for one reason only, and it isn't to talk." There's no quick comeback. The façade is gone as we stumble into my bedroom. Coop makes short work of my clothes, ripping my shirt open, letting the buttons scatter to the floor.

He throws me on the bed, standing back to let me watch him as he strips out of his clothes. The moment he teases me with the zipper of his jeans, I can see he's not wearing any underwear. Fuck, those 'V' muscles that herald a path to nirvana are even more mouthwatering than they were in my dreams. My memory is a pale imitation of the real thing.

"Keep looking at my crotch like you want to devour it, and I might just let you." My stomach starts to somersault at the thought of it. An hour ago, I thought he had slept with someone else last night, as is his right. I'm not his girlfriend, but the relief that I felt when he told me he hasn't been with anyone since me was disconcerting. Now, the idea of taking his big, beautiful cock in my mouth and watching him fall apart beneath me seems somehow forbidden, naughty, and sexy as hell.

"Promises, promises, big boy."

As his jeans slide to the floor, my pulse is racing at the sight of him naked and hard as steel for me. He stands, waiting for me to make the next move, scrubbing his hand over the scruff of his jaw without taking his eyes off me. The rise and fall of his chest tell me he wants this as much as I do.

"What do you want, Zee?" Running his thumb over his bottom lip, I'm mesmerized as he flicks his tongue out to wet the tip. My breath is ragged as I climb to the bottom of the bed, reaching out to bring him closer.

"Your cock." He's the perfect height for a standing blow job. Sitting on the edge of the bed, I wrap my hands around his waist and pull him forward, taking his impressive girth into my mouth.

"Holy shit." I love the low growl that escapes him as I take him deeper, letting my tongue caress his erection—steel encased in velvet-soft skin. His hands slide into my hair in an attempt to slow my pace, but I'm too hungry for him. "You've got to slow down, beautiful. I'm going to blow my load in three seconds flat if you don't stop whatever you're doing with your tongue right now."

I pull away, staring up at him as I wipe my lips. "You don't like my... technique?" I give him a wry smile, knowing full well that he was enjoying it a little too much.

"Your mouth is fucking magical, but I'd like to last longer than a sixteen-year-old with a fistful of lube and the centerfold of *Playboy.*"

"Maybe I want to have that effect on you." I wrap my fist around the base of his cock, guiding the tip back to my lips. Flicking my tongue over the head of his cock, I train my gaze on him, his eyes transfixed by the sight of his cock thrusting in and out of my mouth. It's a powerful feeling to know that he's lost in the pleasure I'm inflicting on his body at this moment.

As I pick up the pace, his groans become a roar.

"Jesus Christ. Slow down, Zee. You've got the suction of a fucking Dyson!" I double down, gripping his ass as I continue to work him hard. "If you don't want me to come in your mouth, you need to stop." Instead, I moan in approval, knowing that it'll send a vibration straight through his cock. I can feel his release pulsing, ready, and uncontrollable.

He looks so goddamn sexy when he's on the brink of losing his mind. He throws his head back, shouting my name as he spirals out of control, crashing over the edge. Each warm spurt of cum fills me with satisfaction, knowing he couldn't hold back and the pleasure was too much for him.

After letting him ride out the aftershocks, I release him, and he slumps down onto the bed, struggling to hold his body weight.

"Holy shit, woman. Why did you do that?"

"Because I wanted to. I guess I'll need to see to myself now, too." I'm happy to let him watch me while he catches his breath.

"Fuck that. Do you think one orgasm is going to stop me from licking every inch of your body? I'm already getting hard again just thinking about the taste of you." My eyes drop to his cock, and sure enough, he's sporting a semi. There's nothing hotter than a guy who's ready to go over and over again.

I shift up the bed before spreading my legs. "Better get to work then, champ." He crawls onto the bed, stalking me, biting his bottom lip in a way that sends a jolt of desire straight to my core.

"Yes, ma'am." Hell, he has the drawl of a southern gentleman, the body of a god, and the mind of a sexual deviant—he might be the perfect combination.

I've been dreaming of his mouth between my thighs all week, and the reality is so much better. He's hungry for me—ravenous—kissing my folds as he would my lips, flicking his tongue over my clit until I can't string together a coherent thought.

He sends me spiraling over the edge multiple times until I crave more. I need to feel him inside me.

"Fuck me, Coop."

"Now who's a veritable Shakespeare?" He meets my gaze with a dark delight that makes every muscle in my body tighten in anticipation.

"Condoms. Nightstand drawer."

"I doubt you have any that are my size, beautiful."

"I'm sure you can find an extra small in there." He laughs as he reaches for the handle.

"You're about to get a spanking rather than a good fuck. You know fine well that an XXXL is a snug fit."

"I must have forgotten. Guess you'll have to remind me."

"And here I thought fucking your mouth would've been reminder enough." He roots around in the drawer, leaving me waiting.

"Nope. My pussy definitely needs a repeat performance to solidify your legacy."

"Fuck!"

"What?"

"There are no condoms in there. Please tell me there's a box in your bathroom?"

"You must have a few in your wallet?"

"Fuck, fuck, fuck! I was going to buy some in the john at the club. I was too distracted by you and your texting to think about anything else and forgot."

"Have you ever had an STD?"

"No. You?"

"No. Are you clean? Do you get tested regularly?"

"Yes and yes."

"Me, too, and I'm on the pill, so fuck me now. I'm not waiting for you to go to the store."

"Are you sure?"

"Yes. Now, fuck me before I change my mind." He grabs me around the waist and flips me onto my front.

"Get up on all fours, Zee." His lips caress my ear as his cock rests heavily against my ass. "If you want to feel how big I am, then I better make sure you get it good and deep... and hard." Holy shit. His voice is an aphrodisiac in and of itself. I do as he asks, grinding my hips up to tease him in the process.

"Is this when I get that spanking you were talking about?"

"Fuck, you're going to be the death of me."

I shoot him a glance over my shoulder. "Hell of a way to go."

He slaps my ass with enough force to sting, at the same time slamming his cock inside of me in one hard thrust. It's fucking glorious, skin to skin. Condoms are great and all, but oh my God, having Coop ride me bareback is such a turn-on I can barely breathe. Wrapping his arm around my waist, he steadies me, taking and claiming my body, driving me wild as he grinds into me.

"Jesus Christ, you feel good. So fucking warm and wet for me. Let me hear you, beautiful. Still want to make jokes about my cock?"

"Coop. Oh God! Harder." His free hand runs the length of my spine, his warm and calloused palms sending shivers through every nerve ending in my body.

"God, you're so fucking tight." Every thrust of his hips is a delicious torture in this position, his balls stroking my clit every time he sinks to the hilt. I grab the pillow, screaming into it as I'm slammed into an intense orgasm, writhing as he continues to set a punishing rhythm, chasing his release.

When he crashes over the edge with me, he rears up, roaring my name. We collapse in a sweaty tangle of limbs, breathing heavily as the realization sinks in—he just fucked me bareback because I begged him to.

"I guess I should be glad I swallowed most of your swimmers earlier." He lets out a chuckle before turning to face me.

"You're on the pill, though. We're covered, right? You said you were on the pill."

"Calm down, Coop. Yes, I'm on the pill. You have not planted your seed deep in the heart of my womb. The jizz comment was a joke, plus it's also true. I was a trooper back there, I swallowed. That's a compliment of the highest order."

"Fucking hot as hell is what it was. I think I showed my gratitude. How do you taste so good? Do you shower in maple syrup or something? Seriously, I could lick you out all day long."

"Sounds like a plan." I pull the bedsheet over myself, but Coop is quick to tug it off me.

"No covering up. I want to look at you."

"You're bossy."

"It's called manly, not bossy."

"Yeah, yeah. You just want to stare at my tits."

"I'm an equal opportunities voyeur. I want to see your tits, your face, your legs, your ass." I turn into his side, resting my head on his chest. His heart is still racing, but there's something strangely relaxing about having his arm around my shoulder.

"The indestructible Zoey... what's your last name?"

"Smooth. Real smooth. It's Porter. Zoey Porter. You really should get a girl's last name before you ride her bareback."

"It's not like you were asking my last name."

"Danford."

He lets out a breathy chuckle. "Not fair. My name is plastered on my jersey. And you probably have my Titans poster in here somewhere, so you can flick one out now and again. Am I right?"

"Not even close. You're right, though. I knew your last name before we met, so I guess I can't fault you on that one."

"I do have a question, though."

"What? Don't get shy now. You just fucked me seven ways till Sunday."

"Why did you let me fuck you without a condom? You barely know me, and you've gone out of your way to avoid me this week. God, I only got to speak to you through a fucking burner phone. What's the deal, Zee? Was it that bad at my place?"

"That's a shitload of questions." I trace circles on his chest, suddenly uncomfortable with the level of intimacy between us.

"Condom? You could've sent me out the door to the local drugstore. Why didn't you?"

"Because I didn't want to wait."

"You've been making me wait all week. You didn't even want to speak to me."

"I changed my mind. It's a woman's prerogative."

"Seriously, Zee. Why did you shut me out? I thought we had a good time."

"Is this where we get all warm and fuzzy and share our feelings? I'm not down for that."

"Fucking hell. Don't worry, I'm not professing my love for you or anything. I just thought after you showing up on my doorstep and fucking me for days on end, I might take you out for dinner or a few drinks. That we could have a few laughs together. I wasn't planning on giving you my letterman jacket and asking you to go steady. You're so combative." He slips out from under me, reaching for his jeans.

"So, you just fuck me and leave?"

"Are you hearing yourself? You literally fucked me and then left, then avoided me like the plague until you thought I was hooking up with some random Instagram wannabee. I figure I'll just get out before you make me feel completely unwelcome. Oh wait, you already did that."

"Don't go. I don't want you to leave. God, your cum is literally trickling down my leg. You're not going to make me chase you to the door with jizz legs, are you?" That gets a hint of a smile, which he quickly shuts down.

"You want more sex. I'm sure you have a few guys on speed dial who would happily service you." His words sting.

"I'm not good at this, okay?"

"No fucking shit, Sherlock."

"I want you to hang out. We can order takeout and drink beer. Watch movies or play the Switch."

"You want to hang out with me? Me? Cooper Danford?" He strides around to my side of the bed and places his hand on my forehead. "Are you feeling okay? You don't have a fever."

"Sure. I have nothing better to do today. We can have some more sex and hang out."

"Well, how could I refuse such a heartfelt and romantic offer? I need to grab some stuff from my place. I don't relish the idea of spending the rest of the day in last night's clothes. How about I head to my place and change, then I can pick us up some food and movies on my way back?"

"Sex, and you bring food? I might need to have you over more often."

He slyly winks at me. "Favorite food, snacks, and movie genre? Go."

"Chinese. I could eat noodles and fried rice all day long. Orange chicken is yummy, but I'll try anything on the menu. Snacks, not a popular choice when you plan on kissing, but I love Funyuns. Twizzlers and Milk Duds are movie must-haves. Movies. Action, superheroes, anything Marvel. I also have a bit of a lady boner for Wonder Woman, so if you want to venture into DC territory, I won't say no. Please don't bring anything sappy or romantic."

"So that's a no on *The Notebook*?"

"Ugh. Shoot me now."

"Okay. You're my kind of girl. Superheroes, Wonder Woman, Funyuns, and Chinese food. Got it. I'll be back in an hour or two." He shrugs on his shirt and leans in, giving me the softest kiss before making his way to the door as if it's the most natural thing in the world.

"Text me if you think of anything else you want from your super-secret burner phone."

"Will do. And Coop..." He turns to face me, and he just looks so stunning. Freshly fucked but with a playful grin.

"Yeah, beautiful?"

"It wouldn't be the worst thing if you brought a change of clothes for tomorrow morning." I leave it hanging in the air between us, and he doesn't answer. He disappears out of my bedroom, and a few seconds later, I hear the front door close.

As I lay back in the bed, my head is spinning. What am I doing? Normally, I'd call Faith and give her some dirty details, but she's the one person I can't talk to about him. She's been riding my ass all week to talk to him. If she found out we were hanging out, she'd be incessant, expecting forevers when I just want to take it a day at a time.

He wanted to take me for a drink. That's all. Not so scary. He's not exactly playing hard to get, and from what I know of his reputation, he isn't a relationship kind of guy. We can have some low-key fun, no strings, and the sex—oh my God, the sex is unbelievable.

I shower and make sure everywhere is shaved to perfection in anticipation of a long day and an even longer night. I can't be bothered with sexy lingerie, so I throw on some Wonder Woman underwear, a pair of comfy shorts, and my favorite hoody. I was expected to come back sooner rather than later, but as time ticks by, I'm starting to wonder if I scared him off with the overnight clothes comment.

It's official. I'm the lamest woman on the planet. I pull out my phone and tap out a quick text.

Me: *Can you get extra fortune cookies at the Chinese place? They are the only acceptable dessert after some high-quality takeout.*

. . .

No answer. Of course, he may have just keeled over somewhere because I contacted him from my actual phone number.

Ten minutes later, the doorbell rings. Butterflies take flight in my stomach, and it's not something I'm used to. Taking a deep breath, I open the door, and my jaw drops to the floor.

"Honey, I'm home." Coop is standing in the doorway with a suitcase. *A suitcase!*

"What the hell are you doing?"

"You said bring clothes for some sleepover action. I brought a few weeks' worth." My pulse begins to race as panic rises in my chest.

"I said one night. That's a pair of boxer shorts and a new t-shirt." I'm gripping the door for dear life when Coop suddenly doubles over laughing.

"You should see your face right now. Totally worth it. Shift out of the way so I can pull in this suitcase full of movies and snacks, your highness. I don't know if I should be pleased with myself that I managed to freak you out or offended that you think I'm *that guy.*"

"Seriously, you brought a suitcase just to make a joke? That's commitment to the prank."

"I got you good. Your face was so pale, I thought you were going to puke. There's one pair of boxer shorts, one pair of socks, a t-shirt, and my toothbrush. That's it, so calm your ass down and take this." He hands me a huge takeout bag from my favorite Chinese place. I take it over to the kitchen counter and open it up to find at least fifty fortune cookies on top of loads of takeout boxes. How much food did he buy?

"You got my text then. Thanks."

"What?"

"I text you to get extra fortune cookies."

"Oh. My phone is in the suitcase. I didn't see it."

"Really?" I kind of love that he's a man after my own heart when it comes to fortune cookies. "You just got fifty fortune cookies for no reason?"

"Not for no reason. I love them. They're part of the joy of eating

Chinese takeout. Anyone who doesn't think they are delicious is crazy. What could be better than good food followed by a handful of cheesy, vague predictions for the future?"

"Right? They're awesome. I can't believe you got them."

"That's nothing. Wait until you see inside this bad boy." He unzips the suitcase and throws open the lid. It's full to bursting with everything I asked for—snacks galore and a layer of DVD boxes.

"You went all out. I'm impressed."

"I also brought a bottle of the pinot noir you liked from my place."

"Did you tell Faith where you were going?"

"Yes, I explained everything. I told her about the epic blow job and the multiple orgasms while I was chowing down between your thighs. She was most interested in the bareback riding and 'jizz legs,' to use your delicate terminology. *Of course, I didn't tell her anything!* They were too busy defiling my guestroom, so I doubt they even noticed that I came and went. Your dirty little secret is safe. They won't know you're slumming it with me this weekend." He throws a ten pack of Funyuns at me.

"You're not a dirty secret. I just don't like how complicated this is already. Hunter is your best friend. Faith is mine. I don't know about you, but I've never turned up on a stranger's door before and then spent the next three days doing the horizontal mambo with them."

"It was pretty strange. Like getting a mail-order three-night stand right to my door. Not going to lie, best fucking one-night-stand I've ever had. No bar full of cattle and swooning fangirls."

"I bet you just hate having women throwing themselves at you."

"Sometimes, it gets tiring. It was a nice change to meet you under the circumstances we did, just having a relaxed few days of sex, and I thought we had some laughs."

"We did. We can. Isn't that what we're doing today? Fun. Friends."

"With benefits."

"Yes. Definitely with the sex benefits. But first, let's pick our first movie and tuck into this Chinese food. It smells amazing." He unloads everything from the suitcase, piling my kitchen island high with snacks.

"I didn't know which kind of Twizzlers you like, so I got every flavor. If you choose those crazy rainbow ones, though, I might have to leave. They are just wrong on so many levels."

"Strawberry all the way."

"That's my girl!" A thrill runs through me at his choice of words, but I quickly push the feeling aside. He dumps at least ten boxes of Milk Duds on the counter.

"One would've been good. You went a little overboard, champ."

"I like to be prepared." He casually adds a 'family size' box of condoms to the mound of supplies.

"Don't you think it's creepy they have a family-size box of condoms? It's supposed to be for family prevention. And if multiple members of a family are sharing a box of condoms, I feel like that's a seriously disturbed family dynamic. Am I wrong?"

"I can say with all honesty that I have *never* thought about that in my life and wasn't anticipating that response. You're definitely not a predictable woman, Zoey Porter."

"Thank you." I busy myself grabbing us a few beers from the fridge. "I'm just going to throw this out there, and you can take it or leave it. I won't be offended."

"Okay..."

"We've already crossed the line on the condom front. I really enjoyed the whole skin-to-skin thing, and we have established that we're both clean and contraception isn't an issue. I'm not averse to the idea of continuing our weekend without gloves. Up to you. If you want to use them, then that's cool." The words tumble out of me, and it takes me a moment to meet his gaze as I hand him his beer.

"I didn't want to assume anything, so I came prepared this time. The thought of getting to fuck you again without any barriers has me hard already."

"Okay, then." Suddenly, I'm shy under the heat of his blazing stare. "Let's eat. What movies did you bring?"

"Every Marvel movie I own, which is all of them. And your girl crush, with her lasso of truth. Take your pick."

"Start at the beginning. Ironman."

"Oh, you mean business. This is going to be a full-on marathon."

"You got the stamina for it, Danford?"

"Stamina is my middle name."

CHAPTER SIX
COOP

LIFE HAS TAKEN an unexpected turn lately. I've been slammed with training and games, but most nights, I've ended up in Zee's bed. From the girl who didn't want to give me the time of day after our initial hook-up, she has softened around the edges. She'll still reiterate to me daily that she's not my girlfriend, but I think that's more for her benefit than mine.

We've moved past this being a few quick and dirty fucks, even if she doesn't want to admit it. We eat together, we talk, and hang out. There's always sex involved, but it's not the only reason I want to be around her. She's funny and smart as a whip, and those fleeting moments when she shows a softer side—God, she's adorable. My next move is convincing her to let me take her on a date in public. I know that's not always an easy step with someone who lives their life in the public eye. Me being seen out with the same girl more than once will spark all kinds of questions.

I can understand that it could be off-putting. Fame is the price I pay to do what I love. The crowd cheering in the stadium is awe-inspiring, but once you get outside and want to get dinner or see a movie, it would be nice to shrug off the public persona and enjoy some anonymity. It's one of the reasons I love traveling outside of the states. No one in Europe gives a shit about the NFL.

Zee is on a different level. She's already jumpy when it comes to how much time we're spending together. Anyone putting a label on it would scare her off completely, but I'm encouraged by the fact that she hasn't sent me packing already. Deep down, she knows that casual sex isn't spending every night with each other. We've both had experience with one-night stands and fuck buddies. Whatever is going on between us is something else.

After a long day of training, I find myself at Zee's place again, and when she opens the door, there's a comfort I find in seeing her smile and having her throw her arms around my neck.

"You look beat. Hard day?"

"Yeah. Coach was on a rampage. Every muscle in my body aches." I drop my overnight bag at the door. I've been living out of it for weeks now, stopping at my house for an hour here and there to grab some underwear.

"So I need to do all the heavy lifting tonight?" She wiggles her eyebrows at me, leading me by the hand down the hallway to her bedroom. I sit down on the edge of the bed, exhausted.

"How was your day?"

"Work was boring. I met Faith for a nice dinner which. She's been attached at the hip with your bestie, so it was fun getting her to myself for a few hours."

"Did she manage not to draw attention?" Faith is a magnet for mayhem. The few occasions that Zee and I have been at events with them, chaos has inevitably ensued. I've never met a girl more prone to accidents in my life.

"She choked on a nacho, and I just about had to give her the Heimlich maneuver. So, just an average evening. I'm sure it will be on social media somewhere by now."

"How do you feel about being paparazzi bait by proxy? You can't really avoid it now that your best friend is in the media. As long as she's with Hunter, people are going to be interested in her, and let's face it, she's incapable of keeping a low profile." I may as well take this opportunity to test the water with her.

"It is what it is. She is happy, she's clumsy as fuck, and I love the crap out of her."

I pull my t-shirt over my head and drop it on the floor before losing the rest of my clothes and getting into bed. Zee quickly follows suit and crawls in next to me, her hands roaming the length of me.

"Zee... can I take you out on a date?"

"What?"

"You know, two adults going out in public, maybe for a meal or drinks. We've been to numerous events with Hunter and Faith, but we weren't exactly 'together' or on a date. I'm your date to their wedding, for God's sake, and yet you still won't admit I'm your boyfriend. I get it's complicated if we're seen somewhere without them. We can't explain it away as being in the same place at the same time because of our friends, but I like you. We've been having a good time, and I want to take you out on a proper date. We've been fucking for months now, but we haven't gone on a bonafide date."

"I don't know."

"What's the worst that could happen? Let me wine and dine you, then I'll take you back to my place and fuck you in every room of the house. We won't be disturbed now that Hunter and Faith don't need to hide out, so I'd like to have you over." She's quiet for a few minutes, her fingers rubbing up and down my chest in slow, measured strokes.

"Going out on a date doesn't mean we're *dating*."

"Yeah, yeah. You don't have to repeat your lack of attachment to me all the time. I get it. I'm your sex toy. Would it kill you to throw me a bone? One dinner. If you have an awful time, we'll never go out again, and I'll give you free rein of my cock until you're fed up with me."

"Fine. One date."

I close my eyes, content that we're taking a small step forward. She doesn't move to jump me the way she normally does. Instead, she nestles into the crook of my chest, the soft scent of her shampoo intoxicating my senses.

"Zee. Why are you so against letting me in?"

"I don't know." Her voice is small and uncertain, something I've never heard in her before.

"This isn't exactly easy for me either. It's uncharted territory, but I enjoy spending time with you."

"Me, too." She drapes her leg over me and wraps her arm around my waist. I breathe her in, letting myself relax with the heat of her body pressed tightly to mine, and for the first time, I fall asleep beside her—no sex. That has never happened before. Not for me, and I'm almost one hundred percent certain that it's a first for her too.

I thought the biggest hurdle would be getting Zee to agree to a date with me, but I didn't think about the fact that I now have to come up with an amazing first date. Hunter has been giving me all kinds of shit about it, but he doesn't have a leg to stand on. His relationship started on a wager, and he's so fucking whipped already. Everything with him and Faith has been at warp speed while I'm going at a fricking snail's pace with Zee.

"You've been seeing each other for a while now, so I don't get why you're wigging out about a date."

"Because Zee likes to think of us as friends with benefits. I want to change that status."

"Whatever label you want to put on it, or not as the case may be, it doesn't change the fact that you're already dating for all intents and purposes."

"Hey, dickweed, if you're not going to say anything useful, just shut the fuck up. I listened to you drone on for months about the will-you-won't-you of your relationship with Faith. Even when the writing was on the wall, you still wanted to pretend that you had a choice, that you could walk away from your feelings for her. Can you give me a semblance of understanding? So I'm not dealing with a virginity wager or navigating a relationship with my mentor's daughter, but I really fucking like this girl, and I want her to want me, too, and not just between the sheets."

"Well, fuck me dead. Cooper Danford is looking for a girlfriend. Wonders will never cease."

"It must be contagious or something. I blame you for this. You had to go and fall in love with Faith and bring Zee crashing into my life. She's a tough nut to crack, and I'm in for a bumpy ride if I want to win her heart."

"Heart? You said a date. You're falling for her?"

"Fuck up, Vaughn. Just tell me this date idea isn't the worst one I've ever had."

"I think it's the *first* you've had. Have you ever taken a girl out, like actually dated her consistently since high school?"

"I wasn't even that guy in high school. I was the star of the football team. You know what that's like. I was a god. I didn't want to be frenching the same girl week after week, not when they were lining up around the bleachers to show me some affection."

"Do I even want to know what age you were when you lost your virginity?"

"Your brain has been fried with all this virginity talk. I'm sure I wasn't a kick in the balls off the same age as you were. My math tutor, junior year of high school. She was a senior, and she definitely knew what she was doing. Fuck me, she rocked that sexy geek-chic look. What about you?"

"I was a junior as well, but so was the girl. It was the cliché junior prom. The afterparty was at my friend's house, and she and I snuck up to the master bedroom while everyone else was seeing how many solo cups they could drain. I lasted about three seconds flat, and I'm one hundred percent certain she didn't get off."

"What did you and Faith do for a first date?"

"We've already established that Faith and I didn't have a conventional beginning. Technically, the first time I was on a date with her, I was crashing her date with someone else. She was out with that douche nozzle, James, and I snaked her right out from under him. It was such a dick move, but love makes us do crazy things, even when we don't realize it's love yet."

"I want to have a night with Zee that doesn't begin with sex and isn't us being out somewhere as your and Faith's fucking entourage. It's great that we can all hang out, but Zee needs to see me as something more than an extension of her friendship with Faith, as more than a convenient appendage."

"Then take sex off the table for a while."

"Have you lost your goddamn mind? Do you not know me at all? Sex is *not* being tabled in any way, shape, or form."

"Then don't piss and moan that all she wants from you is sex."

"I'm going to ignore that statement considering how many times I've listened to you telling me you had to stay away from Faith, only to fuck her and announce it to the entire country."

"Fair point."

"You're of no help to me today. I'm going to go and figure this shit out myself. Later, douche canoe."

I thought Hunter dropping by training was going to be useful, but I'm no further forward. I know things I *don't* want to do. Zee isn't your typical woman. She won't be impressed by coming to a game and watching the crowds cheer for me. I doubt she'd even bat an eyelid if I brought her to the stadium after hours to hang out. Anything related to my job is off-limits, and the standard dinner and drinks date is too basic at this point.

My head isn't in the game as the day wears on, but I finally decide on a plan of action. I have a game tomorrow, but I make a few calls and set up a date for Zoey and me for Sunday.

Me: *Don't make plans for Sunday. I'm taking you out.*

Z: *Aren't you at practice right now?*

Me: *Just finished.*

Z: *You coming over?*

Me: *I can't. Have a game tomorrow, and Coach was riding my ass for my 'lack of energy.' I think you've sexed the football mojo right out of me.*

It takes her a few minutes to respond.

Z: *Good luck tomorrow. I'll be watching. I suppose I can sacrifice a few orgasms for the greater Titans cause.*

Me: *Do you want tickets? You could bring Faith with you. Hunter's seats are right next to mine, so they could both hang with you.*

Z: *Can I get back to you on that? Faith draws a shitload of attention these days.*

Me: *I'll courier you the tickets. If you want to come and bring whoever you want, then it's all good. If not, I'll see you Sunday.*

The sinking pit in my stomach right now makes me uneasy. I knew better than to ask her to come, and yet I find myself disappointed. The thought of having her in the stands cheering for me is annoyingly appealing.

Z: *You could come over after the game. Or I could come to your place?*

Me: *The team wants to go out to celebrate... or commiserate. Hopefully the former. I'll pick you up at one on Sunday.*

Z: *Keep your disco stick in your pants.*

Z: *It's mine.*

Z: *At least for now.*

Me: *Like I'd have the energy to satisfy another woman. You're a demanding little minx.*

Z: *Have a good night. Talk later.*

Me: *FYI. If my cock is off-limits to other women until you're done with me, that's a two-way street. You're mine, beautiful. I'm not sharing.*

She doesn't reply. I'm always the last one to message. It's like a disease—I can't just put the fucking phone down. Maybe I should've invited her to come out with the team after the game, but if she doesn't even want to come and watch, I'm assuming she wouldn't be up for a night on the town.

I'm not going to blow off the guys and beg Zee to snuggle with me. I'm already putting myself out there on Sunday to try and win her over. I can hold onto my dignity for a day or two longer before I hand her my nut sack.

———————

I've been dragging my ass all day. It was nice to sleep in my own bed last night, but it was fucking lonely. If I didn't have a game, I'd have driven to her house at two in the morning and crawled into bed beside her. Thankfully, I stopped myself from being that pathetic. Instead, I tossed and turned until I had to get up and head to the stadium.

Sitting in the locker room, I'm ready to go, but my heart's not in it today. It's not often that I see my job as 'work,' but right now, I do. Lack of sleep has me feeling hungover, and the last thing I want to do is go out there and slam into the opposing side's quarterback over and over again.

I'm the edge rusher. Not as flashy as the star quarterback, but I'm the guy who's going to inflict some damage on the other team's golden boy, whoever he may be. Together, Hunter and I made the Titans unbeatable.

He's been out for a good while now, and his replacement is great, but the dynamics aren't quite the same. There was magic in the air when we were on the playing field. The whole team worked their asses off in training and gave one hundred percent during every game, but teams have moments—eras that go down in history, never to be surpassed.

Today as we head for the tunnel, readying ourselves to run out to the roar of the crowd, I feel like my era has passed. Maybe it's just a lack of sleep or the situation I find myself in with Zee screwing with my head, but I'm just not feeling it.

I follow my teammates, jogging out onto the playing field as the music blares and the fans go wild. My mind is screaming at me not to look, not to be distracted by disappointment before the game even begins, but I do it anyway. I glance over to my seats, and I'll be damned—she's here! A shit-eating grin splits my face as I watch her cheer and clap. She came alone, and I can't take my eyes off her.

Craning my neck around to keep her in my line of sight, I lose track of myself, slamming into the guy in front of me, knocking both of us on our asses.

"What the fuck, Coop?"

There's a collective gasp, followed by an eruption of laughter from the crowd. The rest of the team runs around me as they line up for the national anthem.

"Sorry! My girl's over there, and she looks hot as fuck in my jersey."

"You have a girlfriend?" As we scramble up and over to take our places, I ponder his question.

"That's the plan. Now, let's win this because I just made an ass of myself in front of her, and I have to redeem myself." Suddenly, I'm fired up for this game, hungry for the win.

Call it macho pride, but I want her to see me at my best—strong, fast, and vital to the team. It matters to me. Falling on my ass wasn't the best start, but hey, she had a huge grin on her face when it happened, and that smile is worth a million bucks.

Every so often, I take a moment to glance over to where I know

Zee is watching, inflating my ego as she jumps and screams for every point. The game goes by in a blur, and we emerge victorious, much to my delight and the stadium packed with Titan fans.

Without thinking, I turn to Zee, letting the rest of the team celebrate. I point straight at her until I know she's holding my gaze before balling my hands into fists and slamming them down on my thighs, thrusting my hips forward—sharp and hard, just the way she likes it. The crowd goes wild, and I can see Zee laughing, throwing her head back in a truly carefree moment. The fans surrounding her stop and stare as her face appears on the big screen. I've drawn some unwanted attention for her. *Shit!*

I half expect her to make a run for it, but to my surprise, she grabs her breasts and gives them a playful squeeze before blowing me a kiss. Fuck. Me. Dead. I pull off my helmet and head for the crowd. I need to get to her sooner rather than later. If I disappear into the tunnel, I can guarantee that she's not going to be here when I come back.

The crowd goes wild as I jump the barriers and make my way to where Zee is standing, looking simultaneously horrified and excited. My eyes never leave hers, stalking her like prey. Fans are shouting and clapping, random hands reaching out to touch my sweat-soaked jersey as I weave my way through the sea of people.

The closer I get, the bigger the smile spreading across Zee's face. I don't wait. I don't speak. The second I'm within reach of her, I slide my hands into her hair and pull her in for a kiss. My lips crash down on hers, the crowd losing their minds around us. She hesitates for a fraction of a second before melting against me, her arms wrapping around my waist as we lose ourselves in the moment. Everything else fades into the background, and all I hear and feel are her lips on mine and the thumping beat of her heart galloping in time with mine.

The scent of her perfume intoxicates my senses, but it makes me achingly aware that I smell like a week-old jockstrap right now. I move to pull back, but Zee holds me just a little longer, tugging on my bottom lip with her teeth. Fuck, she's hot.

"So much for incognito," she whispers in my ear.

"Sorry. If you wanted to stay under my radar, you shouldn't have worn my jersey. Do you have any idea how fucking hot you look?"

"Yeah, I do, actually. Your massive boner is digging into my leg." A lighthearted chuckle escapes her, and it's music to my ears.

"Well, shit. Give me a few minutes to calm down. I don't need everyone taking a snapshot of my woody."

"Why? You could just photoshop Mr. Hankey over it." She has mischief in her eyes and a super sexy grin. "You're a different kind of cocktease, Coop."

"You still sore that you didn't get the original pic? If you're nice to me, I might show you the real thing when we get home."

"Don't you have a guys night to go to?"

"Fuck that. I'll throw you over my shoulder right now and take you back to my place. My plans for the evening involve you wearing nothing but this jersey while you ride my face."

"I like that plan." God, the way she looks at me when she's turned on, it's enough to make a grown man beg.

When I finally manage to get my chubby to subside, I grab Zee's hand and pull her through the crowd. Phones are snapping pictures left and right as I steer us toward the barriers and back onto the field. I'm going to have to blindfold her and take her into the locker room with me. The paparazzi are going to descend like vultures if I don't. The guys wouldn't bat an eyelid at her coming into the locker room with me. I'm more concerned about her staring at a locker room full of cock.

As we head into the tunnel, I catch a glimpse of the big screen. Our kiss is being replayed for all to see in case they missed me wading into the crowd and claiming Zee like a man possessed.

So much for playing it casually.

CHAPTER SEVEN
ZEE

OUR FIRST DATE NEVER HAPPENED, or it did, and it consisted of staying at Coop's place and not going out in public. We got to avoid the press and enjoy a naked Sunday. I much prefer eating food off his sexy, mouthwatering abs. In my opinion, restaurants and candlelight are way overrated.

We've been spending a lot of time with Faith and Hunter, which is great in so many ways—I get to hang with my bestie, and Hunter is a good guy. We have so much fun, but the pressure weighs on me. I feel like it's fast-tracking Coop and my relationship, and I can't really deny it any longer. We're dating. It just comes with so many strings attached.

Faith means well, but she can be a little pushy when it comes to my love life lately. She reads into everything, and it doesn't seem to bother Coop. He and I have had a couple of disagreements when it comes to how we handle being out in public together—nothing to write home about—but he's stubborn, and so am I.

I almost missed the Hall of Fame ceremony because I just couldn't face all the attention I knew would come with being there as part of the Faith and Hunter show. In the end, I wanted to be there for her, and I hated being away from Coop. I'm glad I came to my senses, or I would've missed seeing my best friend being proposed to.

Since Hunter popped the question, Faith has weddings on the brain. Heck, I think she'd make it a double wedding with Coop and me if she thought I'd go for it.

I've barely seen Coop this week—being maid of honor is time-consuming. I'm looking forward to it all being over, so I can spend the weekend locked away in my hotel suite with him. He's been off doing best-man stuff, which I assume means they have been drinking and going to strip clubs. Coop says that's not how he's been spending his time the past few days, but I doubt he'd tell me if he was letting some stripper grind her skanky ass on his lap. It's a tradition for a bachelor party.

Faith has been a bundle of nerves, worrying that she might fall flat on her face on the way to the altar, which, let's face it, is a possibility. I bought her some tricked-out Converse to try to mitigate her propensity for ending up on her ass. I swear an elephant is more graceful than my beautiful bestie.

Once I got her to go to sleep, I snuck out of our room and went to see her dad. She says she's okay with them not being at the wedding, but I know her—it would be a gray cloud hanging over the best day of her life.

Thankfully, I was able to talk her dad into coming and walking her down the aisle. It won't fix things between them, but it's a start, and when they finally get back to a good place, her wedding day won't be looming in the background as something they missed out on. Now, all we need to do is get through the ceremony with Faith in one piece, and my job as maid of honor will be a roaring success.

Faith looks stunning as she walks down the aisle on her dad's arm. Her eyes are fixed on Hunter, and he's beaming ear to ear at the sight of her. Coop is standing at his side, but he's not paying attention to the bride. His smoldering gaze is leveled at me. He looks so freaking sexy in a tux, it should be illegal. The stuff I want to do to him right now is definitely illegal in most states.

My breath quickens at the sight of him, my heart thumping so hard I think it's going to jump straight out of my chest. I'm mesmerized by him, only registering Faith as she thrusts her bouquet into my hands. I don't really remember much about the ceremony. It goes by in a blur, and Coop never breaks eye contact with me. Even when he's called upon for rings, he just holds them out for Hunter to take. The guests notice, and a little ripple of laughter spreads through the pews.

When all is said and done, and the 'I dos' are behind us, we follow the bride and groom, Coop's hand on the small of my back, the heat of his large palm causing a spark to ignite deep in my core. I'm not sure I'll be able to wait until we get back to our suite. I might have to be the clichéd bridesmaid getting freaky in the cloakroom.

"You look... stunning, Zee. I'm sporting a semi right now."

"Only a semi? Clearly, I have room for improvement. Would it tip the odds in my favor if I told you I'm going commando under this fancy ass dress?"

"Fuck me."

"I plan to. As soon as we get to the reception."

"That's not quick enough for me, beautiful. We have our own car and a nice privacy screen between that fine ass of yours and the driver." A thrill courses through me at the dark and delicious tone of his voice.

"You can put that mouth of yours to good use."

"Yes, ma'am."

The second we load Faith and her dress into their car, Coop grabs my hand and pulls me toward ours, eager to get a few moments of privacy. He closes the door and barks at the driver.

"How long does it take to get to the reception venue from here?"

"Ten minutes, sir."

"I'm going to need you to triple that time frame for me... at least."

"Don't you have to be there for the photographs of the bridal party, sir?"

"They can start without us. Do me a solid and put that screen up." He does as he's asked, and the moment the privacy screen is in place, Coop slides his hand down my leg, reaching for the hem of my dress.

"So you only need thirty minutes? Am I only getting half an orgasm?" As his hand wanders up the inside of my thigh, I'm rewarded with the catch of his breath when he feels how wet I am for him.

"I'm pretty sure I can make you come a handful of times at least. You're already slick for me."

"Then stop talking and put your money where your mouth is."

"I'm putting my mouth right where you want it. Between your thighs. Now lie back and enjoy." God, he's hot. I do as he asks, lying across the back seat, letting him push my dress up to my waist. His gaze is greedy as he takes in the sight of me with my legs open wide and my pussy desperate for his kiss.

Coop likes to tease me, to drive me to the brink of insanity before he gives me what I want. He enjoys watching me squirm. It takes him a minute to maneuver his body into the right position, even in this generous back seat. There's nothing hotter than a man in a tux nestled between your legs, especially when that man is Cooper Danford.

"Kiss me, Coop." He looks up at me with a sly grin.

"Which lips are you talking about? I know my preference."

"Ugh. That's so not sexy. Referring to vagina lips is never a turn-on."

"You're already turned on. It doesn't matter what I say to you right now, you're going to be riding my face as if your life depends on it." He darts out his tongue, tasting me with a long, torturous lick. He's right. He could say anything right now, and I wouldn't give a shit. As long as he keeps doing what he's doing, I'd listen to him call my pussy whatever he wants. It feels so freaking good.

"Oh God."

"Nothing to do with God, beautiful. If you're screaming anyone's name, it should be mine."

"Shut up and lick me. I'm close." I'm not above begging. It feels so fucking good when his mouth is on me, sucking my clit into his mouth with a cold breath. I don't know how he does it, but it's mind-blowing. As his tongue flicks over my clit, he holds my gaze, reveling in the power he has over my body and my pleasure.

I reach for anything I can get my hands on—something to anchor myself as I buck wildly against Coop's face. I'm so close, and I don't give a crap if the driver can hear me. I don't think a privacy screen is going to do much good as I scream Coop's name, over and over as I crash over the edge. As the aftershocks pulse through me, Coop fumbles with his pants, unzipping his fly and pushing them just low enough for his erection to spring free.

He wastes no time positioning himself at my entrance, driving inside me in one hard, delicious thrust.

"Fuck, you feel so goddamn good, Zee." His lips crash down on mine in a fierce kiss, the taste of my arousal on his tongue. I want him more than my next breath. All rational thought is gone, lost to the sensation of our bodies coming together—writhing—heavy with the need to find release in each other's arms.

The scruff of his jaw is a delight to my senses, a stark contrast to the softness of his lips on mine. I frantically claw at his jacket, desperate to feel his skin on mine. It spurs him on, his hands sliding the straps of my dress off my shoulders, allowing him to pull the bodice down, exposing my breasts.

As he thrusts harder and faster, his lips kiss down my neck, making his way lower until he captures my nipple in his mouth, his teeth grazing my skin. All I can think about is hearing him come as I find my release.

"Coop! Oh shit, Coop! Don't stop." He grunts in reply, hammering into me, sending me spiraling out of control. As I come apart beneath him, he grabs my leg and pulls it up over his shoulder, taking me deeper as my orgasm takes flight.

"Fuck, Zee!" I writhe beneath him, desperate for him to follow me over the edge. The moment he finds his release, euphoria pulses through every cell in my body. We could be anywhere right now, and I wouldn't care. I don't care about anything except Coop and the way our bodies connect.

He takes my mouth in a fierce kiss, attempting to stifle the roar that escapes his chest. My legs are shaking, and I move to extricate my leg from his shoulder, but I jerk as he circles his hips, sending a delicious aftershock straight to my core. The heel of my shoe hits the window, and I hear the glass crack.

"Shit!"

Coop turns his head and watches in abject horror as the glass shatters. I'm all too aware that we're in a moving car, and I'm virtually naked right now. Any driver who passes in the adjacent lane is about to get an eyeful of Coop's bare ass. He's quick to cover me, so I reach between us and attempt to pull his pants up. I can't help but react as his cock slips out, leaving me bereft.

"Holy fuck. How in the hell did you kick the window hard enough to break it? Those things are almost indestructible." He drops his forehead to my chest, catching his breath and thankfully seeing the funny side.

"I must be channeling the bride today. I'm so sorry."

"Don't apologize. I'm just pissed that I didn't get to stay inside you a little longer. And I don't want anyone seeing you in a compromising position."

I bury my head close to his. "The driver is going to have a field day with this."

"I'm more concerned that Hunter is going to beat my ass when we get to the reception. We've all been worrying that Faith would do something ridiculous today, but apparently, that title is reserved for us."

"The reception! Shit. Coop, I'm not wearing any underwear, and I'm chock-full of your spunk."

"Then I guess we're making a detour." He gives me a sly wink. "Don't worry, beautiful, I've got you covered." When he wrestles his cock back into his pants, he lowers the privacy screen just a touch, enough for the driver to hear him—I'm sure he's heard plenty in the past twenty minutes.

"Hey, man, can you stop at the Victoria's Secret downtown?"

The driver doesn't even flinch, his voice completely flat as he nods, saying, "Yes, Mr. Danford."

The second the screen is back in place, giving us a thinly-veiled illusion of privacy, we descend into a fit of laughter. "Oh my God. He's getting the biggest tip of his career for this."

"Yeah, I think I might just buy him a new car. The guy is professional as fuck!"

"So, we're going to buy me underwear?"

"No. *I'm* going to buy you underwear to make sure my guys don't spill out when you're making your maid of honor toast."

"God, the toast. I hate speaking in front of crowds."

Coop leans in and plants a kiss on my cheek. "It's not like you could top the best man speech I'm going to give. It's going to be hilarious. If I were you, I wouldn't want to give a speech that will be measured against a comedic masterpiece."

"Oh, shut up." We pull up outside of Victoria's Secret, which I can see through the now-absent window. "Don't get me a cheesy wire thong. And no granny panties. Something sexy, but that won't give me a VPL under my dress."

"Are you really trying to tell me about lingerie?"

"Yes, because you're a dude, and therefore, you know nothing about uncomfortable underwear."

"Trust me. I got this. I can find you something sexy and comfortable."

"Well, then, you'll have found the unicorn of lingerie. By all means, good luck. It can't be done."

"Oh, ye of little faith. If you haven't learned by now that I'm skilled with lingerie, then I've been doing something wrong."

"You're plenty skilled at tearing it off, but that doesn't mean you can pick it out. I took Faith lingerie shopping right before I turned up on your doorstep. She had no clue what was sexy."

"Why doesn't that surprise me? I bet that was fun."

I start laughing at the memory of sliding under the door to help her. "I'll tell you about it sometime when we're not scrambling to get to their wedding reception."

"Deal." We come to a halt outside the store. "I'll be back in five. Don't break anything else."

"Anyone can see in the car now. How do I avoid attention after you step foot outside the car looking all super-hot Cooper Danford? You're going to draw attention in a tux."

"You think I look super-hot?" He gives me a playful wink and an utterly panty-dropping grin.

"You're insufferable."

When he gets out of the car, he shrugs out of his jacket and hands it to me. "If you want to hide, you can always put this over your head. If it were me, I'd say own it, but I know it'll dent your street cred if you admit I'm your guy." I know he's joking with me, but there's an element of truth and hurt behind his words.

"Go and buy me some panties, and then we can talk." He leans in and steals a kiss before jogging into the store. As I predicted, shoppers who were just going about their day are standing staring, whispering, and pulling out their phones to get a snapshot of the NFL Titan.

I immediately slink down in the back seat, cloaking myself under Coop's jacket. The sound of fans scrambling for autographs and requesting pictures with Coop irks me. I'm not sure why—maybe because I like him more than I care to admit. The thought of other women pawing at him to get a picture—turns out I'm a jealous woman. I didn't know that before now. No guy has ever made me feel real green-eyed-monster jealousy.

It's only been a few minutes when Coop comes sliding back into the car, slamming the windowless door, and telling the driver to get us to the reception. Once we're moving, I emerge from under his jacket and am met with a pair of black panties in Coop's hand.

"Here. If they don't fit or they aren't comfortable, I'll moon the guests at the reception after I give my speech."

I take them from him and slide them on. Damn, he wasn't wrong. These feel good, and they're sexy as hell if I do say so myself.

"As much as I'd love watching you humiliate yourself, you were right. Is this some kind of superpower you have? Buying women the perfect underwear?"

"First, I wouldn't be humiliated showing my ass. I'm hot, and you could bounce a quarter off this ass, so if anything, I'd be proud to bare it to the masses. Hunter would kill me, but I'd make every woman in the room happy. Second, you're the only woman I've ever bought undies for. I just know every last inch of your body. I could navigate your body blindfolded."

"Now that's a thought. I might have to test that theory." A thrill runs through me at the idea of having Coop blindfolded and at my mercy.

"If anyone is getting a blindfold, it's you. Oh, the things I could do to you."

"I'll make a deal with you. Let me do it to you, and I'll let you do it to me."

"Fuck, now you've got my cock twitching again. Is there any scenario in which they wouldn't miss us at the reception if we just went back to my place and got naked?"

"No. You'll have to wait." He adjusts his crotch, clearly uncomfortable with the erection he's now sporting as we pull up to the hotel.

"Great. I'm going to have a chubby in all the wedding photos. You really need to stop being such a turn-on." The look in his eye is all mischief and heat. His idea to skip out on this is so tempting, I have to remind myself that Faith would never forgive me.

Before I get a chance to answer, Hunter opens the car door to greet us.

"Where the fuck have you been? And what the hell did you do to the car? Faith is freaking out that Zee wasn't right behind us." He looks at me before shaking his head. "Can you fix your sex hair and smudged lipstick before you go in front of the camera?"

Oh shit. I smooth down my hair and scramble to find my purse. Hunter is right. When I open my compact, my makeup looks like I took styling tips from the Joker. "Sorry, Hunter. I'll be there in a minute."

Coop reaches over and tucks a stray tendril of hair behind my ear. "I think you look your most beautiful when you're disheveled." He caresses his thumb over my bottom lip, sending a jolt of electricity straight to my core before Hunter grabs his arm and yanks him out of the car. I can hear him berating Coop as he pulls him in the direction of the photographer.

"Can't you keep it in your pants for a day?" Hunter says in an irate tone.

"Afraid not, bro. Have you seen my girlfriend? She's fucking hot. I couldn't help myself."

"I thought you weren't allowed to call her your girlfriend."

"Fuck off, Vaughn. That's a low blow. Just because it's your wedding day doesn't mean I won't kick your ass."

"Sorry, bro. I'm fucking stressed. It's tense with Coach being here. I'm happy for Faith's sake, but he's seriously giving me death stares every time I look at him. I'm relying on you to be my buffer. He still likes you."

"Of course, he does. I'm epic, and I haven't fucked his daughter."

When they're out of earshot, I set about fixing my makeup. The reflection staring back at me is disconcerting. I have kiss-swollen lips, flushed cheeks, and my hair is a riot. Hunter's words play over in my head. Why can't I let myself lean into what Coop and I have together? Faith jumped in with two feet and got everything she's ever wanted and more.

I thought hooking up with the Titan's hottest bachelor would be a great way to pass a weekend. I never thought it could be more, and now I'm scared that I got way more than I bargained for.

Once I fix my makeup, I paint on a cool, calm, and collected smile, ready to celebrate my best friend getting her happily ever after.

The drinks flow, and I dance the night away with Coop, every twist of his hips a dark promise of a hot and heavy weekend in bed. I could get used to the sight of him in a tux. I thought he was hot in his football gear, but hands down, he's the sexiest man alive in a suit. Anyone I date after him is going to be a crushing disappointment. I guess that's the price you pay for hooking up with a football god.

I'm so screwed—literally and figurative.

CHAPTER EIGHT

ZEE

NO. No. No. No. No!

This can't be happening to me. This was supposed to be easy breezy. I've been telling Coop for months that I don't want to be tied down, that it's just not in my DNA. Maybe I should've spent less time discussing my DNA and instead focused on not mixing mine with his. Shit.

I'm like a finely tuned clock—I'm never late. Since the day I got my first period and ran around the school telling anyone who would listen that I was bleeding to death, I've been able to count my cycle with expert precision. I mark my calendar at the beginning of the year, and I have never once been wrong.

I really need to be proven wrong right now.

I'm ten days late. The fact that I didn't even notice until today is proof that I'm in over my head with Coop. I don't mess up. I don't forget things. Sure, I've given some love without a glove over the years, but I'm meticulous about my birth control. I haven't missed a pill. Sure, I occasionally take it late in the day, but I haven't missed a day altogether. There's no way that I'm the tiny percentile—I hope.

The drugstore clerk gave me an excited grin when I bought three pregnancy tests. She wasn't reading the room—I thought I was going to puke. Of course, that could be morning sickness. I'm praying that it was just a gut reaction to the horrifying thought of being pregnant. I can't be. I just can't.

I read the instructions five times before deciding that I need to wait until first thing in the morning to take the test. It says in the early stages, it's more accurate at that time. Like pregnancy is building up in your pee while you sleep. Gross. Oh, the irony—like I'll get a wink of sleep tonight.

Coop is supposed to be coming over after practice, but I wouldn't be able to hide my anxiety from him even for one night, so I fire off a quick text. I feel bad, but I'm not technically lying to him.

Me: *Need to cancel tonight. I have an upset stomach.*

Coop: *I can come take care of you if you want? It doesn't have to be about sex all the time.*

Me: *Thanks, but we are most definitely not in the relationship phase where you see or hear me when I'm sick. Just need a good night's sleep.*

Coop: *I'm sure you're still gorgeous, even when you're hugging the toilet.*

Me: *I'll call you tomorrow.*

Coop: *If you need anything, give me a call. I don't care if it's two in the morning. Just call.*

Me: *Thanks.*

I want to say so much more, but I can't. I'm probably freaking out about nothing. There could be a million other explanations for why I'm late. Even as I think it, I don't believe it. Rereading the instructions, I set all of the test sticks out on the vanity and head to bed. I just want this nightmare to be over with. This will all be cleared up in the morning. Hopefully, I'll wake up and have horrible menstrual cramps and ruined sheets because Aunt Flo has blessed me with her arrival.

When I crawl under the covers, the smell of Coop's cologne lingers from last night. Grabbing his pillow, I clutch it to my chest like a binky. My pathetic yearning makes me want to punch myself repeatedly in the face.

A couple of hours into the longest night of my life, I start wondering if I'll have enough morning pee to do three tests. Or maybe I won't be quick enough. I'm not used to putting my hand between my legs while I'm sitting on the toilet. I finally get up and go in search of a solo cup. I can just pee into that and then dip all the tests in it.

A half-hour after that, I got up again and got a pair of Marigolds from under the kitchen sink. I don't want to pee on my hand by accident. I can ditch the cup and gloves as soon as I'm done.

By three in the morning, I'm thinking about sitting the pee sticks on the counter. That's gross too, and I didn't get the kind with the cap on the top. I should've factored that in when I stood staring at the shelves in the drugstore.

God, who knew taking a pregnancy test was so complicated.

In the end, I stop trying to get to sleep. Sleep and life-changing results are not bedfellows. Instead, I binge-watch episodes of *Grey's Anatomy* until the sun comes up. I'm going to be of zero use at work today.

After waiting all night, I find myself procrastinating as I pace the floor, trying to convince my bladder that it isn't about to burst. When I literally can't wait any longer, I run into the bathroom, grabbing the solo cup before I pee myself. Shit. I waited all damn night, and now I'm so desperate, I don't have time to put on the rubber gloves I left out.

The relief is short-lived as I thrust the cup between my legs. Apparently, there's a knack to this that I don't possess. My hand is now covered in my urine, and I only manage to get about half of it in the cup. Why do movies always portray taking a pregnancy test like it's some mystical, magical moment? Even if you're hoping it's positive, this is a rather unceremonious way to find out.

The universe isn't playing around with the whole '*women get the short end of the stick*' scenario. In this case, we get the short end of a urine-soaked stick. I quickly clean myself up and turn on the shower. Three dipped sticks later, and I jump in the shower in a vain attempt to stop myself from counting the seconds until I have my answer. My heart is hammering against my ribcage the entire time, and under the heat of the water, I feel a cold sense of dread settling in the pit of my stomach.

It's definitely been long enough. My world slows down, and I'm bathed in silence as I turn off the water and step out of the shower. I wish Faith were here. I could get her to look. Although, knowing her, she'd accidentally drop them in the toilet before I got a chance to check them. Or she'd be jumping for joy while chastising me for getting myself into this predicament in the first place.

They're right there.

I take a step closer, one eye squeezed shut as if that's going to shield me from what's coming.

One.

Two.

Three.

All of them positive.

"Fuck."

I called in sick to work. I can't face it. Not today. Coop has training, but I called him and asked if we could get together to talk. His tone immediately turned melancholy when I said it—he thinks I'm going to break up with him. He'll be wishing that's what I called for once he finds out the real reason.

Coop may be the one who has been pushing to label n what we have, but I don't think this is what he had in mind. He was thinking about stepping it up from fuck buddy to girlfriend, not a fun roll in the hay to the mother of his child.

Holy shit. I'm going to be someone's mother. Poor kid. I don't understand how this could've happened. I mean, I know how it happened. I got drunk on cock. After the first time Coop and I made the beast with two backs—bareback—it was game over. We were never going to be satisfied with a rubber between us. And I assured him that I had us covered with contraception. He's going to shit a brick when I tell him, but he has to know.

I spend the day cleaning the apartment, needing some way to channel my nervous energy. The minutes tick by so achingly slow as I wait for Coop to arrive as if he'll care that the apartment is clean and tidy. Armed with my triple positive tests, I sit and stare at them, trying to figure out how to word this. I'm about to set off a grenade in Coop's life, and the press is going to have a field day with this.

When I hear Coop's familiar knock on the door, my stomach drops into my boots. He has this crazy, jovial way he wraps his knuckles on the door, it's almost melodic. I'm so nervous I can barely breathe.

As I turn the lock and open the door, I'm met by Coop's panty-dropping smile, the one that got me into this trouble in the first place.

"Hey, beautiful. Are you feeling better? You look a little pale." The slight hesitance in his voice betrays that killer smile of his.

"I've been better. Come on in, I'm not contagious or anything." He leans in, pressing a gentle kiss to my cheek, his cologne mixed with the fresh scent of his body wash. I love the way he smells when he comes straight from training. He must use a different shower gel or shampoo when he showers in the locker room.

"I'd gladly contract whatever plague you're sporting if it means getting to hang out. I was worried about you last night."

"Can I get you a drink?"

"I can grab it. I know where the refrigerator is. You're the one who isn't feeling good. Can I get you something?"

"A water would be great, thanks." I head over to the couch to where I know the tests are just out of sight. I can't sit down as nervous energy is coursing through my body, my pulse racing. When Coop hands me a bottle of water, I continue to pace the floor. "You should sit down."

"Here we go." He unscrews the cap, taking a long swig of his drink.

"What?"

"We need to talk. You should sit down. The classic lines of a textbook breakup. That's where you're headed, right? You fight me every step of the way. Calling you my girlfriend is a hangable offense. I've been waiting for the other shoe to drop. May as well get it over with. I'm tired, and I have training in the morning. Do you want the breakup anger bang? Is that why you had me come over?"

"I'm pregnant," I blurt it out, nothing like the speech I had planned. I was going to ease into it and tell him I don't expect anything from him. I'm showered with a spray of Coop's beer as he spits it out in surprise.

"Jesus Christ!" He wipes his mouth before staring at me with eyes as big as saucers. "Shit. Let me get a towel or something. I didn't mean to spit in your face." He looks completely dazed as he stumbles over to the counter and grabs some paper towels. As he hands them to me, I can see the rapid rise and fall of his chest. He looks the way I felt this morning when I confirmed my suspicions.

"I told you to sit down."

"Is this a joke? Are you punking me right now? If you are, it's not fucking funny."

"I'm not kidding around."

"Have you taken a test, or are you freaking out 'cause your period is a few days late?"

"I took three tests, and all three came back positive."

"Fuck me. I'm going to be a dad?" He looks to me, his eyes drifting to my stomach. "My swimmers put a baby in there?"

"Again with the eloquence."

"You just shouted at me that you're pregnant. Let's not get into a conversation about being eloquent."

"Sorry. Not quite what I had planned." I grab the tests and shove them at him. "Here. Three tests, three positives." He accepts them, stares at them for a moment, then drops them on the floor.

"Gross!"

"You just realized I had to pee on those, didn't you?" He makes me laugh even in the most serious of moments.

"Yeah."

"So you're grossed out being handed a pee stick, but you'll happily chow down in my lady town for hours at a time?"

"That's totally different. And yes, I'll enthusiastically 'chow down' as you so politely put it. Is that an offer?"

"Be serious for a moment. The sticks you just dropped on the floor have some serious implications. Joking aside, they're important."

"Being handed a urine stick isn't exactly how I imagined finding out I'm going to be a dad. I always thought it would be a cute onesie with 'Daddy" on it or something equally as cute. You've thought about this before? Do you have ovaries I don't know about? Funny. Clearly, I'm super manly because my seed is in there making a baby right now."

"Why would you get a onesie? I had to find out squatting over the toilet. Not an easy thing to do, I might add."

"When did you find out? How far along are you? Do you want to keep it?" He reaches out, pressing his huge hand across my stomach in a gentle caress. "Are you okay?" He's gone from playful to deadly serious in the blink of an eye.

"That's a lot of questions. Give me a minute. I found out this morning, so it's really early. Should I not have told you? I thought it was the right thing to do... telling you. And I'm okay. Feeling a little nauseous, which I had written off as some bad takeout."

"You missed one question." I know what he's asking.

"I know. I'm shellshocked right now, and I think it's a decision we need to make together."

"We can talk about it, and I'll support whatever decision you make, but it's *your* decision at the end of the day. It's your body. I won't force you into anything."

"I want to know where your head is at. This wasn't exactly in our plans."

"We don't have any plans. We don't live together. We haven't said 'I love you.' You barely want to be seen with me in public."

"I..." I don't know what to say. Silence hangs in the space between us.

"If you're asking for my opinion because you think I don't want to have a kid with you, I can answer that right now."

"Okay."

"I want it." My heart is hammering in my chest. "I want you."

"Coop..." He interrupts me with a slow, sensual, soul-shattering kiss.

"Just think about it. I won't pressure you." He pulls back, just enough to hold my gaze, his ice-blue eyes filled with compassion. "This could be great. *We* could be great, Zee." His lips find mine, the soft flick of his tongue melting me from the inside out. Is he right? Could we make this work?

"You're not going to want me when I'm all fat and hormonal. It's not going to be sexy when I'm covered in baby vomit and changing diapers."

"Are you kidding? You're going to have a killer rack for the next eight-ish months. And I've heard that pregnant chicks get super horny. You're already a dirty little minx. I can only imagine how filthy you're going to be when those hormones really kick in."

"Stop!" I say, shoving his shoulder playfully. He gestures a pair of huge breasts, giving me a sly wink and his trademark smile. "This is serious. We're talking about being in each other's lives, whether we're together or not, for the rest of our lives."

"I know it's serious. Being a dad is serious. I should know, my dad was a deadbeat, and he split when I was in the seventh grade, never to be heard from again. I can do this, Zee. I can be a good dad. I can be a good husband."

"Whoa, slow down there, sparky. Husband?"

"Yeah."

"I'm not marrying you because I got knocked up. I don't expect anything from you, and I'm not asking for anything. I'm not that girl, the one who takes a Delorian back to 1955 and needs a ring on her finger."

"You still haven't said if you want to keep the baby... our baby."

"I was an unwanted kid, the surprise my parents never wanted. I've always vowed that I'd never do that."

"So you want to terminate?" As he voices the option without judgment or malice, I know my answer.

"No, I don't want to get rid of it. I want it. Sure, this wasn't planned, but life's timing isn't always what we expect. If you're on board, then yes, I want to have our baby."

He lifts me into his arms, spinning me around with a huge smile on his face. He's genuinely happy. "Yes! I freaking love you, Zoey Porter." A wave of nausea washes over me as he spins me one more time.

"Put me down!" Before my feet touch the ground, I lose the contents of my stomach, which wasn't much to begin with. I run for the bathroom, but it's like locking the barn door after the horses have bolted. There's a trail of vomit from the living room to where I now kneel, retching up bile.

"What can I do?" Ugh. I hate that he's seeing me like this.

"Nothing. Just go."

"I'm not leaving you. I'll go clean the floor. Shout if you need anything."

"No. Do not clean up my vomit. See, this is what I was worried about. The sexy magic is gone already. We've descended into a puke-fest within minutes of you finding out. Just go home. I'll be fine. I can clean up my own messes." Instead of doing as I ask, Coop perches on the edge of the tub, the warmth of his hand tracing circles on my back. It feels so good, but with every gag, I grow more and more uncomfortable.

"It's okay, baby. Deep breaths. I'll go and get you some water."

"Why won't you listen to me? I don't want you here. I don't want you watching me puke. I don't want you watching me hugging the toilet. Just go already." Without another word, he leaves me to my pity party. If this is what I have to look forward to in the coming months, it's going to be worse than I thought. I have a high tolerance for pain, and I don't usually complain, but my Achilles heel is physically being sick. Nausea makes me wallow in self-pity. I don't suppose anyone particularly enjoys it, but I'm a big baby when I puke.

I lay on the bathroom floor for a while, enjoying the cool tile beneath me. Closing my eyes, I try to make the nausea pass through sheer force of will, concentrating on my breathing. I'm not sure how long I lie there, eventually pulling a towel from the linen closet and using it as a pillow. Coop was right to leave when I told him to. I'm in no fit state for company, and I don't want him seeing me like this.

It's not until my stomach settles a little that I hear movement. Either I'm being burglarized, or Coop never left. I'm sort of hoping for the former. I'm a puke-covered mess—a burglar would leave me with a shred of dignity.

The door opens, and there he stands, looking as breathtaking as always.

"Enough is enough. I'm taking you to bed."

"I told you to go."

"Yeah. You say a lot of things. I wasn't going to leave my baby mama in a mess. I cleaned the living room, and I've been waiting for you to come out of here, but there were no signs of life, so here I am." He kneels beside me, reaching his arms underneath me.

"If you call me your baby mama again, I'm going to make sure the next time I blow chunks, that I do it in your direction."

"What would you rather? My pregnant princess? My incredible incubator? Buddha-belly beauty?"

"I want to punch you so hard right now. You're lucky I don't have the energy."

"Sorry. I need to learn not to piss off the pregnant lady. I just want to make you smile."

"I'm gross. I smell like puke."

"Not going to lie, I agree with the smell observation. How about I fill the tub, and we get you smelling better before I tuck you into bed?" He doesn't wait for a reply, letting me lie on the cold floor for a few minutes longer while the water runs. When it's ready, he strips me out of my seriously gross clothes and lifts me into the tub.

"Better?" He doesn't leave but instead lowers the toilet seat and takes up residence, watching me carefully as if I could break at any second.

"Yeah. You didn't have to do this... any of it. Thanks. I appreciate you staying even when I was a total hosebeast." The water feels so good, washing away the wretched day.

"What kind of guy would I be if I left the mother of my child in a pool of her own vomit?"

"You're really enjoying this whole 'my seed is deep inside you' thing, aren't you?"

"What's not to enjoy? You're hot, I dig you, and our kid is going to have some killer genes in the looks department. Hopefully, he has your brains, or he'll be an Adonis with the IQ of a football."

"He? What if it's a girl?" I can't get over how happy he seems. I thought he was going to freak out like me. A soft smile spreads across his stunning features.

"Then she'll be my princess. And I'll have to go to the shooting range more often, so I can pepper the tailgate of any horny teenage boys who want to take her out when she's sixteen."

"How often do you go now?"

"That would be never. I'm good with a football, but I have had no desire to wield a weapon until now. I think you just tripped some protective, primal shit in my DNA."

"Are you really okay with all this, or are you just holding in the freak-out until I'm not in the room with you?"

"I'm good. I just want to make sure you're okay. I want to be in this with you, not standing on the sidelines like some spare part. Will you let me do that? Just admit that you're my girlfriend and let me go out at three in the morning to buy whatever crazy cravings you have. Ice cream and pickles. Apple pie and hot dogs. Anything you want. You're not in this alone, Zee. We're a team now."

I let that sink in as the warm water envelops me. *We're a team now.* Good or bad, this changes everything. We're in each other's lives no matter what.

CHAPTER NINE
COOP

I'M GOING to be a dad. No matter how many times a day I tell myself, it still hasn't sunk in. It's been weeks since Zee found out she's pregnant, but it's still our little secret. She doesn't even want to tell Faith yet. I get it—she says she wants to wait until the first trimester is over.

Another week, and we'll be past the milestone. Zee has had crazy morning sickness. I don't know why they call it that. It should be twenty-four-seven sickness. Of course, that has made it so much more difficult to keep it hidden from Faith and Hunter. I hate not telling Hunter, and I get the impression that he knows something's up, but he hasn't pushed me on it. It's easier with him not being on the team anymore. There's no way I'd have been able to keep it to myself if we were still training day in and day out.

Christmas was the hardest. My liver has taken a beating. Zee is eating for two—I've been drinking for two. Zee insists Faith would know the second she started refusing alcohol. So, I've been intercepting as many drinks as I can on her behalf. It's easy when I'm the one ordering at the bar. When Faith or Hunter have been getting a round of drinks, I've been downing Zee's on the sly. I'm surprised I didn't slip up and tell them the good news in a drunken stupor.

Today is the day we get the three-month scan. If all is well, we've agreed to tell Faith and Hunter. I think I'll be on the wagon with Zee. I've sickened myself with alcohol in my attempts to keep our secret. I need a break!

I offered to pick her up, so we could go to the doctor's office together, but she insisted on just meeting me there. I'm trying to break down her defenses a little at a time, but she's a tough nut to crack.

I make sure to arrive early because I want to be there when Zee arrives. What I didn't factor in is the fact that I'm a dude sitting by myself in an OBGYN waiting room. It doesn't help that most of the people here seem to know who I am. I'm so relieved when Zee walks through the door. She looks radiant—the pregnancy glow is a real thing.

When her eyes find mine, I'm happy to see a genuine smile on her face. After she checks in, she takes a seat next to me, and I lean in for a kiss, but she shies away, her gaze shifting from person to person.

"Everyone in here knows who you are. Best not to draw any more attention," she whispers.

"I think that ship has sailed. Look where we are. I don't exactly make a point of accompanying random women to their OBGYN appointments."

"I don't want this getting out. You should've worn a baseball cap and shades."

"What movies have you been watching? I'd draw more stares being in a doctor's office with shades on. Stop worrying about everyone else and focus on what we're here for."

"It's okay for you. You're a beloved Titan. I'm going to be painted as the woman who tricked you into staying with me."

"Did you trick me? Did you get pregnant on purpose?" I already know the answer. I know Zee better than she'd like to think.

"Of course not. How could you even ask me that?"

"I wasn't. I was simply pointing out that I know, and you know that isn't the case. Haven't you wondered why I never asked how this could've happened? You were on the pill."

"I just assumed that you've been wondering about it. I never intended this at all."

"Trust me, I know you aren't thrilled to be tied to me for the rest of your life. You regularly make it known. If it were any other woman I've slept with, I probably would've questioned her intentions. With you, I'm one hundred percent sure that we're the minuscule number who are the exception to the rule. I like to think that it's fate, no matter how irked you seem to be at having my child growing inside you."

"That's not..." She's about to explain away her obvious disappointment that I'm the guy who knocked her up, but the receptionist calls her name, and it's time to see this baby.

Once the door closes and the prying eyes of the waiting room are behind us, Zee reaches for my hand as we head down the hallway to the exam room.

"So, you're not ashamed for the staff to know we're together? Only the rest of the general public?"

"Can we not have this conversation right now? I'm sorry I hurt your feelings. This is just new territory for me. I'm adjusting."

"It's not exactly old hat to me. I've never knocked anyone up before. And contrary to your aversion to being my girlfriend, I've never had a woman I'm seeing be unwilling to admit she's with me. Are you ashamed of me or something?"

"No. I just know that when this hits the press, they are going to be judging me. It won't be you who gets vilified."

"All the more reason to admit that we're a couple, not just casual fuck buddies. Surely, it would be better if they know that we're in a committed relationship?"

"Are we committed? You're stuck with me. It's not the same thing." I want to walk away right now. It shouldn't be this hard to prove that I'm in this.

"I'm not even answering that question because you already know the answer."

We sit in silence until the technician comes into the room.

"Hi, Zoey, and..." she looks me up and down, "... Cooper Danford. I'm a big fan." This isn't helping my case with Zee that we can be anything less than a high-profile couple in this town. "Let's see how the baby is doing." After the initial recognition of who I am, she switches to being completely professional and tries to set Zee at ease, explaining everything she's doing.

She turns the screen to face us, pointing to a tiny moving person. *Holy shit!* That's my baby.

"Wow." It's all I can manage. Incredible.

"Baby is roughly the size of a fig right now."

Our fight from only moments ago is forgotten at this moment. I reach out and grab Zee's hand, lifting it to my lips and pressing a gentle kiss to her palm. "That's our baby." I can see tears welling in her eyes, but she starts blinking furiously to get rid of them. She's always got to be in complete control of her emotions, and I'm at a loss for why that should be.

"Is everything okay? Does it have all its limbs? Is there a heart-beat?" This is the first time Zee has sounded like an expectant mother. A warmth spreads throughout my body, my heart fit to burst. I'm such a sap when it comes to her.

"Everything looks great. Right on track." She presses a button, and a rhythmic sound fills the room. "And yes, there's a very strong heartbeat."

"That's our baby's heartbeat?" Fuck. I'm going to cry like a pussy in a moment.

"Yes." Her expression changes, and her brow furrows as she moves the wand over Zee's stomach.

"Is everything all right? What's wrong?" Zee squeezes my hand as I question the technician. She looks worried.

"Hold on just a moment." She moves the wand again, tapping buttons on the machine while we anxiously await her response.

"Something's wrong. Oh God, Coop, something is wrong."

"Your baby is fine. Sorry, I didn't mean to worry you unnecessarily. I just wanted to be sure before I said anything." Now I'm definitely worried.

"Then what is it? You're freaking us out over here."

"I thought I heard something when I let you hear the heartbeat. With a little cajoling from the wand movement, I was able to confirm. There's a healthy heartbeat. In fact, there are *two* heartbeats."

"You mean the baby and Zoey, right?"

"No, Mr. Danford. You're having twins. Congratulations."

I'm dumbfounded, rendered speechless, which is very difficult to do.

"Are you sure our baby doesn't just have two heads or four legs? I feel like that would happen to me."

The technician moves the wand over Zee's stomach again. "Come on. Come out, little one." We stare at the screen, waiting. After a few moments, as if on cue, there it is—not one but two babies.

"Well, fuck me."

"I already did, and this is what happened." Zee's eyes are transfixed on the screen with trepidation and wonder.

"Hell, yeah, it did. I put two babies inside you."

"And that was such a tough task. Almost as hard as the fact that I'm going to have to push two babies out of my vagina, obliterating it for all time."

"Why would you say that? Way to ruin my super masculine moment."

"I forgot this is all about you. I'm just the incubator. Is that right?"

"The incredible incubator. Don't forget the superlative!" I lean in and kiss her hard, pouring every emotion I'm feeling into this one small show of support and affection. I don't want her to know that I just about shat my pants when I heard the word *twins*. When I pull back, Zee looks up at me with fear in her eyes.

"How are we going to do this? I'm terrible with babies. How am I going to manage two?"

"*You* won't. *We* will. It's going to be great. You'll see. We got this." My heart is hammering in my chest, and my pulse is racing. "Can we please tell Hunter and Faith now? I think my head will explode if we don't have people to talk to about this. We need allies. We're going to be tied to our household. Two babies against the two of us. Hunter and Faith will give us an advantage."

"You say that like we're a football team."

"On our way, right? Already got two players cooking in that oven of yours." I give her a sly wink and attempt to hide my fears.

"Don't call my uterus an oven."

"What do you want me to call it?" I'm about to start suggesting alternatives, but she cuts me off.

"Why don't we decide that later? None of your smartass remarks are required right now. And to answer your question, yes, I think it's time to bring in the reinforcements. Why don't you invite Faith and Hunter over to your place for dinner? We can tell them tonight."

"Now we're talking!" I quickly type out a message on my phone before she has a chance to change her mind.

Me: *You and Faith, dinner 7pm. My place.*

Hunter: *You have the manners of a feral child. I think what you meant to say is, Hunter, would you and your lovely wife like to join me and my sometimes girlfriend for dinner tonight?*

Me: *Fuck up, numbnuts. Are you coming or not?*

Hunter: *Sure. We'll be there. Anything I should bring? Scotch, wine, dinner?*

Me: *I'm thinking Chinese takeout. I'll text you later about the logistics.*

Hunter: *Okay. Send me a list and I'll just pick it up on the way over.*

Me: *Sounds like a plan. Text you later, fucknuts.*

· · ·

"Your wish is my command, fair maiden. I'll request all your favorite dishes from that great place, I can't remember the name of it. It'll come to me. This will be a quiet night with friends."

"You really think it's going to be quiet after we tell them? I think Faith is going to scream so hard it'll shatter all the glass in the house."

"Well, we'll deal with it. Do you want to tell them, or would you rather I do it?"

"I'll do it."

With the excitement of the scan, Zee was exhausted by the time we got back to my place. I sent her to lay down for a while before Faith and Hunter arrive. She's been out for two hours, a soft snore escaping her now and then. I'm thinking naps are going to become a regular occurrence in the coming months. I mean shit, she's growing two people. *Twins.* How the heck did that happen?

When the doorbell chimes, Zee begins to stir. I've been lying next to her for the past hour, just staring at her. It sounds creepy when I think about it, but I'm just in awe of her. I'm so fucking happy about making babies with her. Sure, this isn't how I thought it would happen, but Zee is definitely the girl for me. The way I see it, this is just an accelerated timeframe. I know Zee doesn't see it that way, so I'm just going to have to convince her.

I open the door and welcome our friends and the mountain of food I had them pick up on the way—all of Zee's favorites. Faith has a bottle of wine in each hand as she brushes past me in search of her partner in crime.

"Zee, where you at? I need a bottle opener."

"She'll be out in a minute. She was taking a nap," I say it before I think to filter myself.

"A nap? You really must have worn her out with your sexcapades. Zee never takes naps."

"Sure, let's say that. I totally wore her out today." It's not technically a lie. I did wear her out with the news of not one but two babies on the way. I still have the scan pictures in my back pocket—two tiny figs.

Hunter and I set everything out on the table, grabbing plates and chopsticks for everyone. Faith immediately goes for the wine glasses while I instinctively head for the ginger ale. It's one of the few things we've found that settles Zee's stomach.

When she emerges from the bedroom, she looks exhausted. Faith pulls her into a bearhug. "I brought your favorite pinot, and your man ordered everything on the menu at the takeout place. I hope you're hungry." There's a moment when Zee's eyes meet mine, and I know exactly what she's thinking. She's about to hurl.

"Faith, can you grab some napkins for me?" With her attention diverted momentarily, I grab the ginger ale and take it to Zee.

"Are you okay?" I whisper under my breath.

"I don't think I can eat." Shit. Zee sitting at a table without shoveling food in her face will be a dead giveaway. The girl can put more food away during dinner than most of the guys on the team. I love that about her. She's not afraid to eat. It sucks when you take a woman out for dinner, and she nurses a single lettuce leaf with a glass of water. There's nothing attractive about that. If anything, it's a total turn-off for me. I don't want someone sitting across from me, staring longingly at my food.

"Is it the smell? What can I do?" She takes a swig of the ginger ale, but she looks pale.

"I just need a minute. Maybe I'll go to the bathroom really quick. Keep them busy. I wasn't planning on telling them the second they came in the door. I need to get through dinner at least."

"Okay, if you're sure. Anything you need, I'm your guy."

"Thank you. You've been so great about all of this, taking it in your stride."

"That's my job."

Faith interrupts us, handing Zee a glass of wine. "What are you two whispering about?"

Zee doesn't respond, but I see the moment she catches a whiff of the alcohol. It turns her stomach, and she thrusts it at me before running down the hall to the bathroom.

"Questionable lunch. She was feeling a little off earlier." I don't think Faith believes me for a second. She gives me a death stare before following after her friend. There's nothing I can say right now without incriminating myself.

Hunter gives me a sideways glance as I take a seat at the dining table. "Everything okay?"

"Sure, why wouldn't it be?"

"I've known you long enough to know when you're bullshitting me, bro."

"Am I that obvious?"

"What's going on?" He has his suspicions, they're written all over his face. I'm not the only one who has a shit poker face.

"Can we just wait on the girls? I'm too tired to spin you a line right now, and I'm worried about my girlfriend. Is there any world in which I can go and check on her without your wife tearing me a new one? She can be pretty scary when she's being protective of Zee."

"Yep, she's a little spitfire. I'd leave them to it, they'll come out when they're ready. In the meantime, you can fill me in on what's going on with the Titans."

"Not much to tell, bro. Everyone is just doing their thing. The new guys are settling in. Yada, yada, yada."

"You don't sound too enthused."

"To be honest, I'm not. It's not the same since you quit on me."

Hunter rubs his eyes, exaggerating every movement. "Boo-fuck-ing-hoo. You miss me? When did you have your vagina installed?"

"Fuck off. You know exactly what I'm talking about. The Titans have had their golden era. We were it. There's just not the same kind of vibe and thirst for the win. Plus, you always made me feel like a fetus, old man river. Now I'm one of the oldest on the team. That shouldn't be a thing... feeling old at twenty-nine."

He rubs his thumb and forefinger together. "Do you hear that?

It's the world's smallest violin playing for you. You do realize that you're complaining about being in your twenties, injury-free, on a multimillion-dollar contract. Wise up and enjoy the ride because pretty soon, it'll be over. A distant memory."

"Do you miss it?"

"I used to before I met Faith. She has a very distinct way of... diverting my attention to other things."

"She's a chaos magnet."

He lets out a little chuckle. "She sure is. How are things with you and Zee? She still trying to ditch you in public? That's got to put a dent in that massive ego of yours."

"You don't know the half of it. I swear I need therapy after being rejected so many times. I'm not exactly used to it. I mean, look at my face. I'm pretty fucking handsome."

"And truly humble," he jibes.

"Bite me, Vaughn."

Faith reappears with Zee following close behind. She shoots me a quick glance, and I know straight off the bat that she's struggling. If she were a cartoon, she'd be green right now.

"Are you sure it's food poisoning, Zee? If you have the plague, and we all get sick, I'm going to be pissed."

"Trust me, Faith, you're not going to catch anything from me. I'm certain of that." I stand and pull the chair out for Zee to sit down. She seems so fragile at the moment, and all I want to do is make it better for her.

Hunter is quick to cut to the chase. "So you invited us over for dinner when Zee is feeling sick from 'food poisoning.' What's going on, guys?"

I look to Zee. She said she wanted to be the one to tell Faith, so I guess we're not getting to eat dinner before this goes down. "Do you want me to tell them?"

Faith looks worried. "Okay, what the hell is going on? You're freaking me out now."

"I'll tell them," Zee says with a reassuring squeeze of my thigh under the table. "I'm up the duff with this guy's spawn."

"You really touch my heart with your heartfelt words, Zee. How could I not want to father your babies?"

Faith jumps up from the table, sending a full plate of chicken chow mein flying into the air. "Oh my God!" I don't know if she's happy or horrified. "You're pregnant? Are you kidding?"

"Nope."

"How? When? I mean... I know *how*. Holy crap. This is huge, Zee."

"Oh, and there's something else. It's twins." My girl really knows how to drop a bomb. I slip my hand into my back pocket and pull out the scan picture.

Faith and Hunter's jaws literally drop at the sight of our tiny offspring. Faith grabs the picture and examines it closely. "I don't see babies. These look like potatoes. We're having potatoes?"

"Yep. Two little Danford potatoes."

"I think you meant to say Porter potatoes. Has a better ring to it." Zee chuckles at her alliteration, but it causes my heart to drop into my stomach. I want my kids to have my name. I want Zee to have my name.

CHAPTER TEN
ZEE

EVERY TIME I check my phone, it stresses me out. I'm starting to show now, and every time I'm seen in public with Faith or Coop, the rumor mill is churning. I thought it was bad after Coop's grand gesture at the Titans' game a few months ago, but that was nothing compared to the scrutiny I'm getting now.

I underestimated just how popular Coop is with the women of Nashville. They've taken to Twitter to badmouth me at every turn. I've officially been labeled as Cooper Danford's 'girlfriend,' 'booty call,' and 'latest conquest,' among other things. There are picture comparisons from when we were first photographed together and of us now. It's clear that I've put on weight, but I'm carrying two babies for God's sake. I'm also eating everything in sight.

I told Coop to cut me off when we're together. I seem to have lost all willpower and replaced it with a super sweet tooth. He's hopeless. If anything, I eat more when he's around. Coop's fans have gone to town, calling me a fat pig, asking if Coop has become a chubby chaser. It's messed up, but now we face a new challenge. I can't pass this off as a few extra burgers anymore. My belly has popped, and I look very much pregnant. You'd have to be an idiot not to notice at this point.

I have to talk Coop off the ledge with every new story about his chubby girlfriend. I hate to see him struggling with all of this because of me. I finally gave in and told him that it wouldn't be the worst thing in the world if he used the word 'girlfriend' concerning me. It made his day—it was quite sweet, actually. Within seconds, he had his phone out, snapping a selfie of us—him kissing my cheek.

Having my best friend constantly in the limelight with Coop's best friend doesn't make it any easier to fade into the background. I have no desire to be in front of the camera or splashed all over social media, especially when I'm turning into a whale. Every time I try to rationalize my feelings for Coop and tell myself I'll be okay if we end up as friends who share DNA with two tiny people, all it takes is one kiss, and I melt like butter. He has some serious skills. For fleeting moments, I let myself believe in the fairy tale—I let myself imagine what happily ever after could look like.

Today, Coop is doing a press conference after his game to announce that we're expecting. It's all I can do to keep my lunch down. Instead of going to the game, I jump in the car and head to my parents' house. I need to tell them before they see it splashed all over the news. My dad has shown more interest in me in recent months than he has my entire life up until now. It's a direct correlation to me being spotted out and about town with a Titan.

I haven't inflicted my parents on Coop yet. He thinks it's because I'm embarrassed to be with him, and as many times as I try to explain that it's the other way round, he doesn't believe me. My parents would make sure I go down in Coop's estimations before the end of a five-minute conversation, and I already feel like a relationship failure. They are the epitome of parents who didn't want their kid. I don't want Coop to draw similarities where there are none. Okay, maybe one—we didn't plan this. But, here's where I differ from my parents— I *want* these babies, and I'll make sure they know that every single day. By the time they're ten, they'll be sick to death of hearing how much I love them.

As I pull up outside the house I grew up in, my stomach sinks, and I wonder if I'm going to be chastised for being an unwed mother. Although, that would require some level of giving a fuck about me. I don't use my key because I don't feel like this is home to me, and I don't think it ever was. Instead, I ring the doorbell and wait until my mom opens the door.

"For God's sake, Zoey, use your key. I'm in the middle of getting ready to go to the country club."

"Nice to see you, too, Mom." I follow her inside with a heavy heart and dread seeping into my bones.

"Well, you could've given me more than an hour's notice that you were coming by. Your father and I have busy lives. We plan our weekends. Just because we're your parents doesn't mean we sit around waiting for you to honor us with your presence."

"No shit."

"There's no need for crude language, Zoey."

"It's Zee, Mom. Not Zoey. No one calls me that."

"Zee is a letter, not a name. I gave birth to you, and I shall call you what I like." She doesn't skip a beat and won't take a minute to sit down and actually talk to me. I follow her around like a lost puppy, begging for scraps of affection.

"Mom, can you just stop for a second so that we can talk? I want to speak with you and Dad."

"Is this about that Danford boy? Your dad said you've been in the news because you're dating some football player. You could've told us that in a text message or a phone call. You really are too dramatic, Zoey. I don't know where you get it from."

"Probably from years of you and Dad giving a grand total of zero fucks about me. Dramatics is the only way to get your attention." She just busies herself even more, so I go in search of my dad. She just mutters under her breath as I leave the room. I don't even know why I bothered coming.

My dad is hiding out in his office with his head in a book—as always.

"Hey, Dad." He grunts in reply, barely acknowledging me. "Can you come into the living room for a moment? I need to talk to you and Mom. It's easier if I don't have to say it twice." He lifts his head, eyeing me with a lackluster stare, reminding me that I'm an inconvenience.

"You need to cut back on the sugar if you want to keep a guy like Cooper Danford interested, Zoey. You're letting yourself go. How you got a guy like him to date you, I'll never know."

"Thanks for the confidence booster. Coop likes me just fine the way I am." I wish Coop were here with me right now. He'd charm the pants off my parents, and I'd have one person on my side.

When I have them both in the same room, my throat goes dry, and I'm about ready to hurl. The morning sickness passed a few weeks ago, but right now, I could blow chunks for sure. They sit, staring at me as I pace up and down, wringing my hands together.

"Well, spit it out, Zoey. Your father and I don't have all day. He has a round of golf to play, and I have a committee meeting to get to."

"I assume you've seen me in the papers recently with Cooper Danford?"

"Yes, yes. We already know about him. Good catch. You really should be trying harder to stay in shape if you want to continue dating him." They are just completely blind when it comes to me.

"When you're done fat-shaming me, I came to tell you before you hear it on the news... I'm pregnant."

"Do you know who the father is?" Are they serious right now?

"No. I regularly participate in gang bangs, so I could only narrow it down to a hundred or so guys. They put out an announcement at the BDSM club I frequent, so hopefully, they can all take a quick DNA test and give me some answers." They stare blankly.

"Are you keeping it?"

"Seriously? No fucks given? Yes, I know who the father is. I've been seeing Cooper for quite some time now, and we're expecting twins."

"So you trapped him?"

I resume pacing, clutching my swollen belly in a protective way. "No, Mother, I didn't. I know you'll find this hard to believe, but he's the one who pursued me. He wants these babies. He wants to build a life and a family with me."

"You'll regret this later, and so will he..." My mom trails off, but I know exactly what she's thinking.

"Like you regret keeping me." Neither of them has a pleasant word to say, and I'm not going to stick around to hear any more of their vitriol. I pull out my keychain and remove the key to this house. I have no desire to come here under duress and subject myself to this shit.

I drop my key on the counter and head for the door.

"Zoey, don't be so dramatic."

"I'm not being dramatic. I just realized that your opinion of me will never change, and I'm done trying. Peace out." As I head out the door, relief washes over me, along with a wave of nausea. I'll not blow chunks in their house. I run for the door and keep my lunch down until I reach the bushes out front—the ones that used to break my fall when I snuck out of the house at night. It seems fitting that my parting gift is a big dose of vomit in their front yard.

When I get to my car, I immediately call Faith as I pull out of the driveway.

"Has he done the press conference yet?" Faith and Hunter went to the game today to show Coop some support. Plus, we factored in the possibility that Faith might have another mishap and divert press attention from our little bundles of news.

"Not yet. Game is almost done. I reckon it will be a good hour before the conference, though. How did it go with your folks?"

"It went just as I expected. They were assholes, and then I puked in the bushes out front of their house. I'm coming to you guys. I should just have come there in the first place. It was a waste of time talking to my mom and dad. They'd be shitty grandparents, anyway. Can I just adopt your Grams as my kids' grandma?"

"I'm sure she'd love that. You know she has a soft spot for Coop after Thanksgiving."

"I should've sent Coop to my parents' house. They would love him. I was lucky enough to have them echo everything Coop's fans have been saying. The essence of the conversation was the fact that I'm a fat slut."

"Zee, I'm sorry. I know what it's like to be on the outs with your folks."

"Yeah, but you had a relationship to tarnish. Your parents were upset out of love. Mine are just indifferent to me. Anyway, I've told them. It's done. Now I need to focus on learning how to be a good parent. I don't ever want my kids to think I don't care about them."

"That would never happen. You're the most loving person I know. You've always had my back. I have no worries about what kind of mom you'll be. These babies are going to be so loved, Zee. Not just by you and Coop, but by Hunter and me. We're family."

"Don't you go skipping ahead of yourself. Coop and I still have so many hurdles to overcome. It might not end up all sunshine and rainbows. I know that, so I don't want you getting your hopes up."

"Okay, I'll make a deal with you. If you make a real effort to open up to Coop and give him a chance at forever, then I'll keep my big trap shut on the subject."

"Faith..."

She cuts me off. "I don't want to hear your excuses. He is a good guy, he's clearly in love with you, and you're having his babies. He deserves at least an opportunity to win your heart."

"God, you're like a Hallmark movie sometimes. It's annoying as shit and makes you impossible to say no to. Although, how do you know that I haven't already professed my love to him?"

"Women aren't the only ones who gossip about their relationships. Coop and Hunter are like clucking hens when they get together. Let's just say it filters back. Regardless of whether you've told him, do you love him?"

"Change the subject, Faith. I'm driving downtown, and I want to pull my car over and puke my guts out. I need a good distraction. Tell me about the game. Is Coop staying focused? The last thing he needs is an angry mob when he's about to announce his impending fatherhood. If they lose, you know it will get blamed on me."

"Girl, he's crushing it. They are up by fourteen right now and dominating the field. Whatever you've done to get him on his A-game, keep doing it. They could be going to the Super Bowl if he keeps this up."

"I guess my swollen ankles and constant pickle breath is a real turn-on for him. I'll be sure to flash him my stretch-mark stomach before the next game."

"Are you totally craving sex? I hear pregnancy can cause some major lady boners in the second trimester."

"I'm pulling into the stadium now. I'll meet you in the conference room after the game."

"No fair. I want details! You got to hear all the sordid details of my deflowering."

"The whole of America got to hear the details of you being devirginized, Faith."

"I can't argue with you there."

"I'll see you shortly. I'm hanging up now." Before she gets a chance to protest, I end the call. She unwittingly hit a nerve. I haven't let Coop see me in my birthday suit since I started to show. The way he has always looked at me—as if I'm the most beautiful woman he's ever laid eyes on—I don't want to lose that. Pretty soon. I'm going to be a mother, and he's not going to see me as the hot, sexy, carefree girl you can fuck every which way.

We've had some lights-out activity since my sex drive has kicked up a notch. For me, that's still nowhere near my sexual appetite before the impregnating and all the puking. Hugging the toilet bowl hardly screams 'come get me, tiger.' It's easier on my dwindling confidence just to put some distance between us. The other side-effect of housing Coop's babies is that every time I look at him, I go all weird and gooey inside. It's disconcerting, and I don't like it. I feel like the Grinch, and my heart is reluctantly growing three sizes. Coop is a Who down in Whoville, except that he's really fucking hot, and he's an NFL god. Maybe not the best analogy, but I claim baby brain twice over. It's going to be a rough day all around.

The press conference is interesting. I hang at the back of the room with Faith and Hunter flanking me on both sides. Coop is just as charming and heartfelt as I expect him to be. He reads a brief statement confirming that he's going to be a daddy and that I am, in fact, his baby mama. He used those exact words, so he'll be getting a punch in the nuts later.

Reporters erupt into a barrage of questions, and there are some not-so-nice comments, but Coop keeps his cool and speaks with conviction. From what I know about him, keeping his cool isn't usually on the menu, but I'm happy he doesn't rise to the bait. Faith is the one I really need to worry about—she's ready to kill every reporter who has a bad word to say about me. She's a one-woman lynch mob! God, I love that girl.

Coop is happy to see me here, and when it's all said and done, he gives them all a show. The second he's done, he makes his way to me, cameras flashing left, right, and center. He slides his hand over my stomach—it's the first thing he does when we're together. He gets this goofy grin on his face that I kind of love. Then he pulls me into his arms and kisses me as if our lives depend on it.

Hunter is the one to step in, and he yanks Coop from my arms, making a path for us to leave safely. Faith is at my front with Hunter, and Coop is at my back. I'm a baby sandwich. I don't think I've ever had three people be so invested in my well-being. That's a sad fact of being Zoey Porter. I let myself drink it in for just a moment, but only for a moment. Faith is the only person I trust implicitly in this world. She won't hurt me or stop loving me, that much I know is true.

A friend like Faith is forever.

Men are a temporary fixture. Their love is fleeting. Sure, Coop thinks he has strong feelings for me right now, but they're not even about me, they are about the babies. Once we're in the thick of parenthood, I'm not going to be as appealing anymore. There's a reason I don't get involved with guys—I don't want to give them the power to break my heart. I've already given Coop more than I'm comfortable with, but there's something about him. He makes me want to believe I could have a happily ever after.

The press conference has stayed with me for days. Coop was so sure of himself, even in the face of ridicule. You have to expect it when we made sure not to be known as a couple in public and then coming out saying we're having twins. I get why they're surprised, and I only have myself to blame. If I had listened to Coop in the beginning, we wouldn't be facing any blowback right now. I'm the gold-digging fame groupie to the press.

I sometimes wonder if I'm defective. I don't get all gooey at the idea of tying myself to one man for the rest of my life. I struggle with the fact that I hate spending a night alone in my bed now. The bigger my belly grows, the more I crave falling asleep in Coop's arms. He's gotten under my skin, and I can't seem to shake it. He's like a barnacle, a super-hot, sexy, mouthwatering barnacle.

"Penny for your thoughts." His voice is so gravelly when he wakes up. It makes me want to mount his morning wood every damn time, especially with these pregnancy hormones running rampant.

"Just that you're a barnacle."

"What?" Shit. I really said that out loud.

"Never mind."

"You just called me a barnacle. I'm not likely to forget about it. Spill. Your mind is a freaky place. Just when I think I'm figuring you out, you come out with some random shit that throws me off."

"I was just thinking about Faith. Our best friends are married.

What does that mean for us? Am I going to lose her as a friend when we stop seeing each other? Like, who gets them in the break-up? Hunter is your best friend. Will I get phased out? Usually, when you split up with someone, you don't see them again. We're always going to be linked by our friends and by our babies. Everyone knows these things end badly. We'll be splitting the kids between households, and that's when animosity sets in. I don't want to lose Faith if we can't make it work."

Coop throws his hand up over his eyes, letting out an exasperated sigh.

"Why are you worrying about shit that hasn't happened? Is there no scenario in your mind where we go the distance?"

"It's just not realistic, but I want our kids to feel loved and wanted. Maybe we should quit while we're ahead? Be friends so that we can be the best parents for these little people growing inside me." My heart hurts at the suggestion, but that's just more confirmation that I should stop this before I get too dependent on Coop.

"Fucking hell, Zee. You're depressing as fuck right now. Just accept that we're giving this a shot, we'll have it all, and will be the happiest people on planet Earth... you, me, and the babies. We're going to be a family, and I'm going to love you. So shut the fuck up about breaking up with me, and let me love you, woman."

"You don't love me, Coop. You love the idea of me. I'm all pregnant with your twins and your mighty seed or whatever you're calling it. That's what you 'love.'"

"Right, because I couldn't possibly be cognizant of my own thoughts and feelings. Jesus, you really are a tough woman to love, but I'm going to do it anyway. Okay?"

"Okay." Even as I say it, I know I can't.

CHAPTER ELEVEN
COOP

TODAY IS THE DAY. I'm going to ask Zee to move in with me. She's going to freak out, and she's probably going to shoot me down, but I want it out there in the ether. I want her to have options, and with every week that passes, we get closer to the babies being born. I want to live in the same house as my children and see them every day.

Zee has been scaling back the amount of time we're spending together over the last few weeks, and I don't like it. I miss her. We speak on the phone every day, but we've gone from spending every night together to every other night, sometimes a few nights in between sleepovers. Listen to me, I sound like a teenage girl. *Please come have a sleepover, Zee. We'll have so much fun. We can watch rom-coms and paint each other's nails.*

I've resorted to asking Faith for some insight on her best friend, but she tells me to keep doing what I'm doing, and Zee will come around. Since the morning she called me a barnacle, I feel like I'm banging my head against a brick wall. The press has been lurking outside her office and following her every move. I tried to have a security guard watch out for her, but she's stubborn as a mule and kept sending him away until he quit.

The attention is hurting us and makes Zee even more aloof than normal. She wants to distance herself from me, which is impossible now that we're having twins. Today, I convinced her to let me take her on that first date we never got around to. A promise of no press and her favorite food of the week got me a firm 'yes.'

As I pull up outside her apartment building, she scurries out of the lobby in a baseball cap, as if that would hide her identity. I was going to go up to get her like a gentleman should, but she insisted on just jumping in the car. She's not exactly able to 'jump' in and out of anything now. She's got the cutest baby bump, and I hate that she's self-conscious about it. She's never looked more beautiful to me.

"Hey, champ. Where are we heading?" She lowers herself into the passenger seat, and I realize the Mustang may not have been the best choice. I should've brought my truck. It would definitely be easier for her to get in and out. Shit. I guess the Mustang isn't going to be family-friendly, especially not with twins. "Earth to Coop. Where are we going?"

Her voice breaks into my anxiety-inducing daydream.

"It's a surprise." I lean in, pressing my lips to her cheek. "You look beautiful today."

"Now I know you're lying. I think the suspension on this car is crying out for mercy with me in the passenger seat. It probably looks lopsided from behind."

"I'd enjoy looking at you lopsided from behind any time."

"Did that sound better in your head than when it came out?" She rolls her eyes and shoves me away.

"Yeah. It totally sounded cute, and it was definitely meant as a compliment. You look amazing."

"I look like a whale. Your nickname for me is going to have to change from beautiful to Shamu. My body is going to be ruined by the time these two arrive." She rubs her belly at the mention of the babies. She likes to portray herself as a hardass, but she's got a big, soft gooey heart. It's obvious to anyone who takes the time to get to know her.

"I forbid you from smack-talking my baby mama. I have impeccable taste, and my genetics wouldn't just commingle with some average girl."

"So, your sperm approves of me? You have a weird way of complimenting a woman, Coop. How have you managed to be such a player up until now?" She clicks her seat belt into place, and I pull into traffic.

"Who says I was a player?"

"Oh, come on! You can't play a player, champ. It takes one to know one."

"Are you playing me now, Zee?"

"Of course not."

"Then afford me the same courtesy. Trust me. I'm in love with you. If there's anyone in this situation who's going to get their heart shattered into a million shards of glass, it's me. Don't think I didn't noticed your distinct lack of reciprocation when I said I loved you for the first time."

She shifts uncomfortably in her seat, staring out the window to avoid my gaze. "You said it in a passing comment. I figured it was a slip of the tongue. You and I aren't 'love' people. We fuck, we enjoy no strings. It's our thing."

"Do I have to bring up the elephant in the car?"

"I already know I'm an elephant. I prefer the term 'thinly challenged.' Rude!" She smiles as she turns to gauge my reaction.

"Ha-freaking-ha. You can label yourself as void of the ability to love someone, but don't lump me in with that. We're way beyond no strings. Our babies have made sure of that. I lo..."

"Don't say it, Coop."

"Why?" I tighten my grip on the steering wheel, my knuckles turning white. "You already know I feel it. Why is it some terrible thing for me to say it out loud?"

"Because I'm not ready."

"Well, you better get ready. We're a family now. I don't care if you don't say it back right now." That's a bare-faced lie, and she knows it. There's pity in her eyes, and it's like a dagger to my heart.

"I don't want you to say it. It's an obligation. You want to make things more stable for the babies, I get it. But I don't want you to love me out of some misguided sense that everything has to be cookie-cutter perfect. Life doesn't work that way."

"It can if you let it."

"I can't. Maybe you should just take me home."

"Zee, can you stop overthinking every little detail? I'm taking you out on this date. We've been seeing each other for a long time by my standards. I don't profess to know everything about successful dating outside the bedroom, but I'm intelligent enough to know it usually involves a first date. We never had that, so we're doing it. Today. You can be grumpy, or you can chill the fuck out and let me romance you a little. If you behave yourself, I'll even throw in a foot rub when we get home. And some naked massage of any other areas you might be in the mood for." That gets a smile out of her.

"Is there food at this place? I'm starving." Her subtle fidgeting with her hands is a giveaway that she's nervous. Why would she be nervous about hanging out with me?

"Would I steer you wrong, beautiful? You'll have all your favorite foods. Anything you're craving today?" As we wind our way through the streets, I reach over and rest my hand on her leg. I want her to relax and have fun today.

"Popcorn, ice cream, and pickles."

"Together? Or separate?" She's had some weird food combinations in the last few months.

"Oh, I didn't think about putting them together. I might try that. Is that too gross?"

"Whatever you want. You're never gross to me. Okay, maybe the pickles in ice cream is kind of gross, but your wish is my command."

"So, are you going to tell me where we're going?"

"Nope."

I put in a call to Anders to see if he could sweet-talk the owner at the local batting cages for me. I want today to be incognito for Zee, so buying the place for a day was the only way I could see pulling it off. I carry a lot of sway in this town, but not when it comes to baseball. Zee is a big sports fan, and she mentioned how excited she is that Nashville is going to be getting its own major league team.

It took all of five minutes for Anders to get the owner of the batting cages to close shop for the day and let me attempt to impress Zee. I had someone bring in every food I could think of for my lovely, pregnant date. When I pull into the parking lot, Zee is grinning from ear to ear.

"Is this our date? The batting cages?"

"Yes. Did I hit a home run, or is this a swing and a miss?"

"Enough with the corny clichés! But yeah, you totally hit a home run. I love baseball."

"I know things about you."

"I guess you do, Coop. I'm impressed."

"Just wait until we get inside." I switch off the engine and quickly jump out and round to Zee's side of the car to help her out. She reluctantly takes my hands and lets me pull her up.

"Next time, can we take the truck? It's not easy for a weeble to get out of this car."

"A weeble? Woman, you need to stop ragging on yourself. We're out to have some fun, and you look amazing." Her lips find mine in a sweet caress.

"Thank you."

"What for?"

"For putting up with me. I'm doing my best, but none of this is easy for me." I slide my hands into her hair, pulling her close as our lips meet, our tongues twisting and tangling, lazy but full of urgency.

"We can go at your pace. I know you're worth the wait." I reluctantly relinquish her lips and drape my arm around her shoulder, pulling her tight to my side.

When we get to the door, there's a sign that says, *Closed for the*

Day on it. "Oh shoot. It's closed." Zee pouts her lips and ruffles her nose. It's so stinking cute.

"Not to us. You don't like being in the public eye, so I got rid of the public. It's just you and me. We have the whole place to ourselves."

"Oh, my God! Really?"

"Yeah. Too flashy?"

"I love it." She squeezes me tight, but her belly gets in the way. It grows by the day, along with my love for her. How could I not love her? She's taking care of our twins, getting them ready to face the world.

"Phew, I thought you'd like it, but I wasn't a hundred percent confident."

"That's so unusual for you. I thought you lived in a constant state of overconfidence."

"What can I say, you've changed me. Now, let's go have some fun."

When we get inside, the place is eerily quiet, but that's what I wanted. The caterer has put on an amazing spread, and Zee's eyes light up when she sees all her favorite foods. She grabs a plate and starts filling it.

"Are you going to keep me company and eat some of this?"

"You don't have to ask me twice. I'm on it, but if I get out of shape, I'm blaming you. You have good reason to eat whatever you like. You're eating for three now. I'm ducking out on training, so I can spend the day with you." I give her a conspiratorial wink and pick up a plate. It all smells delicious. I'm going to be working this off for the next week, but it's worth it to see the grin on Zee's face.

Without prying eyes around to divert our attention, it's so relaxing, like taking a hiatus from our normal life. Zee is enjoying herself without worrying about people snapping pictures or pawing at me for autographs. The conversation is flowing, and little by little, I feel like she's opening up to me. It's rare that Zee lets her barriers down, but I love getting to know her more. She's by far the most interesting, witty, and beautiful woman I've ever met.

"Ready to step up to bat, pretty lady?"

"Yep."

"Don't worry, I'll go easy on you. I bet you bat like a girl."

"You say that like it's an insult, Danford. Hitting 'like a girl' just means that I'm going to embarrass you when I hit a better average than you."

"Them are fighting words. Do you have a competitive streak?"

"Maybe a little. Besides, you keep telling me that I've been bestowed with the hallowed Danford genes, so I guess these little guys are going to give me an edge. I'll be swinging with the weight of three. You better watch out."

"Okay, you're giving me a boner right now talking about my genes being inside you." I'm not even kidding. It's this newfound primal boner. Every time I see her with that sexy bump, I just want to ride her until she's begging me to let her come.

"Everything gives you a boner. I reckon a good steak or the perfect french fries could get a rise out of your cock."

"Hey, don't underestimate the power of a well-cooked steak." I grab a helmet and put it on her head before handing her a bat. "You ready to show me what you've got, hot stuff?"

"I'm ready to beat you! Come on, babies, let's show Daddy what we're made of." As the words leave her mouth, I'm overwhelmed by a wave of—I can't even put it into words. It's like fireworks are going off throughout my body. Hearing her say 'daddy' just warms my heart.

"Big talk. Let's see it, then." I flick the switch for the pitching machine and wait. Zee has this serious look on her face, wiggling her ass as she swings the bat a few times, getting herself into position. It's not until the first ball comes hurtling toward us that I realize this was a really bad idea for a pregnant woman. She hits the ball dead on, sending it soaring. Fuck, she's good. The second comes, and she takes another swing. Two for two. As the third ball flies toward us, she flinches, dropping the bat and grabbing her stomach. The ball is coming straight for her.

I jump in front of her, shielding her from a seventy-five-mile-per-hour curveball. If I were smart, I wouldn't have faced forward. The ball smacks me right in the junk and sends me to the ground in agony.

"Are you okay? You grabbed your stomach. What's wrong?" My words are disjointed, barely above a whisper. Fuck, it stings. I'd rather slam head-on into a monster quarterback any day of the week. Baseball players must have a fucking death wish. A concussion is better than crushed nuts every time.

"Forget about me. Are you all right? That looked like a sore one." I'm now curled up in a fetal position.

"I'm fine."

"Yeah, you look it."

"Flip the switch. Turn the machine off before another ball comes flying at you." I hear it release as if it heard me and wants to put me in my place. I scramble up, moving her out of the way, and reach for the off switch. I get a ball right between the shoulder blades this time. It hurts like a motherfucker, but I'd take it five times over the crotch ball.

Zee starts laughing, her voice echoing in the empty space. "I'm sorry. I shouldn't be laughing. Are you okay?" She leans over, bracing her hands on her knees.

"No, I just got a curveball to my meat and two veg. I'm fucking traumatized."

"Don't make me laugh. I'm going to pee myself. Your spawn are sitting on my bladder."

"Cross your legs, or just... stop laughing at my pain." She actually crosses her legs, her hand reaching out to grab my shoulder to steady herself.

"Oh, man, I'm really sorry. I just can't stop laughing." She's all-out belly laughing at me, a little snort escaping her, which only makes her squeeze her legs together even more.

"I'm glad my excruciating pain amuses you." She stops mid-laugh and clutches her stomach once more, her face sobering. "Zee. What's going on? You're doing that thing again. Are you okay? Are you in pain?"

A wide grin spreads across her face as she lowers to my side and grabs my hand, placing it on her belly. Nothing is happening. "Just wait a..."

Holy shit! What the fuck was that? I can feel something against my palm. "What the hell?"

"Did you feel it?"

"Yes. What the fuck was that?"

"It's your babies kicking for the first time." Her eyes well with tears, and I'm not ashamed to say I'm about to follow suit.

"Are you serious? I thought it was some weird *Aliens* moment." Her stomach moves again with a strong kick against my hand. It's amazing.

"Don't worry, it's not extraterrestrial. Not that I know of."

"Has this happened before?" I stare at her stomach, willing the babies to move more.

"No, this is the first. I've had little fluttering feelings before, but not a real, distinguishable kick. It almost felt like gas. This... this is definitely a little foot."

"It's... wow. Incredible." I lean in, talking to her belly. "Hey, little guys. I'm your daddy." Another kick.

"Keep talking. They're responding to your voice."

"I hate to break this to you so early, but your dad is an idiot. I came up with this great idea for a date, but by the time your mom agreed to come out with me, you guys were taking root. Now, instead of a cute date, I'm the asshole who put a pregnant lady in front of a pitching machine. I think this is the definition of 'hair-brained.' In my defense, your mom has taken a really long time to warm up to me."

"I think it was a wonderful idea for a date."

"I should've come up with something else now that you're pregnant. Doesn't say much about my ability to be a dad when I put you in danger before they even come out."

"Stop being so hard on yourself. And keep talking. They really like your voice, and so do I." Her smile is so genuine, so I continue to ramble to her stomach.

"I'm excited to meet y'all. From your kick, I'm thinking one or both of you are going to make awesome kickers. Tiny Titans." More kicking. It's unlike anything I've ever felt before. They become more real to me at this moment.

"Oh my God, Coop. They do like your voice."

I rub my hand over her stomach, wishing I wasn't in so much pain right now as I take in this massive moment. "You guys might be the only kids I ever have because you kicked your mom, and I had to jump in front of a curveball. I'll teach you about them when you're older, but I think my nuts got the fright of their lives. They may never be the same again."

Zee rests her hand over mine, cradling her stomach. As I stare up into her eyes, she looks different—more beautiful if that's possible.

"Coop..."

"Yeah?"

"If your nuts are intact, don't have kids with anyone else... okay?" If I weren't already literally floored, this would do it—a crack in her ironclad façade. It gives me hope for our future.

"Zee..." I slide a tendril of her hair behind her ear, "... my swimmers are yours. I promise I won't let anyone else use them."

"That's the sweetest and kind of grossest promise anyone has ever made to me. I know I don't have the right to ask you that."

"Stop right there. You have every right. I've told you I'm yours for as long as you'll have me. Contrary to popular belief, I'm not an asshole."

"I never said that."

"I know you didn't. Just let me finish. You and I both know that sex can just be sex, a mutual pressure release valve, fun and hot, and a lot of the time, meaningless. But that's not how I want my life to be. I don't want to be that washed-up has-been who never really got himself a life. We didn't plan this, but the moment you walked in my door, I've been under your spell, even when you didn't want me to be. Maybe you still don't. But I'm here, and I'm all in. I mean all-fucking-in. You don't have to worry about me knocking up another woman. You don't need to worry about me even looking in another woman's direction. Just relax and focus on getting our little family to the end zone, okay?"

Her lips crash down on mine before straddling me on the ground. I'd be totally into it if she hadn't just sat on my sore spot. "Shit! Sorry, beautiful, I'm in agony here." She's about to move off me, and I can tell by the look on her face that she thinks it's because she's 'heavy' right now. Fuck that. I pull her back down, cock be damned.

"I'll move. I don't want to crush..." I don't even let her finish the sentence, focusing on the sensation of her lips on mine and the way she tastes as I make her forget her name with this one kiss. As she relaxes into my touch, her stomach is pressed against me, and one of the babies kicks so hard, I can feel it. So freaky and yet so awe-inspiring.

"I love you, Zoey Porter. Move in with me." This wasn't the way I wanted to broach this subject with her, but my brain short-circuits when I'm around her. I become dumb—or dumber than I already am—and things come out that aren't supposed to.

"I..." It would be cruel to leave her hanging. She's not ready to admit her feelings for me, but at this moment, I know beyond a shadow of a doubt, I'm going to marry Zoey Porter. It might take a year, it might take ten, but someday I'm going to put a ring on her finger.

CHAPTER TWELVE
ZEE

"YOU'RE INSATIABLE, you know that? I thought you were a depraved little minx when we first hooked up. Pregnancy is making you all kinds of naughty. I dig it." Coop's right. I can't get enough of him. The bigger I get, the more sex I want. I can't bear to sleep alone anymore, it's pathetic. I'm definitely making him work when he's in my bed—orgasms before saying goodnight and orgasms before saying good morning.

"Crap! I have to be at work in thirty minutes." I scramble off the bed. I'd say I'm in a hurry, but it's now physically impossible for me to hurry anywhere. If my apartment were on fire, I'd still only be able to waddle down the stairs. Coop points out the logistical nightmare of twins in a small apartment and up three flights of stairs every chance he gets. I haven't given him an answer about moving in with him yet, and it's been weeks since he asked, but if I'm really honest with myself, I want to live with him. I feel like I should do something special when I tell him because I've been such a crappy girlfriend thus far.

It still seems strange to me to say I'm Cooper Danford's girlfriend. He's been so understanding and patient, but I can see it's wearing on him. I want to say the three words I know he longs to hear, but whenever I try to vocalize them, it's as if I go temporarily mute. I want to explain why I feel so unworthy of him or these little lives growing inside me.

"Are we still on for staying at my place tonight? I need to stock up on clothes. The team is ragging on me every day that I now wear the same three outfits all the time. They're not wrong."

"Yes. I'll come by after I finish work. It might be a bit later than normal. I need to come back here and grab an overnight bag after I finish for the day."

"Do you want me to grab your stuff? I don't have to leave right now."

"Thanks for the offer, champ, but I'm fine. I promise I won't be super late. In fact, if you text me what you're in the mood for eating, I can pick it up on the way over."

"Let my very pregnant girlfriend run around town picking up my dinner? And the grand prize for douche canoe of the year goes to Cooper Danford! You get whatever you need for your overnight bag, and let me worry about dinner. If you have any cravings, text me."

"Me picking up takeout gets you all the way to douche canoe of the year? I'd have done it sooner if I thought there were awards involved. Something to tide you over while you wait on a Hall of Fame nomination."

"Burn. That was a low blow. For that, I'm eating the entire stash of pickles you keep in my fridge that you think you've hidden! It's cute, really."

"Aww, man. I totally thought I was hoarding them on the sly." I grab my purse and check my makeup in the mirror before heading to work.

"Do you want me just to pretend I don't know? I can manage the clueless ruse."

"You being clueless is a ruse? But you do it so believably. You should've gone into acting." I can barely keep a straight face. He's easy to wind up, but he gives as good as he gets. There's a laidback give and take to our routine these days, and I enjoy our verbal sparring and jibes.

"You think you're hilarious, don't you? You're lucky I adore everything about you." He strides over to where I stand with my hand on the doorknob. I need to get going, but I hate leaving him.

"You're not so bad yourself, Danford. I'll see you after work. I lo... I'll text you when I'm on my way." He slides his hands into my hair and pulls me in for a slow, sensual, mind-altering kiss. The way his tongue caresses mine makes me want to strip him naked and lick every inch of his body. The smell of his cologne has become such a comfort to me of late—sexy, sultry, and masculine. I breathe him in as he continues to kiss me, reaching the deepest parts of my soul.

"Do you really have to go?" His breath is ragged as he leans his forehead against mine. "Can you call and tell them you'll be late? Morning sickness."

"I don't have morning sickness."

"I know, but all I can think about right now is how desperately I want to hear you scream my name while you come."

"Maybe I can be a little late." I drop my purse and let Coop lead me back to the bedroom. His ministrations are a craving—one I can never fully sate.

By the time he's done with me, I can barely open my eyes. Bone-weary springs to mind. When he has to leave for some press conference, he leaves me curled up in the blankets.

"Do you want me to come back for you later if you're too tired to drive?"

I snuggle down further into the pillows that smell of his cologne. "I'll be okay to drive later. I just need a little cat-nap."

"Cat-nap? I could take a nap nestled tight in your pussy. Does that count?" An exhausted chuckle escapes me.

"You need to work on your romance language!"

"Anything for you, beautiful." He kisses my forehead and runs his hand over my ever-growing belly. "Bye, babies. See you tonight." They wriggle every time they hear his voice.

"The three of us will be over later. I promise."

"Okay. Have a good rest."

After he leaves, I can barely keep my eyes open long enough to tap out a quick text to my boss. Pregnancy hormones, especially when you're growing two babies, is enough to get out of any social occasion. My boss has been great about working with me. I usually push through and get my ass to work no matter how crappy I feel, but today it was nice to let Coop exhaust me in the most delicious of ways, and I drift off into a sated, dreamless sleep.

My heart is beating wildly in my chest as I pull up outside Coop's place. It seems like a lifetime ago that I was standing at his door for the first time with my mouth agape at how holy hot he is. And by the same token, it feels like yesterday.

As I shimmy my belly out from behind the steering wheel, I think I'm going to throw up. Not because I'm pregnant, but because I'm terrified about the grand gesture I'm about to make. I take a few deep breaths and pop the trunk to grab my bag. Before I can lift it out, Coop is out the front door, coming to greet me.

"Hey, beautiful. Perfect timing. I just got back with Chinese takeout and all the fortune cookies you can eat." He pulls me into his arms, barely able to get his arms around me at this point. Two babies equal a whole lot of belly. "Are you feeling okay? Your heart is pounding."

"I'm fine." *I'm not fine.*

"Good. Now I don't have to feel bad about fully appreciating how your breasts look in that top. They could make a grown man weep." I shove his arm, but I have to give him credit where credit's due. He's managed to put me at ease with one little compliment.

"You're going to be sad when they go back to normal size, aren't you?"

"I'll take you and your sexy chest any size, any day, any time. I'm an equal opportunities lover. Now, let me grab your bag, and let's get you inside, fed, and naked. In that order." He goes to the trunk and pulls my case out. "Jesus, Zee, what have you got in here? Rocks?"

"Just the essentials."

"Essentials. This thing weighs a ton. You shouldn't have carried this down from your apartment."

"I took the elevator, and the doorman lifted it into the car if you must know."

"Good. I'll be leaving him a big fat tip the next time I'm at your place. It still doesn't explain why you brought so much for a couple of nights. I have all your creature comforts here, or at least I try to."

"You do."

He slams the trunk shut and wraps his free arm around my shoulder. "Fuck me. You planning on staying for weeks?" He says with a chuckle. "You're lucky I'm so strong and manly." I shrug out from under his arm and step in front of him as he drags my suitcase.

"What if I did want to stay for a bit longer than a few days?"

"You know you're welcome to stay here whenever you want, beautiful. Mi casa es su casa. How long are you thinking? I know it adds time to your work commute, but you know I love having you here."

I take a deep breath, my heart almost galloping out of my chest. "I was thinking... maybe... if you're okay with it... I might stay... permanently. If you still want me."

He stops dead in his tracks, the furrow of his brow concerning me as he searches my face for I don't know what. "If this is a joke, it's not funny, Zee."

"I'm not joking. That night at the batting cages, you asked me to move in. It could've been delirium from taking a baseball to the groin, but on the off-chance that you meant it, I want to give this a try. Us. You, me, and the babies."

Before I can dig a bigger hole for myself, Coop drops my suitcase and sweeps me up into his arms as if I weigh no more than a bag of sugar. "Hell, yes! My baby and my babies under one roof. You won't regret this, Zee. I'm going to make you so fucking happy."

"Put me down. I'm all for celebrating, but spinning a pregnant girl in circles only leads to one thing." He immediately stops, setting me down with as much care as he can muster in his over-excited enthusiasm. I rather unceremoniously puke my guts out on the driveway outside his house—*our* house now. That's going to take some getting used to.

"Shit. I'm so sorry, Zee. Baby daddy fail. I'm just... fuck... I have never been happier than I am right now. This is going to be amazing. We're going to be amazing, I promise."

When I'm done retching, I stare up at him and smile even though my stomach is still churning. He has the goofiest grin on his face.

"This isn't playing out the way it did in my head on the way over." I retch one last time to add to my utter mortification. "There was a lot less of my lunch on your driveway, and I seemed sexy as hell in my head. Imagine Marilyn Monroe saying she wants forever with you."

Coop scoops me up into his arms, leaving my symbolic suitcase in the driveway. "Forever? I'll hold you to that. Marilyn couldn't hold a candle to you, beautiful."

"I'm all gross and pukey. I can walk into the house."

"It's customary to carry you over the threshold when you enter *our* house for the first time."

"That's after weddings."

"Same shit, different shovel." He slyly winks at me, and I can't help but smile.

"Shakespeare, eat your heart out. Who needs a sonnet when I have your romantic declarations?"

"He needed all that fruity language because he wasn't rocking a cock like mine. Tell me you wouldn't rather have my mouth put to better use."

"Please don't make me horny before I've brushed my teeth."

He's amused by the fact that I'm a pukey mess. "Not those lips I'm thinking about kissing, beautiful." Even in my current state, he sends a thrill coursing through me.

"What have I told you about referring to vagina lips? Not cool, buddy. If we're going to be roommates, you really have to stop with that."

"You love it. And I'm going to be the best damn roommate you've ever had." Cradling me in his arms, he heads for the front door.

"Faith is the only person I've lived with other than my family. She set the bar pretty high."

"Can she go down on you until your screaming in ecstasy? Hold on. Don't answer that. I'm having a major spank bank fantasy right now." Only Coop could take me puking up the contents of my stomach and the most nerve-wracking moment of my life and turn it around to make me laugh.

"You wish, champ. No more spank bank for you. If you want to get off, it better be with me."

"What? Is it considered cheating if I'm getting up close and personal with palm and her five sisters?"

"I don't know the rules right now. I'm hormonal, and I am moving in with a boy for the first time as we speak. And I'm all fat and smell like vomit."

Coop sets me down on the couch. "There's one rule in this house, and unless you agree to abide by it, I won't let you move in." My pulse quickens at the sight of his serious expression. Oh God, he's changed his mind about me moving in. Maybe I should've asked first instead of springing this on him. I thought it would be romantic—that didn't quite work out for me.

"You've changed your mind. I shouldn't have come." I'm about to scramble off the couch, but I'm not exactly the most agile human being right now.

"No, crazy lady, I'm going to chalk that ridiculous comment up to hormones. My one and only rule is... don't diss my girlfriend." Relief washes over me. "You don't get to use the word fat when talking about yourself unless you're using P.H. phat. As for the vomit, well, I can't really spin that right now, but I can go and get your suitcase out of the driveway and find your toothbrush for you. Sound good?"

"Yeah. Then can I get a do-over? A non-vomit moment."

"No do-overs, I'm afraid. You said you want forever with me, so I don't care if you blow chunks directly *on* me. This is still in my top three best days ever."

"What are the other two?"

"In third place is the day I got drafted to the NFL. Second place is you telling me you're pregnant, and top spot is this moment right here."

"You really think being forced to live with me and have kids with me is better than the NFL? You've worked your whole life for your career."

"Hands down, you're the best damn thing that has ever happened to me, Zoey Porter. Now just relax while I grab your bags. I really need you to brush your teeth so I can kiss the ever-loving crap out of you."

"Deal."

Coop disappears down the hallway, and the gravity of my decision hits me. I did it. I made a commitment. He's right. I told him I want forever, and yet I still haven't said those three little words.

The babies are awake, their little arms and legs shoving at my organs as they vie for space. I rub my hand over my stomach in an attempt to soothe them. "Hey, little guys... or girls. This is our new home. Not new to Daddy, but for me, it is. When you're ready to come out, this is where you're going to be living. I think you're going to love it. I know your dad is really happy that we'll all be together. I'm happy about it, too. He's going to be the best daddy in the world. I can just tell. Nothing like your grandfather, that's for sure. You'll love him. I know that, too, because I love him. I just haven't told him that. I will. Hopefully. I promise I'm going to try not to be such a mess by the time you're born."

They kick and shove at the sound of my voice. I seem to have the opposite effect on them than Coop. His low, raspy tone is like a lullaby to them and me. As I look around this familiar space, it feels different. I already have so many happy memories here with Coop, along with Faith and Hunter. It warms my heart to think of how many new and exciting memories we'll make here as a family.

When Coop appears with my suitcase, he's sporting the same goofy grin he's had since I got here.

"What are you so happy about?"

"That's a rhetorical question, right? My girl and my babies just moved in. I feel like the king of the world right now, except I'm not on a doomed ship about to drown."

"You've seen *Titanic*? I didn't peg you as a sappy movie guy."

"I may or may not have had what can only be described as an obsession with the Titanic when I was a kid. Did school projects on it, watched every documentary that's ever been made about it. Promise not to laugh."

"Okay."

"The last time I went to Vegas with the team, I told them I was going to meet up with a stripper we met the first night we got there, except I wasn't doing that at all. I went to the Titanic museum in the Luxor Hotel. I didn't give a shit about them knowing, I just didn't want any of them to tag along and ruin it for me. It was fucking epic. I read every plaque and looked at every artifact. I bought souvenirs and everything. Thought I was going to cry like a bitch baby when I saw the section of the hull they recovered from the wreckage."

I sit, stunned for a moment. I'm pretty sure he's the cutest guy who ever lived. Just when I think I've got his number, he surprises me.

'Wow."

"Do you think I'm totally lame now?"

"Just the opposite. I think you're adorable." He looks puzzled. "Now I need my toothbrush because I want to kiss your dorky, adorable face."

"Digging the Titanic is *not* dorky."

"Okay, Jack, but just so you know, I think Rose was an idiot. There was totally room on that floating door for the two of them. She told him she'd never let go and then literally let go of him. What the fuck? How is that true love? I would've hauled you up onto that door if it killed me. No way I'd be letting you die and leave me heartbroken. I'd be so pissed at you if you died."

Coop finds my toiletries and hands me my toothbrush and toothpaste. "Just so you know, I'm taking your annoyance at the prospect of my death as a profession of your love for me."

"Okay."

I may not be able to say the exact words, but I think he knows that I feel it all the same, I hope. Coop helps me to my feet and leads me down the hallway to his bedroom, although I suppose as of tonight, it's now *our* bedroom.

The moment I emerge from the bathroom with minty-fresh breath, Coop pulls me into his arms, his lips finding mine in a soul-destroying kiss. My pulse races with a deep desire to stake my claim on this man. He guides me over to the bed without breaking our kiss. Reaching for the hem of my dress, he runs his hands up my thighs, but I pull back.

"Can you turn the lights off?"

He stares at me for a moment, the spell broken. "Why? I want to see you while I make your toes curl. You're so beautiful, Zee."

"I don't feel it. Not today. Can we just turn the lights off?"

"Do you want me to stop?"

"No, I want you to make love to me, Coop. I want to know what it feels like to be loved by you." I can barely maintain eye contact with him as realization dawns. It's as if he's staring into my soul, and I'm more naked than I've ever been as I stand before him.

I watch the rapid rise and fall of his chest as he searches my face for a sign—of what, I'm not sure. "How is it that I'm the luckiest guy in the world, and yet you don't see what a catch you are?" A lump forms in my throat, and I know I'm going to break down if I don't shove this feeling right down to my boots.

"Stop talking and show me." He does as I ask long into the night, only stopping long enough to feed me the Chinese takeout that was left to go cold in favor of mind-blowing sex. What a way to spend our first night living together. If it's anything to go by, I'm probably going to die before I'm thirty of a sex overdose.

CHAPTER THIRTEEN
COOP

LIFE IS GOOD. It's better than good. It's pretty damn amazing right now. Zee moved in last month, and we've never been better. I was shell-shocked the day she showed up with her suitcase. We hadn't talked about her moving in since I asked her in a rather unceremonious way. She stuttered a few words that day, and I knew we weren't quite singing from the same song sheet. The fact that she didn't wait for me to ask again tells me we're on the same page now.

Zee thought it would be fun to have Faith and Hunter over for dinner the weekend after we moved all her stuff in. There's no simple text messaging between her and her bestie. Everything is a joke or a big reveal. Zee's apartment was originally going to be for her and Faith, but it never really panned out that way. Faith went on the fast track with Hunter and never got a chance to move in properly. That being the case, Zee decided to pull out their lease agreement at dinner and ask her to sign the termination papers.

The moment Faith realized what it meant, all hell broke loose. One thing is for sure, life for Hunter and I will never be dull, not with these two.

I've asked Zee a few times if there's anything she wants to change in the house to put her own stamp on it, but she insists she likes everything just the way it is. I was expecting to be complaining about the introduction of florals all over my house, but Zee, as always, surprises me at every turn.

With everything left as is, it seems odd to me that the house feels so different. There's something about knowing that Zee is here to come home to after a game and lying next to me when we wake up in the morning—it's epic.

I always thought I would feel trapped if I ever moved in with a woman, but the opposite is true. I suspect it's not so much about the cohabitation, but rather the person I'm doing it with. Zee isn't great about opening up and sharing her feelings, and even as I think it, I'm chastising myself for sounding like an episode of Dr. Phil.

Even though Zee hasn't said those three little words to me yet, I don't feel the same urgency to hear them. I know her heart, and she's here every day expressing herself with her actions. I can rest easy in the knowledge that she'll say it when she's good and ready because she definitely feels it.

The gravity of her giving up the lease on her apartment wasn't lost on me. She didn't insist on keeping it as a fallback plan. She's all in, and I respect her more every day as we navigate our way to the beginning of parenthood. We've talked it over and decided we want to be prepared, so we're going for a scan today, and we want to find out the sex of the babies.

I barely make it through practice in one piece. I'm so distracted—excited like a kid on Christmas Eve just waiting for Santa to arrive. I took some hits that are going to hurt in the morning, but I don't care. My focus is firmly set on Zee and the babies.

I've never been to Zee's office, mostly because she said it would be unbearable with everyone wanting autographs. I get where she's coming from, but I also understand the need—probably more than she does—to integrate our lives. I'm not going to just lurk in the shadows, so I finally convinced her to rip off the band-aid today and let me pick her up for the scan.

The second the receptionist sees me, her eyes go wide as saucers, and she grabs the phone. I'm hoping she's just calling Zee to let her know I'm here. If not, I'm about to be the hot topic around the water cooler. She composes herself before greeting me, but her cheeks are flushed, and she's struggling to look me in the eye.

"Hi. I'm Cooper Danford. I'm here to see Zoey Porter."

"I'm a huge fan!" Her composure lasted all of two seconds. "Would you mind giving me your autograph?"

"Yes, he minds. *I* mind." Zee's dulcet tones reverberate around the room.

"Hey, beautiful." I give her a quick kiss and rest my hand on her now sizable baby bump. I wonder if it should be called a 'babies' bump when you're having twins? "You ready to go?" I'm mildly aware of the receptionist sighing behind me.

"Come on back to my office for a minute. I need to grab some stuff to work on tonight. Plus, you won't have to deal with our wildly inappropriate receptionist drooling all over you." My woman is feeling possessive today. I like it. It's pretty sexy.

As I follow her to her office, all eyes are on us. It would be funny if Zee weren't so bothered by it.

"You'd think they've never seen a pregnant chick before." I try to make light of the situation.

"It must be nice to be you. No one is looking down their nose at you, wondering how the hell you snagged a hot catch like me." There's my girl, with a little fire in her belly. "I'm hot! Or I was before I started growing humans."

"Zee, take a breath, baby. Why do you give a fuck what any of those losers think? Besides, this is all in your head. Trust me, no one thinks that I'm too good for you or too hot. I'm the fucking envy of the locker room. All of my friends are wondering how the hell I managed to get you to agree to a date with me."

"It's not in my head. It's on your Twitter feed and all over Instagram."

"Seriously, I'm going to delete my accounts. I'm sick of idiotic keyboard warriors having any kind of sway over your mood."

"You can't do that."

"The fuck I can't! My job is to win games. That's what I get paid for. The rest is just bullshit I put up with to do what I love. I'm sick of it. In fact, can we just stop talking about it. I'm deleting all that crap today. I want to focus on the really amazing part of the day. We're going to find out if we're having boys or girls."

"Or one of each." A small smile returns to her stunning face as she shoves whatever papers she needs into her bag.

"I never even thought about that. I'm pumped! I got totally slammed at practice today. My head was in the clouds."

"Okay, let's do this."

When we head out into the main office space, we're back to being the center of attention. I sling my arm over Zee's shoulder, pulling her tight to my side. I hate when she's uncomfortable because she's with me.

"Wow. Your co-workers are bad at the incognito stares. I think the word blatant was invented for them."

"Don't y'all have better things to do? Haven't you ever seen a pregnant woman and her boyfriend before? Go about your business, people!"

"You heard the woman. Get back to work!" Her anger dissipates as she snuggles in at my side. "You okay, beautiful?"

"I'm good. Happy. There's no one I'd rather do all this stuff with."

"You sure you wouldn't prefer a guy who lives in obscurity? Someone who wouldn't draw attention when you walk down the street or through your own goddamn office."

"Even if you weren't... who you are... you'd still be noticed by every red-blooded woman in America. Famous or not, you're gorgeous. Like stupid handsome. Peak physical, mouthwatering, 'want to mount you every minute of the day' kind of masculine beauty." She's so stinking cute when her pregnancy brain lets loose for a minute or two.

"Well, thank you for the compliments, and rest assured, I'll let you 'mount' me the second we get home, but you missed the point. I meant you might prefer someone who isn't famous, who isn't me." We step into the elevator and head for the lobby. Zee moves up onto her tiptoes and pulls my face down, her lips soft as they meet mine in a sensual caress.

"I know what you meant, Coop. There's no one out there who could ever be better for me than you." I tangle my hands in her hair, deepening our kiss, but the lobby arrives all too soon.

"Let's go find out some genders."

"Are you sure you want to know?" Our OBGYN is enjoying this. We said at the last appointment that we didn't want to find out the gender of the babies, but I'm guessing she's seen this more than a few times, and the majority of parents-to-be cave and want to know. I just think with it being twins, we need to be as prepared as possible before they arrive. The Doc says it's unlikely Zee will get to forty weeks carrying twins, so we have even less time to prepare for twice as many babies.

My stomach is doing somersaults as we wait to hear the Doc say the words. Zee looks at me. "We want to know, right? All that scouts be prepared crap. We need to know."

"If you're having second thoughts, we don't have to find out." I squeeze her hand. I'm desperate to know, especially as we look at the screen and see those little hands and feet moving around. It actually looks like one of them is waving at us. It's insane and adorable, and I'm still struggling to wrap my brain around all of this. Yes, I can see Zee's beautiful big belly, and I can see the scan, watching the babies moving, but it's impossible for me to marry the two in my mind.

"I want to know. I just don't want to find out if it's going to ruin it for you. We're in this together, Coop. Your opinion matters to me."

God, she just slays me at the most inopportune times. I don't want to start bubbling like a baby in the doctor's office.

"I want to know. It would be nice to be able to decorate the nursery in pink or blue or whatever you would like."

"The nursery? Oh God. This is actually happening." She looks from me to the screen and back again like one of those crazy double-takes you see in cartoons. "We're having actual babies. We aren't mature adults, Coop. What if we mess them up? My parents are just awful people. I don't know the first thing about being a good parent." I run my hand over her cheek, hoping to give her some comfort. She's never mentioned her family before. Maybe I should've asked before now, but when I'm with her, no one else matters.

"You're going to be an amazing mom, Zee."

"What about you? Do you have normal parents?"

"My mom is great. Dad went AWOL when I was a kid."

"Oh God! We've only got one parent between us who's worth anything. This is going to be a disaster. And we have two babies coming, Coop. *Two!*"

"Zoey, look at me. Take a deep breath. We're going to take this one step at a time, okay?"

"I'm scared, Coop. What if I'm not cut out for this?"

"We already know all the things *not* to do when you have kids. The shitty parents taught us that much. The rest we'll figure out together. One day at a time. You and me, Zee."

"You and me."

The doctor has been waiting patiently while we freak out, a knowing smile tugging at the corners of her lips. I bet she's seen more meltdowns than she can count. "So, am I telling you, or would you like me to write it down and put it in an envelope?"

Zee looks at me with a huge smile on her face. "Tell us, Doc."

"I'm happy to tell you, you have two very healthy-looking twin boys. Strong heartbeats and right on target for size."

"Size? Like their manhood?" The moment I say it, I regret it.

"No, Mr. Danford. We check head size and limb measurements.

Twins are often smaller, but these two are looking on target for single pregnancy size."

"We're having boys! Zoey Porter, you're amazing." She giggles at my proclamation.

"I haven't really done anything, Coop, other than being impervious to birth control, apparently."

"Are you kidding me? You're making humans as we speak. Tiny little boys. Sons." A lump forms in my throat as I attempt to stop myself from tearing up, but I'm overwhelmed with unwavering love and devotion for this woman and our burgeoning family.

"Congratulations. Let me print you some of these scan pictures, and then we're all done for today. The front desk will get your next appointment booked in before you leave."

Zee gets cleaned up while I eagerly await some new pictures of our sons. *Sons.* I'd have been over the moon with girls or one of each —healthy babies are all I want—but knowing that I'm going to be a father to not one but two little boys, I feel like my heart is going to break free from my chest.

The doctor hands me the scan pictures before leaving us to go see her next patient. As I stare down at the most amazing little shots of our boys, I'm fit to burst. Zee cleans off the gel they use for the ultrasound, and after we check out and get our next appointment details, we make our way to the elevator. I can't stop looking at the scan pictures as we step inside and hit the button for the lobby. They're incredible.

"Have I told you lately how much I love you, Zee?"

"Yes, but I haven't told you."

"That's okay. I..."

"Shut up, Coop. I'm doing a thing here."

"O-kay."

"I'm trying to tell you that I... love you." *I'm speechless.*

I thought I was prepared, that I knew how Zee feels about me, but actually, hearing her say it out loud is more than my brain can process today. My pulse is racing as she holds my gaze.

"Zee."

"I'm sorry it's taken me so long to say it, but I just... I'm scared."

"Of what? Of me?"

"In a way, yes. I wasn't exactly wanted by my parents. I was an accident. So, you can imagine how much of a mindfuck an unplanned pregnancy is for me. I'm not good at talking about my feelings."

I reach out and cup her face in my hands. "You'll open up when you're ready, and I'll be here to listen. I know it took a lot for you to tell me how you feel. I thought I was okay knowing you felt it or were on your way to feeling it. But hearing it... Zee, you've made my life today. Knowing that you're carrying our sons and hearing you say you love me... I'm the luckiest man alive."

My lips crash down on hers, and I have a moment of déjà vu. The last time we kissed like this in an elevator, we rode that thing up and down until I finished riding Zee every which way I could.

"You're thinking about the elevator sex, aren't you?"

I grunt in reply, my cock straining against my pants. She reaches between us, her hand running down over the length of my erection. Fuck, that feels good. I close my eyes, letting my head drop back for just a moment, leaning into her touch.

"Fuck, you need to stop that." If my cock could talk, it would be screaming at me right now.

"Why? You're obviously enjoying it." Her voice has that delicious rasp she gets when she's aroused.

"We're not having sex in an elevator."

"It wouldn't be the first time, and if I recall, it was *extremely* satisfying the last time."

"You're pregnant."

"No shit. So, you don't want to nail the fat chick in a public place?"

"Zee, I'm going to need you not to refer to yourself as fat because it's really starting to piss me off." She's stunning. How does she not realize this?

"Well, I'd hate to piss you off by trying to get you off." She backs away, putting as much distance between us as she can manage in such a confined space.

"You are not fat, you're pregnant, and you are certainly not a random 'chick.' I absolutely want to strip you naked right now and ravage every inch of your body, but I won't. The reason has nothing to do with how physically attracted I am to you right now, which I just want you to know is a fucking truckload of attracted. You're sexier than the first day you showed up on my doorstep."

"That's a lie."

"No, it's not." I close the gap between us, bracing my hands on either side of her—there's nowhere for her to go, and she can't avoid my gaze. "Zee, the only reason you're not naked right now is because I have such reverence for you and for this stunning body you have. I need you to hear this. You're being so hard on yourself, and there's no need for it. You are beautiful. Stunning. I want you so bad my balls are turning blue. So, can we avoid fighting over a non-issue and go straight to the part where I take you home and lose myself in your pleasure until you can't take any more?"

"I like your plan better than mine." I find the sweet spot on her neck, letting the scruff of my jaw tantalize her senses as I kiss her just the way she likes. "Definitely better than mine."

"I have my moments of genius."

The second the elevator doors open to the parking garage, we quickly make our way to the car, both of us desperate to get home.

I'm grateful that the hospital is just a short drive from our house, and today my reasons are twofold. When Zee goes into labor, I'll be able to get her there ASAP. But today, I'm thankful that I can have her home and naked in record time. I always thought the idea of guys being super into their partner during pregnancy was a myth, but now I know this is some primal, caveman shit. She's got my babies inside her, and every time I look at her—really look at her—I fall more in love with her, and I get a major boner. It's a win-win.

Making love to Zee is all-consuming and better than any casual sex I've ever had—more fulfilling. Since she moved in, I think we've christened every room with the exception of the nursery. The thought of having sex in the room where my kids will sleep seems weird. Zee says until it is decorated, it's fair game.

Today is the day we're turning one of the guest rooms into the babies' bedroom, but before I get started, Zee steps out of the bathroom, freshly showered, her hair a cascade of soft waves. She has that look in her eyes, the one that oozes sex appeal. Leaning against the doorjamb in nothing but a towel, my jaw drops, as does her towel.

"Last chance to christen this room, champ. Are you up to the task?" There's a sly grin creeping in at the corners of her lips, and it's such a turn-on to finally see her confidence in the body she currently inhabits.

"Fuck me, you're mouthwatering. I've got an instant boner." I reach between my legs and attempt to adjust myself so it doesn't feel so tight and almost painful as my cock strains against my jeans.

"Then you won't mind letting me ride your face." Jesus, this woman is going to be the death of me in the best possible way.

I stop what I'm doing and stride over to where she stands, naked as a jaybird, and sweep her up into my arms. "You can ride whatever part of my body you want, beautiful, but you're doing it in our bed."

"You're no fun." She pouts as I carry her to our bedroom.

"I'm okay with that. Fun wasn't exactly what I was thinking. You're not going to be laughing when I'm pushing you to the brink of orgasm, holding you there until you can't bear it any longer. Then, and only then, will I slide my cock deep inside you and send you crashing over the edge with me, headlong into a fucking amazing orgasm."

"Mmm. I should shoot you down for not giving in to my room-christening sex."

"Are you going to? You'd be cutting off your nose to spite your face."

"Of course, I'm not. I'm horny as hell. I am going to ride your face for so long, you're going to have lockjaw when I'm done with you."

"Is that supposed to be a punishment? It's an incentive!"

CHAPTER FOURTEEN
ZEE

"YOU'RE JOKING, RIGHT?" Coop looks like a deer in the head-lights as he recoils from me.

"I think I just hurt the babies. Fuck, what if I speared them in the brain or something?" He slides out of bed and shrugs into his jeans.

"What the hell? You didn't finish the job, Coop. I'm horny, and you're leaving me hanging. Why are you getting dressed?"

"I'm taking you to the hospital. We need to get another scan."

"What? You're totally overreacting. So what if the babies moved while we were having sex, it's not a big deal. They kick me all the time."

"I was too rough. I got carried away in the moment. I really think we should get you checked out. Don't babies have a soft spot on their heads? What if I damaged one of them with my cock? Fuck. They're not even born, and I'm messing up." He's serious. I guess I am not getting a spine-tingling orgasm, then.

"Coop, while your cock is big and hard and all kinds of impressive, it can't reach into my uterus. The twins are fine. Stop being ridiculous and come back to bed."

He starts pacing the room, running his fingers through his hair. "I know you're kidding right now, but let's be serious, my cock is massive."

"I can't believe you're saying this with a straight face, Coop. For a start, if you pierced my uterus with your mighty member, you would also have broken my waters. Do you see any liquid?" I throw back the covers in an attempt to entice him back to bed.

"No."

"Then, I'm right. I love you, but you're batshit crazy sometimes. You won't harm the babies by having sex with me. In fact, the doctor said that if I go to term, then sex can help induce labor at that late stage. Right now, you're fine to ravage me as much as possible before we become a family of four."

He takes a seat on the edge of the bed, reaching over to hold my hand. "I don't think I'll ever tire of hearing you say you love me."

"I'm sorry it took me so long."

"Don't apologize, Zee. I'd rather know that you mean it. If you'd just said it because I did, I'd never know if it was your true feelings or whether you were placating me."

"I'm not exactly the kind of woman who placates in any way at all."

"Yep, you're a ball-buster. Thank God we're having boys. I don't think I'd survive in a house with three ball-busters."

"Maybe the next one will be a girl." I don't know why I just said that or where it came from. I'm waiting for Coop to get spooked at the prospect, but he just smiles at me.

"We'll still outnumber you three to two. Besides, I like the idea of being a girl dad, especially if she takes after her mother. You're feisty, and you don't take any shit. I reckon our daughter would follow in your footsteps." I'm waiting to feel panic rise in my chest, but it doesn't come. Instead, a calm warmth spreads through every nerve ending in my body—*contentment.*

It's such a foreign concept to me that I didn't recognize it right away. I take a moment to drink him in. Cooper Danford. As a lifelong Titans fan, I've always appreciated his talent and hard work. As his girlfriend, I love his kindness and how open and honest he is with me. I've given him so many reasons to walk away, but it just makes him love me harder.

"Now, will you come back to bed and finish what you started?"

"Are you sure the babies will be okay? Maybe we should hold off until after they're born?"

"What have you done with the real Coop? The guy I know couldn't go weeks without getting his rocks off."

"Trust me, I don't relish the idea, but now I'm fucking terrified I'll hurt you."

"You haven't. You won't. Stop thinking with your overprotective brain and start thinking with your cock again, please." A slight smile tugs at the corner of his mouth.

"Aren't women the world over telling guys the exact opposite of these sentiments?"

"What can I say? I'm not like other women."

"Don't I know it."

"Listen, the way I see it, we have to enjoy while the getting is good. Who knows what shape my vagina will be in after I birth two Danford babies. Look at you, you're a mountain of a man. These babies are going to obliterate me, and you'll be complaining for the rest of your life that fucking me feels like throwing a rope into a trashcan."

"Wow! That's a graphic and deeply-disturbing picture you paint of our future. Plus, there's surgery now that can restore you to a pre-trashcan vagina, and let's not forget that I can have just as much fun with anal. You'll still be tight as a drum back there, beautiful."

It doesn't matter what's happening, Coop can always make me laugh. He can find the lighthearted side in any situation.

"Yeah, like I'll be letting you anywhere near my ass right after I've given birth to your cute, lovable, tiny spawn."

"Misery loves company, right? At least I'll still have palm and her five sisters to fall back on."

"I hate you right now."

"No, you don't. You love me. You said it out loud, and there are no take-backsies."

"Take-backsies? What are you, eight? I'll love you even more if you take your pants off and fuck me. If I'm going to be severely lacking in the orgasm department for a while, it's really your duty and a kindness to both of us if you just shut up and put that big cock of yours to good use."

"How can I say no to that?" he says with a wickedly delicious and dark tone to his voice.

"You can't." I throw back the sheets and spread my legs, cupping my full, and may I say kick-ass breasts. He doesn't disappoint, the rapid rise and fall of his chest telling me he's powerless to refuse me. As he ravages my body with his gaze, I feel emboldened right now. Seeing myself through his eyes, I feel like the most beautiful woman in the world.

His ministrations aren't rough or frenzied, but the end result is the same, if not more intense because he's so skilled at building my anticipation until I'd sell my soul for the release only he can give me.

We make love long into the night, and as we rest in sated bliss, the unimaginable happens. *I'm mortified!*

"Zee?"

"Yeah?" Please don't have heard. Please have missed it.

"Did you just fart?" Oh God.

"There's no dignity left in pregnancy. Can I just run away and hide now?"

"Well, I'd say you could hide under the covers, but I'd strongly suggest you don't inadvertently Dutch oven yourself right now." I shove his shoulder, my cheeks flushed with embarrassment.

"You're mean."

"I'm mean? You're the one who just disturbed the covers, which goes against the rules of sharing a bed with someone. Now I'm getting a waft of it." He fakes being horrified, but I can tell he's just loving this.

"Just for that, the next time I'm going to totally hold your head under the covers. You have to be nice to me, I have a fragile ego right now, and I'm carrying your babies."

He's trying to keep a straight face and is failing miserably. "I suppose I should be grateful for small mercies. I'm lucky you didn't shit the bed. You didn't, did you? Come to think of it, it sounded a little wet."

"I'm doing take-backsies. I don't love you. I'm beyond mortified, and you can't stop laughing at me." I move to get out of the bed, but he pulls me back in.

"What did I tell you about disturbing the covers!"

"You suck, Cooper Danford."

"And apparently, you blow."

"I'm going to sleep in the guest room." He's got me smiling, and it annoys me that he can change my mood on a dime.

"The hell you are. You're parking your stinky little butt right here with me. We live together now, Zee. It was bound to happen sometime. I'm just glad it wasn't me. How would I have explained to the paramedics that I knocked you out with a one-cheek squeak?"

Okay, he got me. A laugh escapes me as he tucks me into his chest, his warmth warming my back as he drapes his hand over my stomach. This is the way we fall asleep at night, it's super corny, and I love it.

"I love you, beautiful, farts and all."

"Let's never speak of this again."

My OBGYN says I could go into labor anytime now. She thinks it's best for me to have a planned C-section, so we don't have any surprises or problems. She gave us stats on so many scenarios that it was all a bit overwhelming. Coop and I talked it over, and as much as I'd prefer not to have surgery, I want to do what I feel is right for the babies.

Coop has backed me on every decision throughout my pregnancy, but at this point, I can tell he's worried about the birth. I'm focused on the two little lives I have to bring safely into the world. He's got the added burden of worrying about me.

We're meeting up with Faith and Hunter tonight for dinner, and after talking it over with Coop, I'm going to ask Faith if she'll be there with us. I don't want to be on my own while they sew me back up like Frankenstein's monster, and I'm adamant that Coop stays with the babies once they're out. They need to be the priority, and if Faith is there to hold my hand, he won't feel so torn between the twins and me.

Faith has always been my rock, and it only seems fitting that her husband is Coop's steadfast friend. I'm sure he'll come to the hospital and sit in the waiting room in case Faith or Coop need him.

I'm struggling at this late stage to find any clothes that fit. Stretchy pants are my savior, and I'm way past cute maternity tops. These boys are big and heavy. I've taken to wearing Coop's jerseys and shirts, and even they are getting a little snug.

The nursery is finished, and there are two cribs ready and waiting for some babies. When I can't sleep at night due to the worst heart-burn, I go into the room and sit in the rocking chair in the corner. Staring at the cribs, I still find it hard to picture what life is going to look like for us in a few weeks.

Faith and Hunter are already at the restaurant when we arrive, and my bestie is off her feet and hugging me as best she can. Side hugs have become a thing now. No one can reach me from the front anymore.

"Oh my God! You've gotten bigger this week." She cups my belly, dipping down to say hello. "Hey, boys, it's Auntie Faith. I got you some cute clothes today and lots of books."

"Don't say bigger, Faith. Zee will knock you out if you say that again," Coop interjects.

"I mean it in a good way! You look amazing, Zee. Like actually glowing. Pregnancy suits you."

"Yeah, yeah. Tell that to my bladder and my esophagus at three in the morning."

Hunter stands to give me another side hug. "Hey, Zee. Babies giving you a tough time?"

"Yes."

"They already take after their dad, then." He shoves Coop's shoulder, and they do their bromance hug before we all take our seats at the table. Damn, I don't think I can get close enough to eat my dinner. I'm officially over pregnancy in a big way.

Coop sidles up beside me, draping his arm across the back of my chair. "You okay, beautiful?"

"I won't be able to reach my plate."

"I can fix that. The way I see it, you have two options."

"And they are?" He has that little hint of mischief in his voice, so I know he's about to make a joke of some kind.

"Option one, we balance the plate on your stomach. You have your own built-in table."

"That makes me want to stab a fork in your hand. Next option."

"You can sit back, relax, and I'll feed you like Cleopatra. You're my queen, and you know I like to meet *all* of your needs."

"Better." I want to lean over and kiss him for being so sweet, but I'm afraid I'll tip over. "Come here and kiss me, champ."

"Your wish is my command."

"Y'all are so cute," Faith says as she snuggles close to Hunter. "When are you going to tie the knot?"

I kick her under the table. I can still move my ankles. "I'm going to need you to shut up, Faith."

"What? You're having babies. You live together. You're in love and about to be a little family of four. Why do I get a kick in the shin for asking? It's going to happen eventually. Why not now?"

Coop comes to my rescue, as usual. "I've asked. I listened to Beyoncé. I like it, and I want to put a ring on it. She shot me down." He slyly winks at me. I don't think he realizes that wasn't the thing to say to my best friend to get her to shut up.

"What?" Her voice echoes through the restaurant, garnering stares from the other patrons. "He asked you to marry him, and you didn't mention it? And you said no!"

"Okay, can you keep it down to a dull roar? I'm pretty sure the chef heard you. Don't get all bent out of shape. It wasn't a real proposal. There is no ring, and there was no proposal. He mentioned in passing that we could get married the day I peed on three sticks and made us a family. Everyone knows a conception pity proposal doesn't count. You have to mean it and not because of a champion swimmer penetrating an egg in my uterus."

Now they're all staring at me, including Coop. "You didn't think I meant it?"

"What? Don't play around. Faith will think you're serious."

"I am serious."

Hunter looks to his best friend before adding his two cents. "I know Coop, and he wasn't playing around. Sorry, Zee. Three to one, he proposed."

"No. All he said was that he'd be a good husband. That's not a proposal. You can't gang up on the pregnant lady. I'm not in control of my emotions right now. If I start crying in the middle of dinner and end up on someone's Instagram feed ugly crying, I'm coming for all of you."

"What if I did the whole 'down on one knee with a ring' thing? Would you say yes?" Are you kidding me right now? I want to strangle Faith for bringing this up.

"I'm not talking about hypotheticals. That's not how this process works, and that just proves that we're not there yet. You want me to say yes to the idea of a ring and a grand gesture."

"I'm just trying to get a read on you. You're not the easiest woman in the world to woo."

"I think you 'wooed' me just fine. We're having two kids, and I told you I love you. Isn't that enough for now?"

"Hold the phone! You said you love him? That's huge. How did I not know about this? You've been holding out on me, bestie."

I turn to Faith and stare her down. What the hell? She's single-handedly throwing me to the wolves. "Yes, okay. Emotionally stunted, relationship averse me said the words out loud, and I've done it more than once. Not that it's anyone else's business, but if everything needs to be documented for posterity, let me reiterate the fact."

Completely out of character, I stand up and holler. "Listen up, people. I, Zoey Porter, love Titan star, Cooper Danford. I'm carrying his babies, and I love him. That's all. You can go back to enjoying your dinner." I take my seat, and you could hear a pin drop in here right now.

Coop grabs my face and plants an over-the-top kiss on my lips. "Hell, yeah." He pulls back just enough to hold my gaze. "That might have been the sexiest thing you've ever done for me. Would it be terrible if we ditched these two and went home for some naked dinner?"

"Can we wait until after dinner? I've been looking forward to their chicken parmesan all day."

"Okay, but dessert is going to be in a to-go box, so I can eat it off you when we get home."

"Deal." A thrill runs through me at the thought I may be equally excited about the naked part and the dessert. They make the best chocolate fudge cake here.

"And, Zee, you would never be a pity proposal. I'd marry you tomorrow if you'd have me, regardless of the fact that we're having kids together. I want you. I have since the first moment I laid eyes on you. Just remember that, okay?"

I have no words. My brain goes completely blank, and all I can do is nod my head.

Coop wasn't kidding when he said he was going to feed me like Cleopatra. I can see people at the surrounding tables staring, but for once, I just don't care. My boyfriend is amazing, and he's going to be the most wonderful father. I can take a few sideways glances while I enjoy his attention and love for me.

When dinner is finished, and we're enjoying a few laughs, I

decide it's the right time to speak to Faith. "I have something I want to ask you. Don't feel obliged to say yes, and I won't be offended if you'd rather not."

"Spit it out, Zee."

"The OB has scheduled a C-section for two weeks from now."

"Eek! I'm so excited to meet the little guys."

"I want Coop to be able to stay with the babies after they're born, but I'm not going to lie, I'm a little scared about having major surgery. I'd like you to be in the room with me... if you want to... if you're okay with seeing my insides."

My best friend leaps from her seat and rushes to hug me, almost cutting my circulation off entirely. "Yes! Of course, I will. Oh my God. I'm going to be holding your hand the second you become a momma." The smile on her face makes me feel more loved than I deserve.

"Phew, I'm so relieved. Knowing that I'll have you and Coop there is all that's getting me through the fear."

"Don't give in to fear, Zee, we've got your back." I hold her tight before looking to Coop.

"Do you want to tell them the other part?" He's a handsome devil when he smiles, and I adore how genuine it is.

"While we've been trying to get ready for the babies being born, we started talking about who we'd want to look after them if something ever happened to us. You were our first choice, both of you. We'd like you to be the boys' godparents. You can take some time to think it over. I know it's a big ask."

"Are you kidding? We don't need time. Of course, we will. We'd be honored, wouldn't we, Faith?" Hunter's reaction warms my heart. He and Coop are like brothers, and their bond makes them family.

"Yes!" She looks to her husband with so much love, and I know that if the worst happened, they would take care of our babies as if they were their own. It's a lovely end to our evening.

When we pull into the driveway, I'm ready to crawl into bed with my man. He helps me out of the car now that my stomach has its own orbit. "Want me to carry you in? You look exhausted."

"I don't need you in a hospital bed next to me with a hernia."

"Very funny. You're forgetting I have brute strength that most men could only ever dream of."

"How could I forget? You're one of a kind, Coop."

"You know it!" I waddle my way to the door, happy to be home.

"I have an idea to run past you."

"Shoot." Coop is always three steps ahead of me, anticipating my quirky little routines. The second we get inside, he heads straight for the refrigerator and pours me a cool glass of milk and goes in search of my favorite cookies in the pantry.

"I've just realized that my pregnancy cravings have turned me into Santa Claus."

"Does that make me Mrs. Claus, or am I Rudolph?"

"You're a good ride, so I'm going with Rudolph."

As we head into the bedroom, my pulse quickens, and I know I have to say it before I change my mind. Coop hasn't forgotten either.

"So what's this idea you have? If you want to change all the nursery colors with two weeks to go, I'm not doing it. I'll pay someone else."

"The nursery is perfect. You did an amazing job, and I told you to get someone to do it, so you only have yourself to blame for how time-consuming it was."

"Then, what's on your mind, pretty lady?"

Before I give him the bare minimum information about my idea, there's something I need to ask him.

"Coop..." My heart feels like it's hammering against my ribcage right now, and I don't know why I'm so nervous. "Why do you love me? You could have any woman you want. I don't get it. Why me?"

"Is this a trick question?"

"No. I honestly don't understand, and I want to." He reaches out to rub his hand over my baby bump. It's such a simple caress, and yet it makes me feel loved in a way I never have before.

"Are you being serious?"

"Yes. Humor me."

"Okay, well, let's start by taking the fact that you're about to bring my sons into the world out of the equation. I loved you before you peed on the sticks."

"You did?"

"Yes. Was my love for you not evident in how eagerly I pursued you, or in the way our bodies fit like they were made to be together? I love everything about you, Zee. Your smile, your laugh, the way you stood up for Faith when she needed you. I love the little triangle of freckles you have beneath your left eye. Not something most people would notice, but I think they're adorable. You're smart, funny, and you're not afraid to give as good as you get. I even love the way we bicker daily but fall asleep in each other's arms. Shall I go on?"

When I open my mouth to answer, nothing comes out past the lump in my throat, and I burst into tears. "I love you, Coop."

His brow furrows as he searches my face for any inkling of why I'm so upset. "I love you, too, beautiful. What's wrong? Did I say something wrong?"

"No. You said everything right. No one has ever loved me as much as you do. Not even my parents."

He wipes the tears from my cheek with the pad of his thumb. "Talk to me, Zee. What's this all about? You never talk about your folks. All I know is that you said they were shitty parents."

"They don't love me, Coop."

"I'm sure that's not true."

"It is. I'm not a lovable person. They never wanted me. I was a mistake, an unplanned, unwanted mistake. There's something wrong with me. If my own mother and father can't stand to be around me, then what hope do we have? You're going to realize at some point that I'm not someone you can love for the rest of your life."

He cups my face in his hands, forcing me to meet his gaze. "Zee, I need you to listen to me right now. Look at me." I do as he asks, his gaze reflecting my own, wet with unshed tears. "You're the single most amazing person I've ever met. To know you is to love you, and I wake up every day knowing that you're too good for a dumb jock like me, but I plan on earning your love, every minute of every day for the rest of my life."

"But..." His lips find mine, soft but urgent as he pours all of the love he feels for me into this one kiss.

"But nothing. They're wrong, Zee. If they can't see how amazing you are, then it's their loss. Is this why you pushed me away for so long? You thought you weren't worthy of being loved?"

"Yes."

"I'm not going anywhere, Zee. You and me, we're family. I don't care about anything except you and our boys. I love you so much it hurts, and it breaks my heart to think that you don't feel like you deserve to be the center of someone's universe. You're the center of mine. You always will be. Do you hear me? Tell me you understand that my love for you is unconditional."

My lips crash down on his, my soul lighter for having told him everything. Now I know with unshakable certainty that I want to do something for him. I want him to know how much I love him.

"Will you come somewhere with me on Friday afternoon?"

"I'd go anywhere with you, beautiful."

"Good. I'll text you the address and meet you there after I finish up at work. It'll be my last day, and I'll be done by lunchtime."

"Are you going to tell me what we're doing?"

"Nope. It's a surprise. Is that okay?"

"Yes, but can I at least pick you up at work?"

"That's also a no."

"Will I like the surprise?"

"I hope so."

"It's from you, so I think I'll love it. Unless you're playing a prank on me, then I might not dig it."

"It's not a prank. Not by a long shot."

"I trust you. Now, will you let me show you just how much I love you?"

"Does it involve your head between my thighs?"

"Yes." And just like that, he takes me from crying to making me wet for him.

"Then have at it." He gives me a mischievous grin as he slides his fingers under the waistband of my panties. "And Coop... thank you."

"For what? I haven't started yet."

"For everything. For listening. For loving me."

"I'm always going to love you, beautiful. Now lie back and enjoy."

CHAPTER FIFTEEN
COOP

ZEE HAS GOT me distracted today. She's been plotting something all week, and I've been trying to weasel it out of her, but she's being tight-lipped. This morning, she handed me a piece of paper with coordinates on it—not an address—coordinates. Who does she think I am? I use Google Maps to get me around a city I've lived in for years.

I called Hunter to see if Faith knows what her best friend is up to, but he was in the dark too, until today.

"We got a message from your girlfriend this morning telling us to be at some random coordinates this afternoon."

"Seriously? She gave me an envelope this morning with coordinates. I wonder what she's up to. Maybe a fancy lunch before we're parents and never get the time to do anything at a leisurely pace."

"Why wouldn't she just want to do that with you? Why include Faith and me?" He chuckles to himself. "I guess that isn't so strange. Who'd want to actively spend alone time with you? The last time she did that, you knocked her up."

"You're a fucktard, you know that, right? I'm a catch. She's lucky to have me." My response only garners more laughter.

"The reverse is true, bro. You're a lucky son of a bitch that she gave you the time of day, and even then, it took you a while."

"It must be nice to sit up there on your high horse as the conqueror of virginity."

"That's a new one, but I'll take it."

"So, you really have no idea what we're doing?"

"Nope."

"Then how do I know what to wear? Should I wear a suit, or jeans, or somewhere in the middle."

"I'm hanging up now. You just crossed the line from metrosexual to being the biggest girl on the planet. What should you wear? Shut the fuck up with that crap. Wear clothes, that's all the direction you need."

"Great, and here I thought I'd just show up naked. You're zero help."

"And yet you think I'm the best guy to raise your babies if you die. How messed up are you?"

"Thanks, fucknuts. I'll see you at the random coordinates later. I may or may not be naked."

"Later, bro."

Hunter's right, I've crossed a line. I'm standing in my closet having tried on four different outfits. Thankfully, Zee isn't here to witness my demise. Everything I feel for her right now is so heightened. I'm not sure about her being more emotional with pregnancy hormones—I think I'm the one who's acting like I've had an injection of estrogen. She's so fucking amazing, though. I really lucked out. We've got eight days left until our babies are born, and I want to savor every minute. Things are going to get crazy around here for a while, and I'm cognizant of the fact that I need to let Zee know that I'm here, I love her, and we're a team. Be a supportive partner and all that crap it says in the pregnancy books. She's doing all the hard work right now, so I'm looking forward to being useful.

When I've finally settled on jeans and a semi-dressy shirt, I grab my keys and head off to meet Zee and the others.

I've never been to this part of town before, so I park my car within a five-minute walk of the coordinates Zee left me this morning. The air is crisp, and the sun is shining, so I take a moment to drink it all in as I round the corner to my destination. It's then that I see her and drop my phone, listening to it smash on the sidewalk.

"What the hell is going on?" She's standing before me with a huge grin on her face. Hunter and Faith are at her side, sporting some crazy smiles that would freak me out under any other circumstance.

"Hey, Coop." Zee's voice is raspy, just the way I like it when she has a devious plan.

"H-ey. What's going on, Zee? I thought we were going for a fancy lunch or something. A last hurrah before the babies come."

"Well, we can go for a fancy lunch after."

"After what? Zee, you look... wow. I'm actually speechless right now. And I'm totally underdressed."

Hunter chuckles, enjoying my bewilderment. "Shut up about your clothes, snowflake. Listen to the woman."

I can't take my eyes off her. She looks incredible.

"Cooper Danford, you have put up with all of my bullshit and loved me regardless."

"Now, who's being eloquent?"

She takes my hands in hers, and everything around us fades into the background, even my smart-ass best friend. "We're about to go from a team of two to a family of four. I've never been loved by my family, not really. Faith has been my constant since the day we met. Then I turned up on your doorstep, and life has become all kinds of different."

"Is that a bad thing?"

"No. I thought it was for a while, but I needed to get out of my own way and let you love me. It was only then that I was able to love you back. I'm not all fixed and great at this stuff, but..."

"You're better than you think." I squeeze her hands, search her eyes for what she's trying to say.

"I want to be better for you and our boys, our little Danford potatoes."

"Don't you mean Porter potatoes?"

"No. I want them to have their daddy's name." My heart is fit to burst out of my chest, but before I can pull her in for a kiss, she continues. "I was sort of hoping that I could have the same name as them."

"Zee, are you talking about hyphenating? I'm cool with that. I didn't think I was getting a look-in on the name front, so any little part of me in there is amazing."

"God, you can really be dim sometimes, Coop. I'm not asking to hyphenate names. I'm trying, and obviously failing terribly, to ask you to marry me."

My breath catches, and my brain short-circuits. I must be dreaming. Zee, my Zee, is so firmly against the idea of being married to me or being at all conventional in the building of our family.

"Hey, doofus. Your girl just asked you a question. You're supposed to answer. It's customary," Hunter snaps me back to reality.

"I was supposed to do this with a ring and a super special date. I wanted you to have a perfect proposal, one you can't say no to."

"Coop, this is the perfect proposal for me. I don't need a ring or some big show. You show me every day that you're in this with me. It took me a long time to realize that I want this. I want this more than I can put into words. No fanfare, no big dumb wedding." She turns to Faith and Hunter. "Sorry, guys. No offense. I loved your wedding."

"No offense taken. We already know you had a great time at our wedding. The broken car window said it all."

"Okay, hotshot, button it until your best friend says yes. I feel like an ass right about now. If he shoots me down, this is going to go down as my worst idea ever."

Her hands are shaking as they rest in mine. "Zee, there's no scenario in which I say no to this. I think I'd have married you after that first dirty weekend. I've been waiting for you to catch up to where I'm at in our relationship."

"Sorry it took me so long. If you'll have me, we can walk inside the courthouse right now and get hitched. We have two witnesses, and your buddy has two wedding bands tucked in his pocket. What do you think? Want to make an honest woman of me before I birth your kiddos?"

I pull her into my arms and spin her around. I've never felt such unbridled joy in all my life. "Yes!"

"Coop, please stop spinning me when you're happy. I don't want to puke on you today."

I quickly set her down and turn to Hunter. "Did you know about this when I spoke to you earlier?"

"You mean when you were fussing like a girl going to prom about what to wear? No. I had no idea until we got here, and Zee handed me wedding rings."

"So we're doing this right now? Really?"

"Yep. No muss, no fuss, and a marriage license to boot. All you need to do is say 'I do' and sign your name on the dotted line. Oh, and kiss the bride when it's all done."

"Holy shit. I can't believe you kept this a secret all week."

"Well, I wanted it to be special in my own low-key way. Is it okay that we don't have a big wedding?"

"I'd marry you anywhere, anytime, beautiful. Let's do this." As we head up the steps to the courthouse, I find myself laughing. I was so bowled over by how amazing Zee looks in a red, form-fitting gown that I didn't even notice we were standing in front of the courthouse. Her dress shows off her baby bump perfectly, and I can think of no better way to make her my wife. She's not a conventional woman, and she'd never be caught dead in a big poofy white dress.

As we wait outside the office of the Justice of the Peace, I'm not nervous at all, but I can see that Zee is shaking. I wrap my arms around her, resting my lips on her forehead. "I love you so much. I can't wait to be your husband."

"Me, too."

"What changed? I thought you were dead-set against marriage."

"I was. I guess I just needed the right guy." Her voice waivers slightly, but she leans into my touch.

"Zoey Porter and Cooper Danford?" An imposing figure stands in the doorway. I don't know what I expected of a Justice of the Peace —maybe some old, soft-spoken dude—but this guy is huge. He wouldn't be out of place across from me on the football field.

"That's us." I hold my arm out for Zee. "You ready to do this?"

"Yep."

"You okay? Are you having second thoughts?"

"No. Babies are just kicking. Give me a minute to let them settle." She takes my arm, and we head inside the office. It's not how I pictured my wedding day, but nothing with Zee is how I pictured life and love and children. She's definitely the woman I pictured the day I realized I wanted all of that good stuff.

We recite everything the Justice asks us to repeat, and when he asks if we want to say any vows of our own, I'm about to say 'yes' when Zee grabs my shoulder and turns to face the Justice. "We're going to have to skip over the fluffy, personal vows right now."

"I want to say something. It's our wedding day." She looks at me with her death stare.

"Nope. Save it for later. We need to wrap this up."

"Jesus, Zee..." She just about tears my shoulder out of the socket.

"Coop, just say 'I do' and let's go. I'd love to stay and hear all the ways you love me and tell you a million reasons why I love you, but I'm pretty sure my water just broke." I look down, clear fluid pooling at our feet. She's not going to find it funny if I tell her she just ruined a seven-hundred-dollar pair of shoes, is she?

"Holy shit! We've got to get you to the hospital, now." I'm about to lift her into my arms, my mind going a million miles a minute.

"Not until we sign the papers. We're getting married right now."

"Fuck's sake, Zee. This can wait."

"No, it can't. I want to be married to you when these boys are born. Hurry it up... please... sir."

"With the authority granted me by the state of Tennessee, I now pronounce you man and wife. You can kiss the bride or take her to hospital." He shoves papers across his desk. "Sign here."

I scribble my name and hand the pen to Zee, who's struggling to do anything other than breathe. Her signature looks like chicken scratch. I press a quick kiss to her lips and hoist her up into my arms.

"Hunter, my keys are in my back pocket. The truck is parked two blocks south in that parking lot we always use. Go and get it, now."

He doesn't make some wisecrack about having to venture into my pants and takes off at a run. Zee is tense in my arms. She's clearly in pain, but she doesn't make a sound. This wasn't supposed to happen. We have a plan. We have a C-section set for eight days from now. She has a bag packed that we keep by the front door.

"What can I do?" Faith looks as worried as I feel, looking on helplessly at her friend in agony.

"Did you guys drive or take a cab?"

"We drove."

"Okay. Go to my place and get the bag by the door. You can get in through the garage with the code." She presses her head to Zee's, tells her she loves her, and takes off.

"I'll meet you at the hospital. Hang in there, Zee."

I'm supposed to carry my new wife over the threshold, but instead, she's groaning in my arms, and I feel completely useless.

"Oh God, it hurts, Coop. It really fucking hurts."

"I'm going to get you to the hospital, and we'll get you all the good drugs, okay, beautiful? We've got this."

I turn to the Justice, who's staring at the gross wet patch on his office floor. "Can you be a pal and grab my phone out my other back pocket and dial the OBGYN?"

"Certainly."

"Put it on speaker."

It rings for what feels like hours. "Hello, Doctor Garcia's office." Before she can give me the standard spiel, I interrupt.

"Hi, this is Cooper Danford. My wife, Zoey Porter, has just gone into labor. Her waters broke, and we were scheduled for a C-section next week. It's twins."

"I'll call Dr. Garcia right away. Do you need an ambulance?"

"No, I've got my car. I can have her there in ten minutes."

"Okay. Dr. Garcia will be ready when you arrive."

"Will they still be able to do the C-section?"

"It depends on how quickly she's progressing. The doctor will have answers for you after she examines your wife."

"Okay. I'm on my way."

The Justice ends the call and tucks my phone back in my pocket. "Good luck to you both."

"Thanks. Sorry about your floor," I say as I head out the door.

Zee's groans are coming thick and fast. "Coop?"

"Yeah?"

"You just called me your wife. Pretty great, right?" Even in her pain, she finds a way to make me smile.

"Damn straight. You better believe I'm calling you that every day for the rest of our lives."

"Good. And I'm sorry about ruining everything with the icky water breaking."

"You didn't ruin anything. Hands down, this will be the best day of my life. I got to marry the most amazing woman, and now we're going to welcome our sons into the world."

"Is it wrong if I think this is going to be a crappy day? It really fucking hurts."

"You can feel whatever you want, beautiful. We just need to get you through this. I'm going to be with you the whole time, okay?"

"Promise?"

"Cross my heart and hope to die."

"G-ood. Oh shit! It's like one long contraction... I think. Fuck I don't know. The books all say they come and go and gradually get closer. It feels like it's not stopping at all."

I make my way through the lobby, everyone stopping to look at the woman in labor being rushed out of the building. I'm so relieved to see Hunter pulling up in my truck.

"Get in the back with her."

Some random stranger opens the door for us, sympathy for Zee's current state etched in her brow. "Thank you!"

Once we're in, she shuts the door. "Good luck."

Hunter pulls into traffic, weaving his way to the hospital as quickly as possible. Every bump in the road has Zee crying out in pain. If I could trade places with her right now, I would.

"Oh God. Make it stop."

"We're almost there. Just a few more minutes."

"I need the drugs now, Coop."

"Hunter, what the fuck do I do, man?"

"I'll have you there in two minutes. Does the doc know you're on your way?"

"Yeah. Fuck. This was supposed to be happening next week, and it wasn't going to involve contractions."

"I guess your boys are eager to meet you." He's right. No matter how this goes down, we'll be meeting our sons today.

"Zee, think about the twins. You're going to see their little faces today, and I don't care about the names. You can call them whatever you want."

"If I have to shove your huge-headed sons out of my vagina, you better believe I'm naming them." Okay, so we're moving to the angry stage already. I've heard that the language can get pretty colorful when a woman is in labor. I won't take it personally.

"You got it, beautiful."

The second we pull up outside the hospital. I'm relieved to see the doctor standing next to an orderly with a wheelchair. Hunter comes to a grinding halt before jumping out and opening the door. It takes both of us to move her as carefully as possible, but as soon as she's in the wheelchair, we're moving. The doctor asks me all kinds of questions about when her water broke and how far apart are her contractions.

I'm in a daze. "Mr. Danford, how far apart are her contractions?"

Zee's cry kicks my brain into gear. "She said they aren't stopping, so there's no time in between."

"Okay. We'll get her upstairs and find out what's going on with these babies."

"We're here, beautiful. The doctor is going to give you all the good drugs to take the pain away."

She glares at me. My wife's loving gaze has been replaced by something much darker. "This is all your fault, Cooper Danford. Damn you and your magical penis all the way to hell!"

Wow! I'm not going to lie, I am taking this pretty personally.

The OB rests her hand on my arm. "Don't worry, Mr. Danford, she doesn't mean it."

"I do mean it! My vagina is going to be broken, and it's all because I couldn't stay away from the wondrous Titan cock. Oh God, it hurts."

"I promise she'll like you again later."

"Just take care of her, Doc. She's my whole world."

"WE'RE NEVER HAVING sex again, do you hear me?" God, he's annoying. These drugs aren't kicking in fast enough, and Coop is trying to soothe me, but the things I usually love make me want to rip his nuts off.

"I hear you. The whole hospital probably heard that." I know he's going for levity, but I seriously need Faith to get here. She knows what do to when I'm upset or sore or hormonal.

"Where the hell is Faith?"

"She went to get your bag from the house. She'll be here any second." He looks to the OB, who's all up in my cooch right now.

"Well, Zoey, it seems we're going to have a vaginal delivery today."

Coop is about to move down to see what she's looking at, but I grab his arm with all the strength I can muster. "Do *not* look down there. It will put you off me for life."

"You just said we're never having sex again, what do I have to lose?" He gives me a wink and that stupid panty-melting grin that got me in trouble in the first place.

"Your balls, Cooper. You have your balls to lose if you take a step closer to lady town. Now stay in line with my head, or you're getting thrown out of this room."

"Well, okay, then. Point taken. Is there anything I can do for you, anything I can get for you?"

"Firstly, you can stop pawing my hair like I'm a stray dog. And second, you can go down the hall and get a vasectomy. And while you're there, can you please, for the love of God, find Faith?"

"That's a hard no on the snip, but I'll go and see if Faith has arrived yet."

"If you could wait a moment, we need to discuss what's happening right now," the doctor says with solemnity in her voice.

"Okay." I take Zee's hand in mine, anguished by how much pain she's in.

"Unfortunately, baby A is already well on his way. It's called a precipitous birth."

"So what does that mean?"

"It means that this little guy is coming out the natural way."

"And what about baby B?"

"We'll assess as we go. Many second babies need to be born via C-section because they are not in the correct position, but there are also instances of the second baby engaging just fine."

"So we could be looking at an emergency C-section for him?"

"Yes."

"Okay. I'll go and find Faith." As he moves to leave, I tighten my grip on his hand.

"No. I don't want you to go." This has all become scary, and my annoyance with Coop has flipped on a dime. "I need you here with me. I'm scared."

He leans in, kissing my forehead, the scent of his cologne soothing me if only for a moment. "Then, I'm not going anywhere."

I turn my attention to the OB. "When are you going to do the epidural?"

"You're too far along. This baby is coming in the next ten minutes."

"What?" This can't be right, I'm supposed to be completely numb when these babies come out of me. If the contractions are this painful, I'm not going to be able to push them out.

"You're having back-to-back contractions. I just checked, and you are fully dilated. I've given you something to take the edge off, but I'm about to start telling you when to push, Zoey."

"Oh crap. I can't do this."

"You can, and you will. Now, when I say 'push,' I want you to bear down and push as hard as you can. When I say stop, you stop and use the breathing exercises from birthing class."

"I didn't go to the damn classes. You said I was having a C-section."

"Okay." She turns to Coop. "You're going to coach her through this. In between pushes, I want you to breathe with her so she can follow what you're doing. Two quick breaths in, then a long breath out. And just repeat that pattern."

"Like this?" Coop does as she asks, and she gives him a nod. "Okay. We can do this."

"Now, Daddy, I want you to get up on the bed and sit at Zoey's back. We need her in an almost sitting position."

He kicks off his shoes and scrambles up behind me, my back now resting against his chest. Holy shit, this is painful. He takes my hands, telling me to squeeze as hard as I need.

"Okay, Zoey. It's time to push. Take a deep breath..." I breathe in, my whole body shaking. "... and push."

I squeeze Coop's hands as I push with everything I have. "Holy shit, that hurts." He sounds serious. He better not be moaning about a fucking hand squeeze right now.

"Are you fucking kidding me? Suck it up, Coop. I'm pushing the equivalent of a watermelon out of my goddamn vajayjay!"

"Sorry, baby. You're doing great." The doctor tells me to stop pushing, but all my body wants to do is push. It's an overwhelming feeling and almost impossible to stop, but Coop starts doing the breathing she told him about. "Breathe with me, beautiful. Focus on the rise and fall of my chest."

"I can't. All I can focus on is the pain. I need to push."

"He's right, Zoey. Focus in on his breathing. Mimic it." How is she so calm right now? After a minute, she starts directing the midwife to get ready and turns her attention back to me. "Okay, another big push for me, Zoey."

Five minutes of breathing and pushing, and I'm exhausted. I have no strength left. "I can't do it."

"Zoey, the baby's head is right there. One more push, and it'll be out. You've got this. Take a big deep breath and give me all you've got. You're seconds away from meeting your son."

I brace myself against Coop, trying to channel whatever strength he can give me in this moment. I take a deep breath and push with everything I have. I hear screaming, but it takes a moment to realize it's coming from me. I feel like I'm on fire, the agony almost over-whelming.

"The head's out. Do you want to see, Mr. Danford?"

"Ye..."

"Hell, no! Stay where you are. You're not seeing my vagina with a head coming out of it. That's too much." Just as I say the words, Faith comes barreling into the room.

"I'm here! I'm here. Did I miss it?" She stops dead in her tracks. "Oh my God! My eyes! Jesus Christ." She covers her eyes and turns away. "Why isn't there a sign on the door to warn people? What I just saw will haunt me forever."

"Faith! Open your damn eyes and get over here. I don't need you falling and banging your head right now. I'm sort of busy, pushing a baby out of my body!" She scurries over to my side with her eyes firmly on the floor.

I think Coop is happy he's not the only one being shouted at right now. "You know they do actually have a sign on the door saying that it's occupied with a woman in labor? It sort of infers that you might see some messed-up stuff." I squeeze his hand with all my might.

"Will the two of you just shut the hell up? I'm exhausted, and I have a head hanging out of me. The miracle of birth is fucking painful, and I hate both of you right now because you aren't in agony."

"I think you've broken two of my fingers if that makes you feel any better."

"Not really."

"I'll just shut up now."

"Good idea. You and your swimmers are banned from my body for... ever." Then I turn my attention to Faith, whose face has drained of all color. "And you, when your vagina hangs in the balance, I'm going to start shouting about how it offends my eyes."

"Sorry, bestie. I was prepared for a C-section."

"No shit! So was I, but here I am..."

The doctor interrupts our bickering. "Okay, time to welcome this baby boy into the world, Zoey. One more big push, and he'll be out."

"You've got this, beautiful. We're about to see our son for the first time."

I muster strength from the very depths of my soul, and I push. I've never felt so relieved in my life as I do the moment I feel my son being born. "Is he okay? It's too early. Is he breathing?" Before I can say another word, the most beautiful sound echoes around the room. Our son lets out a cry, and Faith bursts into tears beside me.

"You're a mom. Zee, you're a mommy."

The doctor lays our son on my chest, his tiny body so amazing, I have no words. Coop kisses my head and reaches over to run his fingers over our son's cheek. "Hey, little guy. We've been waiting to meet you. You gave your mom a rough time of it, but that's just the way us Danford men are."

I can't contain the overwhelming love that washes over me at the sight of our baby boy. He's perfect, and he looks just like his daddy. He's a tiny little Cooper.

"Zoey Danford, I fucking love the crap out of you."

I cover the tiniest ear I've ever seen. "Don't swear in front of the baby."

He laughs and nuzzles into my neck. "Already an amazing momma."

"Sorry to interrupt the party, but we have another baby to deliver." My stomach is in knots. For just a moment, the pain dissipates as I gaze at the most miraculous human being I've ever seen.

Coop says what I'm thinking but too afraid to ask. "Will it need to be a C-section, Doc?"

I can feel her examining me, and I'm holding my breath. I thought I wanted to be whisked away to the operating room, but as painful as giving birth is, the thought of having to relinquish this little guy for even a moment makes me anxious.

"No. Baby B is getting ready to make his way into the world. This is going to be easier than the first one, Zoey. Your body knows exactly what to do, and when you feel the urge to push, push. Can someone take the baby while Momma gets his little brother out safe and sound?"

"Coop, you take him. I want you to be the first to hold him after me."

"Really?"

"Of course. Faith can take your place, right?"

"Yes!" Faith props me up while Coop climbs down off the bed.

They clamp the cord and hand Coop the scissors to cut it. He screws up his face, and it's so cute. "That felt weird."

The midwife hands him a blanket and tells him how to lift the baby from my chest. His eyes are glassy with unshed tears. As he lifts our son into his arms, I burst into tears watching them come face to face for the first time.

"Hey, I'm your daddy." He sways from side to side, his eyes fixed on the tiny bundle in his arms. "Your mommy is the most amazing woman I've ever met. She cooked you from smaller than a grain of sand. That's pretty great, right? I know you're probably wondering where your brother is right now. You've been roommates for months.

He's going to be here soon." When he finally tears his gaze away from the baby and looks into my eyes, there's so much love between us I can barely contain it. "Zee, he's incredible."

"Oh God. I need to push." Faith has taken Coop's place, and as grateful as I am, I feel the loss of his comforting strength behind me.

"You've got this, bestie." She slides her hands into mine. "Let's meet our second little guy."

I can see Coop is torn as he watches me brace myself to push, but seeing our son in his arms is all the incentive I need. I've got this.

"That's great, Zoey. One last big push." It still hurts like a motherfucker, but this time I know the joy that comes after. The second he's out, he lets his little lungs fly, rewarding me with a big beautiful cry. The doctor lays him on my chest and asks if Coop would like to cut the cord. He slowly lowers our son onto my chest next to his brother, and then he makes the cut.

"We need to deliver the placenta, but you've done all the hard work, Zoey. You did great. Two healthy boys and minimal tearing considering you just gave birth twice."

"Tearing?"

"It's normal. Once we get the placenta out, I'll stitch you up, and we'll get you settled in with these beautiful boys of yours."

"Can you make it good and tight? I don't want to have a wizard's sleeve down there."

Faith bursts out laughing behind me. "Wizard's sleeve?"

"Laugh it up. It's not your vagina that's like an echo chamber." I look down at our boys. They are identical. I know that sounds silly when I knew I was having twins, but I thought there would be something slightly different about both of them. Not the case. I have two mini Coops, and they are so beautiful.

Coop introduces himself to baby B, and I think my ovaries just exploded. "Hey, little man. Welcome to the family. Your brother is going to lord it over you that he was born ten minutes before you, but that's okay, I'm sure you'll milk being the youngest at times. I am your daddy, and the person giving you some amazing, warm snuggles right now is your mommy. I know how comforting her breasts can be to lie on, so I know you're comfy. When you're ready, then you can come give me some cuddles."

"You guys are parents. That's so crazy." Coop helps Faith get down off the bed and props me up with pillows. "I'm going to go tell Hunter the good news and let you guys have a minute to enjoy your new additions to the family. I'm so proud of you, Zee."

"Thanks. Love you."

"Back at ya." She disappears out the door, and Coop leans in, pressing his lips to mine.

"I love you, Zee. I can't believe you just did that. People talk about men being strong, but there's no way I could do what you just did. Women are the real men. We're all just a bunch of wusses compared to y'all."

"We did it. They're here. Look at them. They are so perfect."

"You're perfect."

"I must look such a mess right now. Try not to remember me like this when you think back to this day."

"Are you kidding? You've never looked more stunning. You've given me everything I ever wanted in a single day. I became a husband and a father today."

"Oh crap. You realize this means we're never going to get to celebrate our wedding anniversary, right?"

"I'll be celebrating being married to you every damn day for the rest of my life." The aches and pains of my body fade into the background as I bask in our newborn family. I don't think I've ever been as content as I feel at this moment.

"I'll hold you to that."

"You better."

———

"They won't latch on. What am I doing wrong?" It's been three days since the boys were born, and I have no maternal instinct superpowers. I'm pretty sure the boys prefer Coop over me, and they don't want to drink my weird pre-milk, milky stuff. What's it called? Colostomy? No, that's not right. That's when you have a poop bag attached to you. It definitely starts with the letter C. *Colostrum.*

"You're not doing anything wrong, beautiful. The nurse said it can take some time and especially while you're waiting for your milk to come in properly."

"God, you make me sound like a cow."

"You're anything but. If anything, the boys are in the wrong. I'd never pass up a chance to get up close and personal with your breasts. And seriously, Zee, they look... wowser."

"Creepy much? We're talking about nutrition for our children. Perv."

"There it is."

"What?" I say, rolling my eyes at him.

"That smile of yours. How are you feeling other than the feeding?"

"Like a truck ran over my vagina." He winces at my words. Call a spade a spade—giving birth is brutal.

"Can I change the subject right now, or does that make me an asshole?"

"Please, change the subject."

"We've been calling these two baby A and baby B for three days. Any chance we're going to agree on names any time soon? I feel like the nurses are judging us."

"You're right. We can't keep calling them A and B. How about you pick a name for A, and I'll pick one for B?"

"I like the sound of that."

"Would it be too kitschy to give them names that start with the letters A and B?"

"Oh, I like that. So, names that begin with A. Let me see. Agamemnon?" Trust Coop to make a joke of naming human beings. He always makes me laugh, but my muscles protest every time I so much as chuckle right now.

"Don't make me laugh. It hurts."

"Sorry, baby. So that's a no on Agamemnon?"

"Be serious. Agamemnon Danford? Could you imagine the beatings he'd get at school for a name like that?"

"Even the thought of someone attempting to bully them in the distant future gives me rage."

"Yep. We're parents now. We're going to be worried until the day we die."

"How about Achilles?"

"Sure. They can be Achilles and Brutus Danford."

"Brutus. Nice one. If we don't go historical, what about fruits? Apple and Blueberry Porter-Danford."

"Winner, winner, chicken dinner."

"Oh, I've got it. Adolf."

"We could slick his little tufty hair into that side parting and use my eyeliner to give him a mustache."

"Can we please do that for Halloween? That would be amazing. Could you imagine taking him trick or treating in that get-up?"

"We're bad parents, aren't we?"

"Fine. What boring names do you suggest?" He winks at me and gives each of the boys a peck on the cheek as they lay on my chest, *not* latching onto me.

"Al Falfa and Billy Bob."

"Oh my, God. Brilliant." I let myself relax and enjoy just being here with Coop and the boys. "We could go with names that match. Ben and Jerry. Tom and Jerry. Jimmy and Chonga."

"Wait."

"What's wrong?"

I don't move a muscle—don't make a peep. I stare at Coop, willing him to read my mind and not make a sound.

"They're drinking. Or suckling. Whatever it is, they are both doing it." I whisper, scared they'll stop if I talk too loud.

"Good job, Mommy. Tiny high-fives, little dudes."

"Right. Serious names only. They should have names."

"What about, Aiden?"

"Aiden Danford. I actually really like that." I rub my finger over his little hand. "Hey, baby A, what do you think of Aiden?" His skin is so soft, and as I say the name, he flexes his hand and grabs my finger.

"Did you see that? He responded to it."

"I did. Hey, Aiden." His cute suckling noises are adorable. "Good job, Daddy."

"So what do you think for baby B?" I love the way he stares at the boys with such devotion.

"I like Blake. What do you think?"

"Aiden and Blake. They sound good together. So we're settled? They have real names now."

"I guess so. I'd like to give them middle names, and as Aiden was born first, I think he should be Aiden Cooper Danford."

"Really?" Coop looks about ready to cry at the suggestion. "Wow. I wasn't expecting that. I was thinking about adding your name. Maybe that could be Blake's middle name? Blake Porter Danford."

"Now you're going to make me cry."

"What? You don't like the idea?"

"No. I love it, and I'm all hormones, baby love, and husband love, and I can't control the water that keeps leaking out of my eyes." He wraps his arm around me, letting me have a moment, but we're interrupted when the door opens, and Dr. Garcia walks in.

"How are we feeling today?"

"I'm good. Sore, but good. The babies are finally eating... or drinking."

"And do we have names yet?"

"We literally just decided. Meet Aiden Cooper Danford and Blake Porter Danford."

"Lovely choices. So, how do you feel about taking Aiden and Blake home?"

"What?"

CHAPTER SEVENTEEN
COOP

A CRY RINGS out in the quiet darkness of our bedroom, and it's quickly followed by a second wail. Adrenaline courses through my body as I'm propelled out of bed.

"What the hell." I stub my toe on the foot of the bed. "Son of a..."

"I'm up. I'm up." I don't need to see Zee to know she's exhausted. She can barely form a coherent sentence. There's a reason people don't tell you what it's like when you bring a baby home from the hospital. Aside from the fact that I checked the car seats were properly fitted and the boys were secure about twenty times before I pulled out of the parking lot, I drove at an average speed of three miles per hour the entire way home. A fifteen-minute car ride took a good forty-five minutes. Then add in the fact that every bump in the road caused my wife an inordinate amount of pain as she heals.

That was a week ago, and we've gotten about one hour of sleep between us—I'm not even exaggerating. I've had times in my life when college finals were looming or training was grueling, and I thought I knew what tired felt like. Now I realize I was a pussy.

Bone-weary. That's the only way I can think of to describe the way I feel. The boys have no concept of night and day, and they want to be fed every two seconds. Poor Zee is in a constant state of undress with one or both of them latched on. I've had to hold her upright at times, as she's just too tired to hold her own bodyweight.

I stumble around in the dark, hopping on one foot after smacking it against the bed. "Alexa, turn the fucking lights on."

I didn't quite catch that. You have various devices with the word lights.

If it's possible to think artificial intelligence is a raging cunt, it's Alexa. "Alexa, turn bedroom lights on.

Okay.

Imagine waking up in the middle of the road in the dead of night, and an eighteen-wheeler shines their high beams in your eyes. That's how this feels.

"Aiden, Blake, shh. Daddy's here."

"They don't want you. The tiny vampires want to drain me."

"Hey, beautiful. I'll bring them over." Blake is more chill than his brother, so I always pick Aiden up first. He's a trickster and a demanding little man. It's amazing to see how different they are in temperament.

I lay Aiden on her chest and take a second to kiss her. We haven't had a moment to think, eat, or shower. It's all go, all the time, and if by some miracle they're both asleep at the same time, you better believe we collapse on the couch or the bed. I actually fell asleep on the toilet the other day. Being startled awake by a screaming baby when you're on the throne is the only legitimate place you can say you were so startled you shit yourself. Not pretty, but nothing is sacred anymore.

"Love you, beautiful."

"Love you, too, champ."

I lift Blake into my arms and take a minute to marvel at his tiny features and the way he sucks on his tongue when he wants to be fed. Everyone says they are my double, but I see Zee in them. Aiden definitely has her spunk, and they both have her eyes.

Blake lets me snuggle him for a few minutes before he gets fussy for his momma. I know it's time to hand him over when he starts trying to gnaw on my nipples. There's no milk coming out of there, little buddy.

When the boys are comfy on the feeding cushion, tucked close to their mommy, the room goes quiet once more, and I crawl back into bed, straddling Zee so she can lean her body back on my chest. Even in my state of exhaustion, I love these moments with them. The four of us cuddled up together.

"Coop."

"Yeah?"

"Are we ever going to sleep again?" It would be funny if she didn't sound so frazzled and serious.

"Yes. At some point, these guys will give us a break and sleep for a solid four hours between feeds. That's what the books say."

"The books lied about so many things. They talk about the joy of natural birth. Scandalous lies. I'm sitting on a rubber ring for my sad and broken wizard's sleeve. I have spit-up in my hair. I don't remember the last time I showered, and my nipples feel like someone has taken a cheese grater to them."

"One of the guys on the team who has five kids told me that he and his wife call the first six weeks after birth, 'suicide watch.' That the sleep deprivation had them on the brink of going insane, but it passes. He promised it passes, and you get to enjoy it more. They've done it five times, so they must be right. Right?"

She gives a lackluster chuckle. "I think sanity left them a long time ago. Five kids. That's what you call a glutton for punishment."

"Plus, we have two babies at once. I don't know what it's like only to have one, but I'm making an educated guess that this is harder."

We sit in silence for a few minutes, listening to the babies' soft breaths and adorable sucking noises, and all the hard stuff just seems insignificant. "It's pretty amazing, though. They're amazing. I didn't know I had this capacity for love, so much love that I feel like my chest is going to explode, and not just from the overabundance of milk."

"Yeah. It's incredible. I'd give my left nut for a full night's sleep right now, but I wouldn't change them for the world. I'm in awe of you, Zee. When I see you with them, like this, I seriously wonder what I did to deserve this life I have with the three of you."

"Well, it was mostly to do with your epic disco stick. And then you kind of grew on me."

"Like a barnacle. Yeah, you mentioned that. I don't care if I'm a crusty barnacle, you're stuck with me now."

"And happily so." She lets her head fall back, closing her eyes as the babies feed, resting for a few precious moments. I can't close my eyes, mesmerized by my own little family. Any tiredness is worth it. I'll take three minutes of sleep a day if it means I get to be with Zee and the boys.

Zee doesn't stir when the boys are done feeding. I carefully lift them one at a time, rubbing their backs until they let out a tiny burp, change their diapers as quickly as possible, and then settle them back in their cribs and tuck Zee under the covers.

I ask Alexa to switch off the lights and then take a quick glance at my alarm clock—3:01 a.m. Closing my eyes, I let the exhaustion carry me away to a dreamless sleep, if only for a short while.

I'm catapulted awake an hour and twenty minutes later, ready to go through the same routine again. By the time I get them back down, it's five in the morning, and I hope beyond hope we can get through to sunrise without another feed, but the boys have other ideas.

The alarm clock reads 5:59 a.m. when Aiden starts fussing. Blake is off in the land of nod, so I creep out into the living room with Aiden and pace the floor with his tiny body resting like a starfish on my chest as I sway back and forth, humming the lullaby my mom used to sing me when I was a kid.

My mom is flying in from Denver next week to meet the babies and Zee for the first time. She's seen them on FaceTime, but it's not the same. As I walk the floor, hoping that Zee can get a few uninterrupted hours of sleep, I'm relieved at the thought of reinforcements arriving to help us through the next few weeks.

I may be a twenty-nine-year-old husband and father, but I'm still comforted by the thought of seeing my mom and sharing my wonderful family with her.

———

When the doorbell rings, Zee starts running around the living room like a headless chicken, trying to tidy the evidence of our whirlwind life over the past few weeks. She's got spit-up on her shirt, and there's still a faint smell of Blake's diaper blowout twenty minutes ago.

"Babe, no amount of Febreze is going to mask Satan's diaper. My mom won't care about any of this. Just chill."

"I've never met your mother, and all she has to go on is the fact that we hooked up, got knocked up, and rocked up to a wedding she didn't get to attend. Oh, and the wedding was my idea, so the blame lays squarely on my shoulders."

"She'll love you."

"I don't exactly have a great track record with parents. If my own don't even like me, I doubt your mom will."

"Well, you have a stellar record with Danfords. Aiden, Blake, and I adore you, and I promise my mom will, too. And no one gives a shit about my dad. He could be dead for all I know."

"That's sad, Coop. Remember, I'm still swimming in new-momma hormones."

"Don't give that loser the time of day. I don't. I have all the family I need."

"Are Faith and Hunter coming over? Everyone loves them. Maybe they can talk me up. Be my backup."

"Not that you need it, but yes, they are going to come over later and bring dinner with them. Oh, and Faith said she's bringing a whole bunch of our laundry that I didn't even know she swiped when they were here the other day."

"She's a legend. I looked at the pile of onesies and vests the other day and resigned myself to the idea of trashing them and buying new clothes for the boys. My God, they can spit up or have a blowout in five outfits a day."

"Okay. I can't leave my mom standing on the doorstep forever. Are you ready?"

"As I'll ever be."

Just as I'm about to open the front door, Aiden starts fussing, and Zee is quick to hightail it toward him before he wakes Blake.

I twist the doorhandle and throw back the door, pulling my mom into my arms. "Mom, it's so great to see you."

She wraps her arms around my waist, squeezing me the same way she did when I was five. "My boy! I can't believe you're a daddy. And a husband."

"It's been pretty full-on around here lately."

"I bet. You were enough of a handful when you were a baby, I can't imagine having two of you. Now enough chatter, where are my grandbabies and my new daughter-in-law?"

"Aiden was fussy, so Zee is trying to get him settled."

My mom bustles past me, her super spidey grandmother senses on high alert. I grab her bags and follow her into the living room, and I'm filled with pride at the sight of Zee swaying and singing to Aiden with pure adoration in her eyes. That's my family.

"Mom, I'd like you to meet my wife, Zee. I mean, Zoey Porter. Now Danford."

My mom clasps her hands over her mouth as she lays eyes on one of her grandsons for the first time. "Hi, Zoey, I'm Jennifer. And who's that tiny bundle of joy in your arms?"

Zee is forcing a smile. She's nervous, and with anyone else, she can mask it, but I know her too well. "Nice to meet you, Jennifer. This is Aiden Cooper Danford."

I move to her side, leaning in to give Aiden a little kiss on the cheek. "What do you think, Mom? Does he look like I did when I was a baby?" I watch as my mom's eyes well with tears.

"He's the spitting image of you when you were born." As if

responding to the sound of my mom's voice, Aiden opens his sleepy eyes. "Oh, but he has his mother's eyes. He is so precious."

"Would you like to hold him?" I wasn't sure if Zee would be comfortable with a veritable stranger taking our son from her arms, so I'm glad she's the one to ask, and it means a lot to me. I want them to get along.

"Are you sure? I don't want to upset his routine or snatch him out of your arms, dear."

"He's your grandson. Of course, it's okay." She gently hands him off to my mom, enjoying seeing someone besides us loving on him.

"He's so perfect. Look at his little nose and those pouty lips. He's going to be a heartbreaker when he's older." She's in love. It's a surreal moment to see my mom—the woman who raised me—cradling my son in her arms.

"Wait until you see the two of them together." As if on cue, Blake starts to stir, and Zee gives me that look—the you-jinxed-it look.

"Sounds like you won't have to wait. I'll go get him."

"It's not a two-way monitor. I promise."

"Yeah, yeah," she quips as she disappears down the hall to our bedroom.

The second Zee is out of earshot, my mom levels her verdict. "I like her. The way you look at her... I've been waiting years to see you fall in love."

"She's incredible, Mom. I've never been happier. And the boys..."

"It's a love no one can prepare you for."

"Exactly. I look at them, and it's like a full-body reaction. Like I could stare at them all day long and never get bored."

Zee appears with Blake in her arms, and I no longer have my mom's attention. I'm guessing this is something I'm now going to have to get used to since she has grandbabies to enjoy.

"Hey, Blake. Are you ready to meet your grandma?" Zee is so sweet when she talks to the babies, and as she sits down next to my mom to let her see Blake, my heart just melts.

"Oh my goodness, another handsome boy. They really are identical. How do you tell them apart?"

"They already have such different personalities and their own little mannerisms. It's crazy." Zee and I don't dress them the same, which I know is a big thing with multiples, but we want them to be individuals. They're going to be referred to as 'the twins' the second they get out there in the world, at school, and I don't want that to be a negative for them. They are going to be in the public eye until I'm done with football, and I can shield them as much as possible, but it's difficult to do my job and keep my private life completely private.

My mom and Zee fall into natural conversation, getting to know each other and bond over the boys, so I try to give them some space and set about cleaning up the baby grenade that seems to have gone off in our kitchen.

It's insane how much stuff you need to take care of one tiny little human. Doing it in stereo leaves us chasing our tails by the end of every day. Two babies, two parents. If Zee is feeding one, then I'm changing the other. If she's dealing with diapers, I'm doing bath time.

No one prepares you for the diapers. You think it's going to be one or two baby wipes and you're done. I swear to God, I've used in excess of twenty wipes on one blowout. There's no recovering a onesie when either of the boys has had a diaper malfunction. I'm not cleaning that shit—literally, a ton of shit. It's unbelievable that such a tiny person can create so much shit.

When I'm done making the place presentable, I take my mom's bags up to the guest room, enjoying the sound of her and Zee laughing in the living room. By the time I'm done, Hunter and Faith have arrived with clean laundry and plenty of food.

We create a production line during dinner, rotating baby duties so we can all eat before the food goes cold. Zee feeds the boys, Faith burps them, and I change diapers. Even Uncle Hunter helps out, getting the boys into fresh onesies for bedtime. He's surprisingly good with them. I for sure thought he was going to suck at it, but he melts just like the rest of us when the boys are making little cooing noises. I wouldn't be surprised if he and Faith start making mini Vaughns sometime soon.

With the boys cleaned up and ready for bed, my mom does the honors of snuggling them until they fall asleep. She has a perma-grin, ignoring the rest of us while she marvels at her grandbabies. It feels strange sitting at the dinner table with Zee, Hunter, and Faith.

They have been our saviors since we got home from the hospital. If it weren't for them, Zee and I would've died of malnutrition by this point. The dynamics of our friendships have changed ever so slightly but in the best of ways. Without any of Zee's family in the picture, and me just having my mom, Hunter and Faith have gone above and beyond to help us find our feet.

Hunter has felt like a brother to me for years, and I know Zee and Faith are closer than sisters. But now that they're married and we're married with twins, our sense of family is stronger than ever. Faith was right there with us in the delivery room, and she reminds us of the mental scarring she endured out of love. She's become family to me in such a short space of time, and I know Zee feels the same way about Hunter.

We couldn't have asked for better friends or more fitting godparents for the boys.

My mom knows Hunter pretty well after our time at the Titans, and he charms the pants off her just like he does with every other woman on the planet. If he could bottle that shit, he'd be even richer than he is now.

While the boys are snoozing and we're all chatting in the living room, Zee and I are struggling to keep our eyes open, dropping in and out of conversations, missing at least half of what's being said.

"Why don't you two go and get some rest?" Even at twenty-nine, my mom hasn't stopped mothering me.

"I'm fine." My words would be more convincing if my head didn't drop right after I said them. I hate that feeling of nodding off and startling yourself. It seems to be a common occurrence these days.

"You're both exhausted. You should get some sleep before the boys need to be fed again. It's true what they say... when baby sleeps, you sleep."

"That would be great if they slept for more than five seconds."

"Well, what are you waiting for? Go to bed. That's an order."

Hunter and Faith second her sentiments. "She's right, bro. You look like ass. Zee still looks beautiful, but you look older than me now." I can always count on Hunter.

"Let's not get ridiculous. You look ancient. Even in my current state, I'm a damn sight easier on the eye than you."

"Go to bed, old man. I'll swing by tomorrow with some groceries. Text me if you need anything."

"You're a gentleman and a scholar, Vaughn."

"I know. You owe me big time."

"I'll pay up when you have kids."

Faith is quick to interject. "After what I saw in the delivery room, I'm thinking a puppy is going to be the closest we get to a kid any time soon."

"Probably for the best. You don't want to perpetuate the Vaughn gene pool. One is enough for us to handle."

My mom just shakes her head. "You boys never grow up, do you? Off to bed and take your lovely wife with you."

When I try to rouse Zee, she's out for the count, so I scoop her into my arms. "Come on, beautiful. Time for bed." She barely registers, but her body relaxes, her head resting on my chest. As I lay her down on our bed, I'm careful not to disturb the boys in their cribs.

I don't bother changing her into PJs, tucking the covers around her before stripping down to my boxers and crawling in beside her. It only takes three seconds for me to join Zee in a deep, dreamless sleep.

CHAPTER EIGHTEEN
ZEE

HAVING Coop's mom here has been a godsend. If I thought she'd move in with us, I'd ask her in a heartbeat. Three adults outnumber twins—I like those odds.

I've already adopted Jennifer as my mom. She's so warm and inviting, and above all else, she's supportive. I can see where Coop gets his kind heart from. We've had so many wonderful conversations in the time she's been here, and she dotes on the boys. I'm picking up loads of tips on caring for my babies, and she never thrusts her opinions on me. She has a way of making you feel—enough. I get the same feeling of genuine acceptance that Coop has given me since the moment we met.

Whenever the subject of my parents comes up, I sidestep it. After what happened the day I told them I was pregnant, they've shown no interest in how I'm doing. Like the idiot I am, I let them know when the boys were born. They said they can't come and meet them right now as they're heading off on a month-long trip around Europe. Who thinks a vacation is more important than meeting their grandkids?

I never understood my parents, and now that I'm a mother, I

understand them even less. I can't imagine ever being indifferent to Aiden and Blake. They are the sun, the moon, and the stars.

How could they be so cruel? I look down into the faces of these two little babies—our babies—and I can't imagine not wanting them. I don't understand how they could've been so heartless. Was I a terrible baby? Or a nuisance of a child? I've always believed it's something to do with me, but as I snuggle a baby in each arm, I know with unwavering certainty that it wasn't my fault. For the first time in my life, I understand that none of this was a failure on my part as a daughter. It was theirs, and theirs alone.

Today, Coop's mom has to get back to Denver, and I can see she's having a hard time saying goodbye to the boys. Even in the short space of time she's been here, they've changed so much.

"I wish I didn't have to go. I'm going to miss you all so much."

"We're going to miss you, too. I hope you'll come back and see us again soon." I was dreading meeting Coop's mom for the first time, and yet here I stand, sad to see her leaving.

"Just try and stop me. I'll be coming to see you so often you'll be eager to get rid of me."

"I doubt that."

She pulls me into her arms, and a lump forms in my throat. "I'm so happy my son has found such a lovely woman to spend his life with. You're good for him, and I can see that you love my boy as fiercely as he loves you."

"I do."

"Thank you, Zoey, for making my son happy and giving me two beautiful grandbabies. I'm so thrilled to have more family to love."

"They are pretty darn lovable." I can bask in the joy of my sweet twin boys, beaming with pride while they sleep soundly. The second they stir, it's a different ballgame. I love them so much it hurts, but I'm in a perpetual state of exhaustion. It's weird, though. I miss them while they sleep, staring at them in awe, marveling at how full my heart is, overflowing with love. When they're awake and fussing for milk or refusing to give in to sleep, I'm wishing they would close their eyes, if only for an hour. It's a constant push and pull, but I wouldn't change a thing.

"It's not just the boys who've been added to my family. *You* are part of the family now, Zoey. I always wanted a daughter, and I hope we'll make many happy memories together in the future." Her words catch me off guard. I didn't expect Jennifer to welcome me with open arms, after all, my relationship with her son has been so fast. I was prepared for her to resent the fact that we got married in a courthouse without her. But her warmth and willingness to give me a chance overwhelms me, and I can't hold back the tears.

"Thank you."

"Are you okay, dear? Did I say something to upset you? It wasn't my intention."

Damn these hormones. I'm a loose cannon of tears and snot. "I'm fine. You've just been so kind to me. I wasn't expecting it." Her expression looks puzzled.

"What were you expecting? A monster-in-law?" She gives me a warm smile.

"I guess I thought you'd be more like my mom. Indifferent." The sympathy in her gaze only fuels my ugly cry.

"Oh, Zoey. No mother should ever be indifferent to their child, but I see that you already know that. You're anything but indifferent when it comes to those babies."

"What if I become a terrible mother? I've never had a good role model."

"I know a good mother when I see one. You are and will be, a wonderful mom, Zoey. The fact that it worries you is a testament to how much you care. Trust your gut, and I know you'll be just fine. Now dry those eyes."

"Thank you, Jennifer."

Coop comes strolling into the living room like he wasn't just standing in the hallway listening to our conversation. Wrapping his arm around my shoulder, he pulls me close, pressing a kiss to my cheek. "I was right about her, Mom, wasn't I?"

"Yep. She's a keeper."

"You spoke to your mom about me?" I lean into his side, shy all of a sudden.

"He did," his mom speaks up. "He called me the week after he met you and told me he'd met the most incredible woman. He said he'd met the woman he was going to marry."

I'm stunned. I had no idea he felt that way about me after our three-day one-night stand. So many moments flash through my mind, seeing them as if for the first time through a new lens.

"Mom, that was supposed to be a secret between us."

"Well, I don't see why it matters now. You're married, after all."

"Yeah, but now she thinks I was some creepy stalker dude." Only Coop would spin insta-love into a stalker situation.

"Now? I've always known you were a stalker. I told you, you're my barnacle."

"Do I even want to know?" Jennifer asks with a chuckle. She and Coop have the same laugh—conspiratorial.

"Probably not."

"You ready to go, Mom? We better get going to the airport."

"As ready as I'll ever be. Let me just smush my little grandsons one more time."

"There's always time for twin snuggles."

Today, I have the same gnawing worry knotted in my chest that I had the day we drove home from the hospital with the twins. We've been safe in our little bubble for a month now, finding our feet and getting through the days and nights like zombies. Luckily, Coop's had time off from the Titans to get used to our new normal, but it's time for him to get back to work, and I'm dreading being outnumbered by the boys. I can't even think about what happens when it's time for me to return to work, which is imminent.

I've gotten used to spending all of my time with Coop and the twins, and I love it. Before I gave birth, I was constantly worrying that I'd feel trapped or that Coop would just bug the shit out of me. I've never been that woman who spends all her time with a guy, but he makes life together feel so effortless. We bicker daily about a million little things, but we never go to sleep on an argument. One of the few kernels of wisdom my mom cared enough to bestow on me.

"Are you sure you want to bring the boys to practice?"

"Yes. You want to introduce them to the team, why not today?"

"I'm just worried about you having to get them ready, loaded up in the car, and then what if you have to deal with the press on the way in?" He's not wrong. All of those things have been going around and around in my head since Aiden woke me up at four in the morning.

"Faith is going to come and help me, and Hunter said he'd meet us at the stadium to get past any paparazzi. We've got our bases covered. If you'd rather we do it a different day and let you stay focused on training, then we'll hold off."

"Are you kidding? I'd love to have you there and let the guys meet Aiden and Blake. I'm proud as a peacock." His panty-melting smile makes all my fears fade away.

"Then it's settled. I've got this."

When he heads out the door, the silence is deafening. I'm crossing my fingers, hoping the boys will stay asleep until Faith arrives to help. I've never been alone with the twins before, building my confidence as a mom knowing support is in the next room.

Faith knows better than to ring the doorbell now, so she just comes inside with the stealth of a cat burglar. "Hey, Zee," she whispers.

"Hey, girl. I finished feeding them about twenty minutes ago, so they should be good for Auntie Faith while I grab a quick shower. Is that okay?"

"Of course. Go, enjoy. I'm happy here with my two favorite little guys. Do you want me to get their diaper bags ready?"

I run over to her and throw my arms around her neck. "If I

haven't told you lately, I freaking love you. I couldn't have gotten through all of this without you."

"I can't breathe." She croaks out as I strangle her with a hug.

"Sorry, didn't mean to crush your windpipe."

"Go shower. You need it." She scrunches her nose, mocking my PJs with milk spit-up on the shoulder.

"I'm going."

With the boys in good hands, I make the most of my time. While the shower heats up, I take a long hard look at myself in the mirror. My once toned body looks like a Salvador Dalí painting. Nothing is quite where it used to be. My boobs are huge from breastfeeding, and my stomach has stretch marks after housing not one but two human beings for months. I don't exactly look at my lady bits, but I know they had to be stitched, so in my mind, it's now Frankenstein's vagina.

This is the first time I've stood naked in front of the mirror and assessed the damage. It's as if someone else is staring back at me—familiar but not quite me. I'm worried Coop won't be as attracted to this new version of me. Sure, I can get back into shape, but there are parts of me that have fundamentally changed, and no amount of diet and exercise is going to fix them.

Stepping under the oversized showerhead, I let the steaming water rain down on me, soothing my aching muscles. It takes all my energy to lather the shampoo in my hair. I've never experienced the type of exhaustion I've felt since the twins were born. There's no time to recover from the assault on your body from giving birth. It's an everyday miracle—women are just supposed to suck it up and hit the ground running. No one tells you that beforehand.

As I cover my body in shower gel, washing away the grime of more days than I care to admit, I think of Coop. I can't imagine how he's going to feel after practice on so little sleep. He's so wonderful with the boys—a real hands-on daddy. I knew he would be, but I fall more in love with him every day as I watch him navigate our new normal.

Coop and I started with such a visceral physical connection. I feel the lack of it now with every nerve ending in my body. I want so much to lose myself in him and find myself again—Zoey, the woman. I have so many labels now, and I crave a few hours just to be me.

Running my hands over my newfound curves, I close my eyes and let myself remember the way Coop's hands feel as they roam my body, enjoying every inch, kissing his way down my neck, lower and lower until he spreads my legs wide and buries his face between my thighs. God, I miss orgasms, even though I'm too tired to have them.

I let my hand slide between my legs, my fingers ghosting a gentle caress over my clit. A thrill runs through me, and relief that whatever trauma happened down there giving birth hasn't made me numb. It feels good. My fingers circle my clit as I tease myself, needing to feel a momentary pleasure, even if it's at my own hand.

I imagine it's Coop, pushing me toward sweet release, but just as I'm about to reach that peak, Faith starts banging on the door. "Zee, Blake has done some kind of evil in his diaper, and Aiden is crying. Are you almost ready?"

"I'll be out in a minute."

"Okay, thank God. I don't know how such a cute kid can do something that smells this bad. It's all over his onesie."

"Yep, it's pretty nasty. Just coming." Sadly, I'm not *coming* in the best sense of the word. I quickly turn off the shower and towel dry myself. So much for making myself look good for Coop. I throw my clothes on and put my soaking wet hair in a messy bun before going back on mommy duty with baby doody. I suppose I should consider it a win if I manage to get out of the house without baby bodily fluids somewhere on my person.

The living room is chaos. Faith is holding Blake at arm's length, trying not to get covered in poop while singing to Aiden to try and soothe him.

"Okay, give me the poopy baby. You see to Aiden."

"God bless you, Zee. I thought I was going to vomit in my mouth at the smell." She hands Blake to me, and I can see she wasn't exaggerating. Blake has shit soaking through his onesie, up his back and down his legs. This is a blowout on steroids.

"I think your daddy has a point, Blake. There's no saving an outfit after a blowout like this. In the trash it goes." I manage to get his clothes off without flicking poop all over the living room, but the second I take it off, he starts wriggling, making a snow angel of shit on the changing table. Gagging repeatedly, I get to work with the wipes, just trying to get him clean enough to bathe. "You're lucky you're so cute, little man." He gives me a funny crooked smile and looks exactly like Coop when he's up to mischief.

"Should I call Hunter and tell him we'll be late?"

"No. We can do this. We're two smart, college-educated women. We can get two babies from one destination to another. If you get Aiden into his car seat, I'll give Blake a quick bath, and we'll be good to go."

"Okay. We can do this, can't we, Aid? Yes, we can." Faith talks to the babies with a cutesy tone to her voice, and it warms my heart to see her loving on them.

I get to work, praying we can still get to Coop's practice on time. He's looking forward to introducing the new Danfords to the team.

"You made it!" Coop looks so happy when he sees me standing on the sidelines with the babies in their tandem stroller. God, he looks good back in his football gear.

There's no way I could've pulled this off without Faith and Hunter. Hunter went all Brando Godfather on the press, telling them to keep their distance unless they wanted to lose access to the team press conferences. I don't think he has the authority to do that, but he sold it pretty well. We got inside without cameras flashing in our faces.

Faith drove my car here so I could attempt to tame my hair and throw on some makeup. I wanted to look nice for Coop, but he's getting the hot-mess version. With a huge smile on his face, he jogs over to us, and I expect him to go straight for the babies, but I'm pleasantly surprised when he grabs my face in his hands, his lips finding mine. For a moment, I forget where we are or that people are watching.

A jolt of electricity courses through my body as he kisses me like he's starved for the taste of me. My earlier arousal in the shower pales in comparison to the thrill of his tongue tantalizing my senses. When he pulls back, I don't want to let him go. I've missed this so much. "You have no idea how much I missed you today, beautiful."

"It's only been a few hours."

"I know, but it felt like forever. I've gotten used to being with you and the boys." He darts his tongue out to lick the seam of my lips. "You look smokin' hot, by the way. Total MILF." As his lips descend on mine once more, all I can do is groan, which only seems to spur him on. I'm lost to the sensation, only brought back to the moment when one of the team shouts in our direction.

"Get a room, lovebirds."

"That's how they got into this in the first place!" Hunter interjects.

"Jealous, Vaughn?" Coop always wants the last word.

"Scared is more like it. Keep your ladies at a distance, guys, Coop might impregnate them by proximity alone."

"Very funny. Only lesser men scoff at the masculinity needed to have twin boys." A soft laugh ripples through the team before they take a collective step closer to the stroller.

"Yes, you're super manly. None of this had anything to do with me. I just carried and birthed them." I give him a playful shove and a conspiratorial wink.

"Guys, I know you've all met Zee before, but I still want to introduce her for the first time as my wife, mother of my boys, and general kick-ass female."

All eyes are on me, and I don't particularly enjoy it, but now I have the perfect excuse to divert attention from me. "Hey, guys. I know you get enough of Coop to last a lifetime, so I apologize in advance for creating two carbon copies of him. Meet Aiden and Blake Danford, the tiny Titans."

"I love that. Tiny Titans." Coop beams with pride as everyone gathers round to meet our sons. Seeing how happy he is makes the pandemonium of trying to get here worthwhile.

Faith sidles up beside me as Hunter joins the fray of onlookers.

"It's like an ovary implodium." She chuckles to herself.

"What? You know that's not a word, right?"

"A whole team of hunky football players oohing and aahing over babies. Just the sight of it makes me broody."

"I'm feeling no brood. My vagina is too close to the wreckage. Two is good. I'm done."

"Really? You wouldn't want to try for a girl? Imagine Coop and Hunter fussing over a baby girl. They'd be wrapped around her little finger in seconds."

"Yeah, but they can be cooing over *your* baby girl. Take one for the team. My lady bits can't handle a third."

"I don't think I'm cut out for pregnancy or motherhood."

"Neither was I, and yet here I stand, married with two kids. When did that happen?"

"In between some stellar orgasms would be my bet." Trust Faith to call a spade a spade.

"God, I don't remember the last time I had an orgasm."

"Seriously? You need to get back on that train." She wiggles her eyebrows at me—such a dork—an adorable dork nonetheless.

"I'll get right on that between changing diapers, having babies gnaw on my nips, and getting zero sleep."

"There's always time for an orgasm. Aren't you frustrated?"

"Honestly, until this week, it hasn't been a problem. In fact, it's been the furthest thing from my mind."

"But the way Coop just kissed you, that man is ready to ravage his wife again."

"Technically, we haven't done it as man and wife. I went into labor on our wedding day."

"Holy shit, Zee. You haven't consummated your marriage. Do you know you could technically get it annulled?"

"I don't think I could play the consummation card. They'd be alerted to the fact that we consummated plenty beforehand when they see the kids in the stroller."

"It doesn't count if it was before the wedding."

"Why are we talking about annulling my marriage?"

"What the hell?" Coop must have overhead because he leaves the guys hanging, striding to my side. "What did I just hear? Annulment? What the fuck?"

"Calm down, champ. If you must know..." I lean in to whisper the full details to him without everyone else overhearing. When I'm done, he slides his hands into my hair and kisses me as if his life depends on it.

"We're remedying that as soon as you're ready."

"Could we do other stuff in the meantime? I'm starting to get a craving for Coop attention."

"Say the word. I've been trying to be sensitive to your needs. I'm dying over here. I have straight-up been ready to mount you since the day after we had the boys."

"I don't believe that for a second. Me in a hospital bed looking like I'd been in a fight with a Mack truck wasn't sexy."

"Babe, I'm rocking a semi right now just thinking about getting you under me again."

"Maybe we can find some alone time when you get home tonight? Foreplay."

"Does that mean I'm getting a blowjob?"

"If you play your cards right."

Coop isn't one to wait around. "Okay, guys, you've seen the babies, let's call it a day. I need to get my wife home."

"We don't have to go yet. Enjoy your time with the team."

"They've met the boys. They'll see them again soon. Plus, they would totally understand my predicament."

"You've got a one-track mind."

"Every guy in the world has a one-track mind. Watch." Oh my God, I know what he's about to do, and the words are out before I can stop him. "Guys, you don't mind me skipping out, do you? I haven't had any action in over a month, and the wife just gave me hope of a BJ. You understand, right?"

"You didn't just do that!"

"Hell-fucking-yes I did. My balls are blue. It's a kindness. They have literally been slowing me down today. I'm fit to burst."

The guys are all laughing their asses off, telling him to get out of here. My face must be redder than a Santa suit right about now. "I'm going to kill you when we get home."

"As long as your weapon of choice is your lips wrapped around my cock, then I'll die a happy man."

CHAPTER NINETEEN
COOP

THE BOYS ARE two months old today, which means Zee and I have been married for two months. Under normal circumstances, I'd have fucked her seven ways till Sunday every day of our marriage. We'd have had a honeymoon on some private, secluded island where clothes were unnecessary. Instead, I haven't actually made love to my wife yet.

Since Zee gave me the green light for foreplay, and the twins seem to have become wise to my intentions toward their mother. They've become astute cockblockers at every turn. Whenever I get close to undressing Zee or getting a glimpse of her in the shower, one of them starts fussing. I swear they have a sixth sense.

We've had one or two moments where we got close, but life is a whole different pace in our house these days. We sped right through dating, moving in, making babies, and getting married. Nothing about our relationship has been conventional, so I guess why start now, right?

I wanted to take Zee out on a date, but with her breastfeeding, it's not that easy, and she's not ready to leave the boys with anyone yet. I get it—she's in full-on mommy mode. I'm down on the list of priorities right now, and I'm okay with that. She's amazing, and we have our whole lives to find time for ourselves and enjoy our family.

My buddy, Anders, called me, wanting to make good on my promise to hang with him next time he was in town. Oh, how life has changed since then. The last time I saw him, I was trying to get Zee to give me the time of day. I was fucking miserable. She had me by the balls before she even knew she wanted my balls. That's not the saying, but fuck it. She likes my balls, and she'd probably find my analogy funny.

"You should go and hang out with your friend. I'm good."

"I don't really want to go out without you. I know that makes me sound like a dweeb, but I'm tired, and if I'm going to go out on the town, I want to do it with my wife on my arm. Plus, Anders is a good friend, and I'd like to introduce you. I want to show off my sexy, hot wife."

"Next time. Once I'm not our sons' only food source, we can hit the town. I promise."

"I'm going to hold you to that."

"Okay, so tell him you'll be there tonight."

"Only if you're sure."

"Yes. I'm going to be hanging with the other men in my life. Actually, they remind me a little of you." She gives me a playful grin. I do love to see her smile.

"I'm jealous now."

"I like to keep you on your toes. Now go and get ready before I change my mind."

"One thing you can never be accused of is letting things get boring! I have a feeling I'll be kept on my toes until I'm ninety."

"You know it, champ." I love seeing the feisty side of Zee. It's tough to keep it fresh when you're up to your neck in dirty diapers.

"Okay, I won't be out crazy late." I pull her into my arms, kissing her neck, drinking in the soft scent of her perfume.

"Don't start something you can't finish, Danford." When a moan of pleasure escapes her, all I want to do is take her to our bedroom and turn that moan into a scream.

"I'll finish it right now. Just say the word."

"You've got somewhere to be." She shrugs out of my arms, an all-too-familiar event of late. She's not ready.

"Okay. I'll see you later. If you need me, just call. I can be back here in twenty minutes. You could always ask Faith to come over. I text Hunter, and he's going to meet me at the bar."

"I'm capable of dealing with the twins on my own. You need to stop worrying about me. Go, have fun. It's one night. You're blowing this out of proportion."

She gives me a quick peck on the cheek and reaches for my keys. She may as well just shove me out the front door.

"Hey, bro. How the hell are you?" Anders is propping up the bar when I arrive, surrounded by a predictable harem of women hoping to warm his bed tonight.

"I'm good, man. How are you? Good to see you."

"What are you drinking?" I can barely hear him above the thumping beat, and the fact that it bugs me makes me feel old as fuck.

"I'm just going to grab a water." He looks at me like I have two heads.

"What have you done with the real Cooper Danford? Water? Get the fuck out."

Hunter appears at my side, just in time to give me shit about it as well. "He's gone soft, Beck. He's all decaf coffee and jammies by ten these days." He amuses himself at my expense.

"Laugh it up, dickweed. If you had two tiny humans who refuse to sleep, you'd be off the hard stuff, too."

"Come on. I'm only in town for one night, and you owe me a proper drink after skipping out on me last time."

"Yeah, Coop, let loose for a night." Hunter jumps on the bandwagon.

"What the hell? You regularly witness the mayhem in my house. You know I'll be fucked if I 'let loose.'"

He claps me on the shoulder. "That's the only kind of fuck you're getting any time soon. May as well enjoy it."

Anders throws his head back, getting a good old laugh at my lack of action.

"Low blow, brother. It's not a laughing matter at this point. This might be the longest I've gone without sex since I was eighteen. I'm dying."

"So, this is the girl you were mooning over, right?"

"Yep."

"I never thought I'd see you settle down and get married with two kids. You need to at least have one drink. We have to toast to you becoming a dad and a husband."

"Fine, one drink."

While he orders a round of bourbon, I pull Hunter aside. "Do not let me get shitfaced."

"Relax, Coop. Zee already text me with strict orders that you better chill out and have some fun. You've got a cool wife and a night off from daddy duty. What's the worst that could happen?"

"She did?"

"Yeah. She loves you."

"I guess a couple of drinks won't hurt." *Famous last words.*

It's been a while since I've been accosted by fans. It's impossible to avoid when you happen to be hanging out with two of the biggest sports personalities around. Anders is three sheets to the wind, staring into the bottom of an empty bottle of Jack Daniels after a couple of hours. He looks suspiciously similar to me the last time I was out with him—checking his phone every five minutes and ignoring the advances of at least a dozen eager baseball groupies.

Hunter is adept at fending off women these days. Everyone in this town knows and adores his Lady Fumble.

Me? I've been signing autographs and showing anyone and everyone cute pictures of my wife and kids. I'm that guy. *Lame!* I thought it would give the clear signal that I am not up for a hook-up, but apparently being a dad is a major turn-on. I've been handed at least six napkins with lipstick marks and phone numbers. One chick even offers to blow me in the restroom.

This shit just doesn't appeal to me anymore. I take a few photos with fans just to get rid of them, and there's always one who tries to steal a kiss. I manage to sidestep her, so she'll have to make do with a blurred photo of me getting the fuck away from her. That's when I know it's time to go home.

"I'm going to hit the road, guys. I'm already the worse for wear."

"Lightweight." Anders is slurring his words at this point.

"Nothing lightweight about having a hot wife to go home to."

He pulls me in for a hug. "I fucking admire you, Coop. You've got it all. I want that."

"Then I suggest you call whoever has you checking your phone tonight."

"You're like the Dalia Lama of relationships, bro. That shit is deep."

I turn to Hunter, who's laughing his ass off. "Will you make sure he gets back to his hotel room? He's drunk as a skunk."

"Can do. You good to get home?"

"Yeah. I'll get a cab. I can come back for the car tomorrow."

"Cool. Give the boys a hug from Uncle Hunter. I'll catch up with you on Sunday. We still on for dinner?"

"Yes. When are you going to knock up that wife of yours? I see the way you are with Aiden and Blake."

"That's a conversation for another night." That's not a no. Vaughn's considering it. I know him too well for a placating answer to hold any weight with me.

"Later, bro."

I pour myself into a cab and head home, more than ready to crawl into bed next to Zee. I shoot her a quick text to let her know I'm on my way. It's later than I thought, but unfortunately, I know she'll be awake. We can't seem to get the boys to realize that the middle of the night isn't party time.

When the cab pulls up in our driveway, I'm already regretting my decision to drink tonight. Drinking makes me horny, and my wife makes me horny, but she has yet to invite me back to the promised land. I guess I'll crack one off in the bathroom before I go to sleep. My balls fucking ache. I really need the release, even if it's an unsatisfactory one.

The lights are out as I creep inside, but I can hear Zee humming gently through the baby monitor. I grab a bottle of water from the refrigerator, take two aspirin and head back to our bedroom.

I stand in the doorway, watching her as she settles Aiden in his crib. "Hey, beautiful."

"Hey, champ. Did you have a good night?"

"It was okay. I missed you guys."

"We missed you, too." She takes my hand and leads me out into the living room. "I don't want to wake them. When you drink, you can't control the volume of your voice. It's cute, but if you wake the babies, I'll have to throat punch you."

"You think I'm cute?" My head is swimming. It's been too long since I had any hard liquor. I knew it was a bad idea.

"You're okay." She winks at me.

"God, you're sexy."

"Now I know you're drunk."

I grab her hand as she moves to start folding the never-ending pile of laundry. "Don't do that. Don't put yourself down. You've been doing it since you fell pregnant."

"No, I haven't."

"That was half-hearted. You know I'm right. It's been lights-out sex since you started to show. And now, you won't let me anywhere near you."

"I have baby spit-up in my hair, and I live in sweatpants. It's not exactly sexy."

"You're sexy to me, spit-up and all."

"That's the booze talking."

"Answer me this... have we not had sex because you're still healing, or is that just what you're telling yourself because you have some crazy notion that I don't find you attractive anymore?"

Her gaze drops to the floor, telling me everything I need to know. "Does it matter?"

"Fuck yes, it matters. If you still need time to heal, then I'm fine to crack one out in my morning shower until you're ready. If it's because you think you're not sexy, then I have a real fucking problem with that, Zee."

"You won't like what you see. I have stretch marks, and I haven't lost all the baby weight. God, *I* don't like seeing myself in the mirror." Now she's just pissing me off. I stride over to her, backing her against the wall, bracing my arms on either side of her.

"When are you going to realize that I'm so in love with you I can barely breathe? I'm not some shallow prick who can't see past a few stretch marks. I'm the father of your kids, and I love every last inch of you. Those stretch marks are hot as fuck."

"Be serious, Coop. You've been drinking, so I reckon you're talking with your cock."

"My cock adores you. That's no secret." I kiss her neck with featherlight caresses, and I love hearing her breath catch in response —she's aroused, whether she wants to admit it or not.

"Will you even remember this in the morning?"

"I remember every time I've seduced you. Every time I've worshiped your body with mine."

"What if it doesn't feel the same? I don't want you to be disappointed." She drops her head on my shoulder.

"I could never be disappointed by you. Every curve of your body turns me on. I'm in love with your stretch marks because they are a testament to the fact that you gave birth to our sons. I'm in awe of everything about you. When are you going to understand?" I slide my hand down the side of her body, the curve of her full breasts making me hard as steel.

"I'm scared."

"I've got you. Tell me you're not turned on right now, and I'll walk away."

"You know how I feel."

"I don't. You've been through a lot lately, and I need to hear you say the words. I won't do anything without your say-so." Her movements are stilted and unsure—not what I'm used to from her. When her hand slips between us, her fingers trace the hard length of me, and she moans in response, her lips finding mine in a passionate kiss.

There's nothing friendly or hesitant in the way her tongue twists and tangles with mine.

"Say it, Zee. You have to say it because if I start, I'm not going to be able to stop. I'm desperate to feel you beneath me... my wife."

Her hands roam frantically before fisting in my hair, pulling me hard against her. "Fuck me, Coop."

"Are you sure?" If she says no, I think I might die. I'm praying to every God I can think of for her to say yes.

"I want you."

"You have no idea how badly I've wanted to hear you say that." I reach for the hem of her t-shirt, eager to feel her soft, supple skin on mine. My mind fractures into a million tiny pieces—sensory overload. If I don't calm down, I'm going to shoot my load before I even get her naked.

"Oh God, I've missed you." To hear those words fall from her lips is more than I can handle. She messes around with my pants, trying to unzip them, but I'm too impatient. I'm done trying to wrestle her out of her clothes. I grab the fabric of her t-shirt and rip the damn thing off before making short work of her bra.

With her back against the living room wall, I cup her breasts, now more voluptuous than they've ever been. "Holy Mother of God. Your breasts are fucking perfect." I have no earthly idea why she's self-conscious. She feels incredible. I only wish the lights were on in here to get a proper look at her, but I'm not going to push her.

I kiss my way down her neck, my cock aching to be inside her. My memories of the noises she makes when she's aroused pale in comparison to the real thing. I nibble, kiss, and nip my way to her breasts before sucking her nipple into my mouth. Holy shit, I'm going to lose it any second. I try to calm myself with a few sports statistics, but I can't get enough of her. Fisting her hands in my hair, she cries out for me to continue, so I move to her other nipple, taking it into my mouth in one long suck.

What the fuck?

Liquid fills my mouth, and it takes me a second to realize what's happening. I gag, pulling away and spitting Zee's breastmilk on the floor. "Fuck. I'm sorry, Zee. I didn't mean to milk you. I completely forgot that could happen. It's not like it's happened before."

"Oh my, God. I'm so embarrassed." She moves to grab her shirt off the floor, but there's no way I'm letting a little breast milk deter me.

"Don't you dare cover yourself up. I'm going to grab a glass of water, and when I get back, you better be naked."

"You don't have to do that, Coop. It's not exactly a turn-on."

"Strip. I won't tell you again." She needs a firm push right now because I know she's frustrated.

I quickly run to the kitchen and swig a full bottle of water. I just couldn't keep that taste in my mouth. It freaks me out, but not enough to kill my raging boner. I'm throwing off clothes as I make my way back across the room. It's so fucking dark in here, the only thing that alerts me to Zee's state of undress is the fact that I trip over her leggings discarded on the floor.

I swear I'm as giddy as a teenage boy who's just discovered what his junk is capable of. I stub my toe on the edge of the sofa, but fuck it, I'm not going to torpedo my chances with a broken toe. I've played with worse.

When I can make out Zee's shape, I reach out and pull her into my arms, my lips crashing down on hers with an urgency I can't tame or harness in any way.

She tastes sweet like lip gloss and sex—sultry and altogether delicious. "Bedroom now." I can't even form a coherent sentence right now.

"The babies are in there."

"Guest room?" I suggest as my hands caress down her side, cupping her sumptuous ass, ready to carry her up the damn stairs.

"We won't hear them if they need us."

"Then where?" I can't hide my frustration, desperation clawing at every nerve ending in my body.

"Couch. Ottoman. The goddamn floor, Coop." Ottoman it is. I find my way in the dark, lowering her onto the plush suede oversized ottoman in the center of our living room.

"I want to see you."

"Shut up, Coop. Just fuck me. You don't need the lights to guide you. I know it's been a while, but you know your way around." She's not wrong, and I'll take whatever she's ready for.

"Yes, ma'am." *Thank fuck!* We're finally going to consummate our marriage. It's back-to-front and upside down, but we've arrived at the same place in the end—our happily ever after.

Her body feels so good, I'm in sensory overload. I want to kiss every inch of her all at once. I crave teasing her for hours on end, drawing every ounce of pleasure I can wring from her body, but at the same time, I want to fuck her hard and fast, throwing us both headlong into a long-overdue release we both need.

I need at least a taste of her, my lips following the trail of my hands caressing between her thighs, and she doesn't disappoint. She's wet for me, which only makes her arousal on my tongue that much sweeter.

"Fuck, you taste so good. I've missed this." I dart my tongue out to flick her clit, just the way she likes it, my hands braced on either side of her thighs.

"Oh God, Coop. Yes." My name on her lips is a litany I've been starved of. I quicken my pace, lapping at her, enjoying her body once again.

"That's it, beautiful. Let me hear you come."

"Coop, open the drapes." *What?* I know it's been a while, but she's lost her edge on the dirty talking. She's usually such a dirty little minx, but whatever, I'm too turned on to care about dirty talk anyway. She could recite the phonebook to me right now, and I'd still be sporting a major boner.

I spread her legs wider, parting her lips, sliding my tongue from her entrance to her clit. "Like this? You like that?"

"What are you doing down there? I said open the drapes, not peel back my flaps."

The penny drops.

"I thought you were using a euphemism. *Opening the drapes. Your drapes.*"

"Eww, no! In what universe is that sexy?"

"It's not, but you feel amazing, and I don't care if you say something ridiculous. I'm horny, and you're hot."

"I meant it literally. You said you wish you could see me. I'm not ready for lights, but some well-placed moonlight would be okay. When I said open the drapes, I meant the living room drapes."

"Oh, thank God. It was by far the worst euphemism I've heard in my life."

"Maybe we should just try this another day?"

"No! My balls are going to explode if we don't do this now, and you were so close to getting some sweet release. If I killed the mood for sex, at least let me make you feel good."

"Coop, open the drapes." Her voice has taken on that sultry rasp I love so much. I jump to my feet and scramble over to the window, almost tearing the damn drapes off the pole. The second the soft moonlight hits her body, I'm left speechless.

"You're so beautiful, Zoey Danford."

"You're not so bad yourself, champ. I've missed that beautiful big cock of yours. Get over here." No arguments from me. I'm quick to get back between her legs, pulling out my A-game oral skills until she's screaming my name and begging for me to fuck her.

It takes all my self-control not to slam into her. Slow and steady wins the race. I gently ease into her, but I can feel the tension in her body. "Are you okay?"

"Keep going."

"If it's hurting you, we can stop." She's wincing as I say it, and that can't be a good sign.

"Maybe if we switch position? Doggy style. It will take the pressure off where I had stitches." As I pull out long enough to let her move, I'm bereft. She's so warm and inviting, my cock is aching for her. "Okay, try now."

She's on her knees, leaning over the ottoman, her perfectly plump ass looking so inviting. I ease back in, caressing her curves as I go. "Better?"

"Yes." Thank you, Jesus.

I begin to move, circling my hips, careful not to be too rough. It's not as easy as it sounds. With every forward thrust, the ottoman keeps moving. *Fucking wheels!* By the time I hit a steady rhythm, we're almost on the other side of the room. I can't get any purchase to get over the finish line.

"For fuck's sake."

"What's wrong?"

"This furniture. I'm fucking you clear across the room. We need a damn bed."

"Stand up."

"What?"

"I'm too sore now, and my knees are raw from our sex on roller skates." Kill me now. "Just stand up."

I reluctantly pull out, cursing the universe for my eternal blue balls. Zee doesn't give me a chance to catch my breath. She takes my aching erection into her mouth, her lips sliding up and down the length of me, her tongue swirling over the tip of my cock.

"*Holy fuck.*" I last all of about three seconds before she milks me for all I'm worth. I crash over the edge, my orgasm ripping through my body like a tsunami of pent-up frustration. The dam has burst, and I find sweet release, roaring my wife's name. "Zee, baby, oh my God! Thank you. Thank you. Thank you."

A cry rings out through the baby monitor.

"I think your screaming orgasm just woke the babies."

"Is it wrong if I say it was totally worth it? I swear you're even hotter than before." She looks up at me, still on her knees, naked and oh so stunning.

"Thank you for making me feel desirable again. For reminding me I can be sexy," she says, reaching for her clothes to go see to the boys.

I crouch down, pressing my lips to hers. "I'm always going to desire you, Zee. You're the love of my life."

EPILOGUE
ZEE

THE NIGHT I ended up on Cooper Danford's doorstep changed my whole world. I never expected a weekend roll in the hay to turn into forever. As much as I fought him every step of the way, Coop got under my skin. He burrowed his way into my heart and wouldn't let go. Now, I have a husband and two kids, and a life I never knew I wanted.

Our little family of four is the center of my world, and I wouldn't change a thing. It took me a long time to let Coop love me and to let myself love him in return. It's not easy to open yourself up to someone when you've grown up knowing that the people who brought you into the world didn't really want you.

The irony of my path isn't lost on me. When I fought against my feelings for Coop, the universe saw fit to test my heart and soul. Kids weren't on my radar. I suppose that's not strictly true. They were very much on my radar as something I never wanted. I didn't think I was capable or worthy of being a mother. The thought that I could make another human being feel the way my mom made me feel growing up scared me to death. And yet, the moment I saw those positive pregnancy tests, I knew I'd keep the baby—babies as it turned out.

I certainly wasn't prepared for Coop being all in with me after such a short space of time, or that I would end up proposing to him. If you'd told me even six months before that day, I'd have bet my apartment on the fact that I would *never* get married.

Life has been pretty amazing over the past few months. Aiden and Blake are finally sleeping through the night. Coop and I survived the sleep deprivation and came out the other side stronger. We may have aged a good five years each, but we made it through.

I've always been confident in my own skin, guarded with my heart, but not with my body. I didn't realize how much stock I put in being young and hot. Losing that confidence during the pregnancy and even more so afterward knocked me for six. Staring in the mirror and seeing someone you don't recognize is hard.

Coop never faltered—not once. Seeing myself through his eyes helped me embrace the woman I've become in a less-than-perfect body. If anything, he seems more aroused by me now than he was before. If the boys are asleep, Coop's ready to get down and dirty.

I'm not going to lie. I was happy to get the babies sleeping in their own room and out of our bedroom. It's hard to get your freak on when you're bunking with two kids. Even that small milestone has had a huge impact on Coop and me. We've been able to physically reconnect, and little by little, I've embraced my inner sex siren again. It's a tough job being the woman to sate every sexual desire of a Titan, but someone's got to do it, right?

Coop's mom decided to move closer, so she could watch the boys growing up, which has been amazing. Between her, Faith, and Hunter, we have a great support network. I went back to work part-time, but I'm not sure that's going to last long. Life is hectic and wonderful.

I took the boys to meet my parents, and they said all the right things that grandparents should, but they don't want to make space in their lives for us, and I'm okay with it. It was for my benefit, not theirs —I wanted my mom to see that I'm *nothing* like her.

Tonight is our six-month anniversary, and Coop insisted that we go out for dinner on a proper date with no babies. His mom is watching the boys, and I've glammed up and poured myself into a dress I know Coop will love. We were going to have dinner with Faith and Hunter, but I called her earlier and told her I needed some alone time with my husband.

On the car ride to the restaurant, I can tell Coop is hot for my dress. He can't keep his hands to himself, and I love it. He's definitely getting lucky tonight, and he knows it. By the time we reach our destination, I think both of us would gladly sneak off to a hotel and have super-loud sex all night.

When we've ordered our meals, and the waiter has brought us drinks, Coop reaches into his jacket pocket. "I got you a gift. I know it's only six months, but I wasn't going to wait a year, so I hope you like it."

He has a blue Tiffany box in his hand, and when he opens it, a huge diamond engagement ring just about blinds me, it sparkles so much. "Coop..."

"I know, I know. You're not flashy, and we're already married, but you never gave me the chance to propose."

"Are you sad about it?"

"Are you kidding me? You asking me to marry you was perfect. I knew you weren't doing it out of obligation or because you felt you should say yes to me because of the twins. It meant so much more, knowing how hard you fought against falling in love with me."

"We're not exactly into doing things the traditional route, are we?"

"No, ma'am. So, I feel pretty good about giving you an engagement ring after the wedding. At least I know you're not going to turn me down. If you don't like the ring, we can change it."

"It's beautiful, Coop."

"Not too flashy?"

"I'd say just the right amount of flash and sparkle." His face lights up, and he takes the ring out of the box to let me try it on. I wrestle my wedding ring off to let him put it on, but it's a little snug.

"Damn. I thought I had gotten the size perfect. I took that sapphire ring you wear a lot to the store to make sure I got the right size. Fucked that up."

"No, you didn't." He holds my hand up, the ring almost over my knuckle, but not quite. God, my fingers look like sausages tonight.

"Your finger begs to differ. Shit. I can get it resized this week. Sorry, Zee. I wanted tonight to be perfect."

"It is. You don't need to get it altered. I can wear it on a chain until it fits."

"What? It needs to be sized. I don't want you wearing it on a chain."

"Coop, listen to me. I love the ring. I love being married to you, and I love the life we're building together. If we've learned anything since we met, it's that life can be... unpredictable."

"Yeah, but a ring isn't unpredictable. In fact, it's very predictable. I should've just taken you to pick it out."

The waiter arrives with our food, but Coop is still muttering under his breath.

"I have a surprise for you, too."

"Hopefully, yours is more successful than mine."

"That all depends on how you look at it." I reach into my purse and bring out a long, thin box wrapped in a white ribbon. "Open it, but don't place it on the table."

"O-kay." He unties the ribbon and slides open the lid, his expression puzzled. "I thought you threw these out? Am I supposed to frame this or something? I'm feeling better about my wrongly sized gift right about now. Besides, I thought these things faded over time."

"They do."

"I'm confused. What do you want me to do with this?"

"Coop, I took that this morning." His eyes go wide as saucers.

"Seriously? Is this why the ring doesn't fit?"

"Yep. I'm pregnant. You officially have the most efficient sperm on the planet."

"Holy shit."

"Good holy shit or bad holy shit?"

He jumps out of his chair and sweeps me up into his arms before announcing our news to the entire restaurant.

"It's a hell, yeah, holy shit! Did you hear that, everyone? My swimmers are fucking Olympians. We're having a baby." His lips crash down on mine in a fierce kiss, and I know that we're in for another life-altering adventure. Sometimes the best-laid plans go out the window, making way for the most amazing moments of your life. When it comes to Coop and me, those moments come from the best lay and zero plans.

THE END

SOCIAL MEDIA

www.instagram.com/evahainingauthor

www.facebook.com/evahainingauthor

www.twitter.com/evahaining

www.amazon.com/author/evahaining

www.bookbub.com/profile/eva-haining

https://www.goodreads.com/author/show/20271110.Eva_Haining

https://vm.tiktok.com/MedmE5rj

http://www.evahaining.com/newsletter

www.evahaining.com

ABOUT THE AUTHOR

I'm happiest when wandering through the uncharted territory of my imagination. You'll find me curled up with my laptop, browsing the books at the local library, or enjoying the smell of a new book, taking great delight in cracking the spine and writing in the margins!

Eva is a native Scot but lives in Texas with her husband, two kids, and a whizzy little fur baby with the most ridiculous ears. She first fell in love with British literature while majoring in Linguistics, 17th Century Poetry, and Shakespeare at University. She is an avid reader and lifelong notebook hoarder. In 2014, she finally put her extensive collection to good use and started writing her first novel. Previously published with Prism Heart Press under a pen name, Eva decided to branch out on her own and lend her name to her full back catalogue! She is currently working on some exciting new projects.

ACKNOWLEDGMENTS

As always, my eternal love and gratitude goes to my husband, Simon. It's not easy being married to me, and yet you take it in your stride. When I feel like I can't keep giving my all in a struggle to find a little corner of readers who enjoy my work, you're always ready with words of encouragement, and unwavering faith in my talent. I couldn't do any of this without you. I love you so much, from now until eternity.

Ria – Coop has been a journey. I didn't think I'd top Jasper for you, but Coop was such a character, and he doesn't want to be second best! You've claimed this guy as yours, and I'm thrilled to have worked on this book with you.

I consider myself very blessed to have a great team of beta readers who support me with enthusiasm. Thank you from the bottom of my heart.

A big thank you to my editor, Nicki Kuzn. This is a great start to 2021 and I look forward to some exciting projects this year.

Last, but by no means least, I want to thank my readers. Your continued support through such a tumultuous few years is so humbling. Without you, I wouldn't be seeing my dreams and months of hard work come to fruition. Thank you so much for giving me a place in this world.

Made in the USA
Coppell, TX
27 September 2024